REIGN OF THE WITCH QUEEN
BOOK 1

ANDREA ROSE

*This book is dedicated to my mother, Eleanor Fenichel.
She left this world for the next before she could read
A Crown of Light and Shadow. It was a blessing to tell her
this story that day in the hospital. It was a good day, and
I will hold those moments in my heart for the rest of my life.
She was my worst critic and my greatest supporter.
Forever in my heart.*

*Special thanks to my husband, Dave for always believing in
me. None of this would have happened without you.*

Table of Contents

Reign of the Witch Queen   7

Chapter 1   9
Chapter 2   23
Chapter 3   35
Chapter 4   51
Chapter 5   65
Chapter 6   79
Chapter 7   93
Chapter 8   109
Chapter 9   127
Chapter 10   145
Chapter 11   161
Chapter 12   179
Chapter 13   193
Chapter 14   207
Chapter 15   219
Chapter 16   233
Chapter 17   247
Chapter 18   261
Chapter 19   273
Chapter 20   287
Chapter 21   301
Chapter 22   315
Chapter 23   329
Chapter 24   343
Chapter 25   361
Chapter 26   375

Also by Andrea Rose   395
About the Author   401

REIGN OF THE WITCH QUEEN

In the beginning, there were two worlds.
The human world is bound by earth, fire, water, and air.
The elven world glows with the fifth element, magic.
Over time, the sister worlds split from each other,
and humans forgot about the elves.

Centuries passed, and the elven world thrived until a beautiful and selfish witch came into power. Using her magic to dominate rather than to lead the elven people of Domhan, she cast a spell to keep men from ever assuming power. The old gods twisted her spell, and no female elves have been born since.

Darker and darker the witch queen became, until many fled the great city. Those who remained were transformed into her army of shadow demons.

Without female elves to continue their race, the elves living in fear of discovery will die out while Domhan falls into darkness. The only hope is a prophecy claiming that the human world holds the key. Only with the three earthly women and the sons of Riordan can the Watchers' Gate be opened. Inside lies the magic that can stop the witch queen.

The time has come for the three elven brothers to follow the prophecy.

Chapter One

HARPER

I've been driving around for two weeks with an expired driver's license. I'd like to say it's unlike me to let things go, but that would be a big fat lie. I'm the queen of procrastination.

It's not entirely my fault. The thought of sitting in a New Jersey Driver's Motor Vehicle office like one of a hundred head of cattle being shoved from one queue to another forced me into my illegal driving. Yup, I just blamed bureaucracy for my bad behavior, and I'd do it again.

After over an hour of being shuffled through lines, having my picture taken, and a thorough examination of every document since my birth that proves who I am, I'm waiting in a gallery of small chairs that must have been some kind of torture device in another life.

The guy behind me had tuna fish for lunch.

The woman next to me fixes her boobs every five seconds

by reaching into her low-cut, yellow blouse and manually pulling them up and in. She smells of stale cigarette smoke and cheap perfume. Fixing her lipstick for the third time in the half hour I've been sitting here, she gives me a wink.

There's a woman with three kids, all in varying states of come apart.

I don't blame them. I want to melt down too. Honestly, I feel for the woman. Imagining having three kids under the age of ten is like imagining my life as anything but an utter mess.

A black screen with red digital numbers hangs on the wall above the six openings where the clerks' desks are situated. The current number is 162, and the middle light in the one is out, making it look like a vertical dash. My ticket is 175. I tuck it into my pocket.

I'm going to die here. Right here in this giant, gray-walled room in a horrible chair with the smell of canned tuna fish as my last memory. This is hell.

"163," the bald clerk with round, blue-tinted, wire-framed glasses drones as if we're inconveniencing him.

The mother of three jumps up, dragging the smallest of the kids with her to the window. While the child whines, she hands the clerk her paperwork.

I'm a little jealous of that kid and the other two running around the tall table where people are filling out mounds of red-tape-related forms.

The room gets completely silent like places do before a rock star belts out the first note of his biggest hit.

The kids are frozen in place.

The boob lady has one hand in her blouse and her face is twisted in a bright-red-lipped scowl.

I stand and turn slowly and find every person in this hell-hole statue-like. Even the tuna guy stopped stinking.

"What the fuck is happening?" I step around the boob lady and the teenage boy sitting next to her, tuck my paperwork into my oversize purse, and step into the aisle. "Hel-looo... What the fuck is wrong with everyone?"

From my right comes a whooshing sound, and the papers from the forms table fly in every direction. A pinpoint of light appears in the middle of the cinder-block wall. It widens until swirls appear and the wind pulls at my hair.

My heart is pounding so hard I'm close to hyperventilating. "I'm dead. I died in the fucking DMV. That's not fucking fair."

A hazy figure appears in the swirling light, then grows bigger, taking on the outline of a man.

I swear to god, Thor jumps down from the opening to the painted-gray concrete floor of the most boring place on Earth. Thor! Blond hair like sunshine, bright blue eyes, a sharp angular jaw, and shoulders as wide as the Jefferson Memorial bridge. Pointed ears poke through his gorgeous long locks. A sheathed sword is attached to his belt. A sword! No beard, but otherwise...

He winces, then his gaze intensifies, and he pulls his lips into a tight line. He shakes his head as if to clear it. When he spots me, he narrows those piercing eyes. "Harper Craig, you must come with me," he says with a heavy brogue.

Legs shaking and heart in my throat, I make a mad dash for the door. I don't care if he *is* Thor, I'm not being killed by him or some swirling light thing. Though, I'm probably already dead.

I keep running. Outside, everyone is frozen. Maybe I'm

going to hell. I mean, I've never given the prospect much thought, but I've been a nice person. I should at least get a chance for heaven or whatever.

I jump into my Toyota Corolla and drop my purse on the passenger seat. The car has seen better days, but it's reliable, and I'm too lazy to shop for a new car. Nothing happens when I turn the key. I mean, not even a click.

Thor opens the passenger door. "It won't work. We're outside of time. I've got to take you through the gate before it closes, Harper."

I wrap my hand around the tire iron I keep on the floor, pull it out, and jab at him. "You're not taking me anywhere. How do you know my name?"

My ears burn with a loud shriek.

"Shite!" Grabbing my tire iron, he pushes my bag to the side and sits in the passenger seat. "You've done it now."

I cover my head and brace for the blow.

"Do you think I'd strike you?" Indignation fills his voice, as if I'm out of line.

Peeking under my arm, I'm ready to open the door and run. "Don't say that as if I'm the crazy one. You came through a solid wall, have pointed ears, look like Thor, and you're trying to kidnap me."

He blinks several times. Touching his ears, he smiles.

I'm not going to lie. That smile could melt the most bitter woman's—or man's—heart. I have to push that aside because I'm probably having some kind of psychotic episode, though the idea that I'm dead is still on the table.

With a shake of his head, his hair hides his ears. He mutters a few words I don't understand, and he almost looks normal. "I suppose those will stand out here. Who is Thor?"

I don't mention that he's too beautiful to not stand out, even without pointed ears. "Thor is the god of thunder."

Cocking his head, he taps his fingers on the dashboard. "I've not heard of that deity, nor am I a god, and my name is Aaran Riordan. Your vehicle will start now. We'll need to go to the Labrador Coast."

When exactly did the world go mad? Oh right, when Thor jumped out of a hole in the wall at the DMV. I grab the strap of my purse, give it a hard tug until it's free, get out of the car, and head back inside.

Before I reach the double glass doors, he grabs my arm. "Where are you going?"

I give his hand a long look.

He must see the fire building inside me because he lets go.

"I'm going to get my driver's license renewed, then I'm going home. I'm sure the fuck not going to Newfoundland with a crazy man who can't possibly exist. I'm willing to accept that I'm having some kind of psychotic break, but I'm not going along with the fantasy." I step inside and check the number, 173. Good, at least I didn't miss my turn. I sit on the last chair in the back row.

Several people are picking papers up off the floor and everyone looks a little confused by the state of the room. The wall is solid again.

Doing my best to keep my breathing steady, I ignore Aaran when he sits next to me. His sword is gone, and that probably means I left my car unlocked and there's a fucking sword in my Corolla.

At least three women, including boobs and lipstick, turn to give him a good look.

I don't blame them. If he were real, he'd be gorgeous, but he can't be real because people don't show up in vortexes and demand I go with them. People don't freeze as if time has stopped. I'm not insane. All is well.

Repeating these things over and over in my head helps, but the impossible man is still next to me.

When my number gets called by a lady with long spiral curls and thick glasses, I jump up and run to her little window. Digging in my pocket, I come up empty. "I lost my ticket, but I've been here for hours."

"Yeah, whatever wind blew through, everyone lost their tickets, hon." As if rogue winds blow through central New Jersey buildings all the time, she takes my paperwork and looks at each paper one by one, then types something into her computer.

Unable to resist, I look over my shoulder. Aaran's chair is empty. He's standing near the door, leaning against the wall. In brown pants and a white shirt, he could be anyone coming off a hard day's work.

"Okay."

The clerk startles me. I spin back to her.

She gives Aaran a look and smiles, then hands me back my paperwork. "It's twenty-four dollars. Will that be cash or credit?"

"I have cash." I pull the money out of my purse and hand it over. I can feel his eyes on the back of my head. Why doesn't he go away?

"Okay, Miss Craig, here's a dollar change and your new license. Thank you for your patience and sorry about the mess." She smiles.

"Thank you. Have a nice day." I walk away, barely

hearing her say, "You too," as I tuck everything in my purse and rush to the door.

"Did you get what you need?" Aaran follows me out.

At my car, I turn to him. "You are not real. I don't know what you are, but you are not real, so go away."

He steps back, and his bright blue eyes are wide. "I'm real enough."

"Leave me alone. I'm a normal girl with a normal life. I don't do drugs, and I generally only drink on weekends. I can't recall being in a situation where someone could have slipped me something, but clearly, that's what must have happened. I'm going home and lying down until this passes." I get in my car and start the engine.

Before I can pull away, Aaran gets in the passenger side. "I'm not a phantom or dream, Harper. You're not mad." For the first time, he sounds sympathetic rather than commanding.

"Sane people don't see holes open in the wall, then have hot men step out of them. Maybe it's been so long since I've had sex that I conjured you for a quick thrill." I shake my head and pull out of the parking lot. To get on Route 1, I drive down an access road behind the mall. Then I get on Quaker Bridge Road and take the ramp. Traffic is miserable in both directions, but I get off at the next exit, make the jug handle, and turn left to cross Route 1. Then I take back roads to my condo.

"Will you give me a chance to explain?" It would be easier to ignore him if his voice wasn't like a meadow in springtime.

I'm turning into a poet, for the love of all. "What's to

explain? You stepped out of a wall, demanded I come to help you, and now you want me to go to Canada."

I stop in my parking space, turn off the car, and get out.

Unsurprisingly, he follows with his sword in hand.

As I climb the stairs, I try to find the moment when my mind must have snapped. Did the DMV *literally* drive me over the edge? "I don't suppose I can get you to just go away?"

"I'm sorry you're upset. Maybe there were better ways to go about this, but the magic only works for so long. I came through and hoped you'd just go back with me. I suppose that was a naive notion. My mother told me this world has no knowledge of magic. I can't leave you. We need your help." He stands very close as I open the door.

Not bothering to lock him out, I drop my keys in the dish on the half table and toe off my shoes.

Stepping out of his boots, he watches me like people watch a cornered dog. "Your home is nice. This living off the ground and attached to others is odd, but I can see the ease of it. No fields to plow or gardens to tend." He looks out the window at the lake.

It's a nice area just outside Princeton. My neighbors are all lawyers and professionals. "My father died and left me a lot of money. Now my mother is quite ill. I'm not going anywhere."

His eyes are warm with emotion when he turns. "I'm sorry, Harper."

"I have a decent job doing logistics, and it's close to home." I have no idea why I'm telling him any of this. Maybe if I talk, he'll either make sense or disappear.

I flop onto my soft gray sectional. "I took the afternoon

off to get my license renewed. It expired two weeks ago. I could have sent all the information in and done it by mail, but I'm a procrastinator and let it lapse."

"What's the penalty if you're caught driving without this *license*?" He rolls the word as if it's a foreign language, and sits on the ottoman at the far end of the couch.

I shrug. "I'd probably get a ticket and have to pay a fine. Maybe, if I made eyes at a cute officer, I'd get off with a warning and a command to take care of it immediately."

The way he smiles is too sexy. "I'm sure you're lovely enough to avoid a fine."

"Why me, what's in Canada, how did you make that vortex, and what help do you need? Start with, why me?" If he's not going to leave, I may as well play along with my delusion.

His eyes shine as if lit from the inside. "It's a very long story, and you might not understand." He shakes his head, and the tips of his ears peek out.

"If I'm *not* crazy, then you're not human?" I get up and cross the large living space to an open kitchen. I grab half a bottle of wine from the fridge and pull the cork. "Do they drink wine where you're from?"

"Indeed, on occasion." There's that smile again.

Damn him.

Taking two stemless glasses from the cabinet, I keep waiting for him to dissolve into thin air, but he's still on my couch, and his sword is leaning against my front door frame when I return with the wine-filled glasses. "Either tell your long story or get out."

The silence is thick with whatever decision he's making. With a nod, he takes the glass. "Try to keep your mind open,

Harper. This is going to sound stranger than what you already saw."

Easing down, I sit carefully so that I don't spill my wine. I drink half of it. "Give me the abridged version. I don't have any more wine in the house."

He sips and smiles at the white wine. He takes a long swallow and puts his glass on the coffee table. "I'm not human. You have that right. I'm elven. My world has been tied to yours since the beginning of time. Long ago, our peoples mingled, but that was a time nearly forgotten."

Should I throw him out or keep listening? I keep a baseball bat in the coat closet near the door. I could force him to leave.

"While it's never been one of my gifts, some elves can read the thoughts of others. Oddly, I know you're considering bashing me over the head with a bat, whatever that is. It doesn't sound as if I would like it." He looks amused rather than angry.

"It's only sensible." I drink the rest of my wine and cradle my empty glass.

Even his laugh is perfect. It's like music. "I don't know why the worlds were separated, but long ago, when humans and elves mingled, children were born. The elven magic has been passed down through the centuries, and three women living in this time have that magic. My world is in trouble, and my two brothers and I were sent here to find those three women and ask them to help save us."

What am I supposed to say to that? I stare at his handsome not-quite-human face and wonder if perhaps I'm sane and it's he who's mad.

"You asked why you? That's the answer, Harper. You are

one of three women who can save us." His hands are fisted on his knees, then he relaxes them and rubs them over his thighs. It's the first sign that he's nervous.

"What are we saving you from?" May as well get the full story so I know what to tell my therapist.

He gets up and paces from one end of my living room to the other. In my modern condo, he looks out of place. I can picture him in a cottage with handmade cabinets. My white shaker-style cabinets and black counters don't suit him at all. His home would have a butcher block and a rocking chair.

"I live in a house that has stone counters. It's my mother and father's house. There are a few rocking chairs."

"That's very inconvenient and intrusive." I use my best scolding voice.

Oddly, he bows. "I'm just making sure you're not going to scratch my eyes out. I don't mean to invade your privacy. Also, I've never been able to read anyone's thoughts before. It's new."

"If I promise not to beat you with a bat or claw you, will you stay out of my head?"

Another bow. "Of course."

"You have a deal then." I get up and offer him my hand.

As he wraps his fingers around mine, I feel the weight of his responsibilities and his fear of failure. I jerk my hand away. It's not the first time I've touched someone and known more about them than I wanted to, but it hasn't happened in a long time. I sit. "Tell your story, but if it gets too long and too crazy, we're going down to the bar."

"You have a pub in the building?"

"Not in the building, but around the corner." My condo

is part of a planned neighborhood, complete with restaurants, shops, and an Irish pub. It's trendy and convenient.

Sitting next to me, he says, "We may need that pub, but let me get the brunt of it out."

Having felt his sincere worry and doubt, I no longer wonder if he's a figment or a lunatic. Whatever he is, he's sincere.

"Before I start, can I ask you something?"

I nod.

"When you touched me, I felt a flash of knowing. You felt it too, I think. Have you felt it before?" The late-day sun shines through the sliding patio door and frames him in a glow of gold and orange. Maybe it's a sign.

"Not for a long time, but when I was young, I could sense things about people. My grandma said it was the sight. She had it too. My mom said to keep it to myself or people would lock me away in an asylum. Her description of such places silenced me well enough, and most of the time, I avoid skin-to-skin contact. I guess over time, whatever it was, stopped."

He shakes his head and covers my hand with his. His fingers are rough with calluses. "You have a lot of gifts you've yet to discover, Harper."

I'm flooded with kindness and sympathy and pull my hand away. "I'm just an ordinary woman with good instincts about people. Don't dramatize it."

While blocking the setting sun, Aaran looks me in the eyes. "The witch queen rules my world and brings darkness to everything she touches."

Chapter Two

AARAN

On one hand, I have to bring this woman to Domhan. On the other, I long to leave her in peace.

She should live a life where no one wants to destroy what she is. Unfortunately, that time has passed. The witch queen knows about the prophecy of three, and she'll be hunting human women as soon as she learns the magic necessary to come here. Human magic is different from elven, and that knowledge is lost in time.

"Several generations ago, the witch queen cast a spell to make herself ruler and keep men from having power." There's a lot to tell about the witch queen, but Harper said to keep it short, so I move on. "The spell worked, but it had an unexpected cost."

As Harper sits up and watches me with her green eyes full of curiosity, her hair shimmers in the sunlight. I've never seen hair like hers. Some would call it brown, but it shines with streaks of red and blond and draws a man in for a touch. "What happened?"

I resist the urge. "My mother hoped that my youngest brother would be a girl, but another babe born six months earlier was the last female elf born in Domhan."

She blinks those soulful eyes. "How old is your brother?"

"Thirty suns. My mother was pregnant when the curse was cast." I hope both my brothers survived the portal magic and found their women more malleable than Harper. That thought makes me smile. I can't help liking this strong, sad, beautiful woman. It does me no good to care. I need her help, not her affection.

"Is that years? The number of times the Earth goes around the sun?" She wrinkles her nose.

"Yes. You call it years." I remember from my training. My brothers and I had to learn as much as we could about this world before we made the trip.

She stands and props her hands on the curve of her hips. Now those eyes flash at me. "Your youngest brother is thirty years old. How freaking old are you?"

"I'm thirty-seven." Unsure why she's so animated, I keep my seat and let her hover over me.

"You look much younger. Is there some fountain of youth over there?" She waves her hands, as if Domhan might be in the air outside the windows, then turns and walks to the kitchen. After taking a glass from the cupboard, she fills it from a spout in the door of a metal cabinet, then drinks it down. Clearly, she's agitated, but I can't imagine why.

"Elves don't age as quickly as humans. We live much longer as well." What else am I supposed to say?

Those full lips of hers twist in what might be annoyance,

and I can't help finding it adorable. "Tell your story. You said it's been thirty years since a female baby was born in your world. That seems pretty serious." She drinks more water and leans on the counter, which sits in the middle of her kitchen, with a sink in the center.

Everything about the way these humans live is foreign to me, but Mother warned me it would be. She and Father came here years ago to look for answers to the curse, but they didn't have the prophecy yet. They couldn't know what exactly they sought. "It's going to get a lot more serious. It will mean the end of our people. Some have already gone begging to the witch queen for help, only to be turned into creatures in her army." I swallow down the bile of that betrayal and push on. "My parents took a large group to the walled city of Tús Nua. It's not the only elven settlement, but it's by far the largest. We cast wards to keep the witch queen out, but those won't last forever. The oracle protects the western continent, but even that magic is fading. We need to break the curse and depose the queen.

"For years, we searched for some clue about how to do it and finally found a prophecy which required time to decipher. Three human women have the magic to open the Watchers' Gate."

She cocks her head and sighs. "And I'm one of these women?"

"That was what the oracle said. And since you were the only one pulled out of time today, I'd say they were accurate." I get up because I feel strange sitting when she's standing. "I'm sorry, Harper, but we need you, or an entire race will die, and Domhan will fall into darkness."

"And why should I care?" The softness in her voice betrays that she does care, despite the question.

"Our worlds are connected. The witch queen will find her way here and destroy this world too. It might not be in your lifetime, but eventually, she will dim your sun with her evil." All I can do now is wait while this human woman decides the fate of everything I love. The problem is, I can't even blame her for saying no.

"You know, this all sounds insane, and it's too much to process after that whole jumping out of a hole-in-the-wall thing. I'm going to change into jeans and go to the bar." She looks down at her black slacks and pink blouse. Without waiting for a reply, she turns and goes down a hallway. A door closes and locks.

Everything about this house, connected to other houses, is foreign to me. The sink is white like the flat cabinets with their black handles. It's the first time I've seen cupboard doors made from just one slab of wood. I open the door where she got water and peer inside the device. Its metal front catches the light from a chandelier, and it has glass shelves. We have something similar, a cold box powered by magic to keep milk, meat, and cheese from spoiling. I'm again struck by the differences between our worlds. The wooden floors are the only similarity, but these are stained dark brown. The food is in packages. Mother told me about the markets here that are super, and you can buy all the food in one place.

Harper seems to live alone, but the large room has a dining table with six chairs. All the living space is in one room so you can see from the kitchen to the couch. It's strange but rather nice.

I sit until I hear the door open again, then I get to my feet.

Sparing me the briefest glance, she grabs her bag from the hook near the door.

Not to be left behind, and admittedly curious about the pub, I follow fast on her heels. I work a quick glamour to hide my ears. Between that and leaving my sword behind, I feel a little exposed.

In heeled boots and denim pants that hug her round ass and make my mouth water, she walks at a clip down the block. At the corner is a well-lit area with people outside laughing and smoking. Harper says hello to a man with a beard who waves and calls her name.

I hold the door open for her to enter. The bar is a rectangle with alcohol bottles in the center, four bartenders, and beer taps, two on either side. The sun is just setting, and the place is crowded, with only two stools empty at the far end.

Past the bar is a dance floor and stage. Music is playing, but there are no musicians. This is the first place that feels a bit more like home and reminds me of the pub in Tús Nua.

Harper sits and leans toward a woman who puts a pink drink in front of her without her being asked. "Thanks, Ashley."

The blonde gives me a long look. "Who's your friend?"

"Aaran, this is my friend Ashley. Ashley, Aaran, who I met at the DMV today." Harper's voice is flat, and she sips the drink.

"Well, I never have this kind of luck at the DMV, girl. Aaran, what are you drinking?" Ashley smiles, showing off straight white teeth and an easy manner.

As much as the pub is similar to home, I have no idea what the pink drink is, but I know what I'd order at home and hope they have something like it. "Whiskey, please, lass."

"Are you from Scotland? I have some decent scotch." Ashley picks up a bottle from behind her with scrolled writing on the label.

The man with the beard from outside slaps me on the back. "You're in America now, try our bourbon. I promise you won't regret it. I'll even buy."

I give Ashley a nod and turn to the man with the beard. "I'm Aaran Riordan." I offer my hand.

"Greg Peterson." His shake is firm. "Harper, Ashley, and I went to school together."

The bourbon arrives in two fancy glasses. I inspect the crystal, wondering if I can drink from this without breaking it.

Laughing, Greg says, "We start with the good stuff and sip it. Next, we'll move on to shots once our taste buds are numb."

So, I sip, and it's good. It's very good, and I sip until we're several shots in and I know everything about Greg and a woman named Liz who broke his heart.

I check on Harper every few minutes, and she smiles from time to time, but her sadness is so deep it never leaves her.

Two hours later, I'm singing old folk songs, and my eyes are blurry.

Watching from the bar, Harper shakes her head. She pays the bill and heads out the door. I stumble twice as I rush to follow her and curse myself for getting drunk when I have work to do. Still, I manage to make it to her house before she closes the door.

She goes down the hall and comes back with her arms full of linens. "You can sleep on the couch. The bathroom is in the hallway. Don't throw up on my floor."

I take the pile and start to make a bed out of the couch. "Thank you. You are very kind."

Putting a large glass of water on the coffee table, she says, "I don't believe your story, but it's clear to me that you do. I don't know who or what you are, but I saw what I saw today. I have to take care of my mother, so I'm not going anywhere with you. Sorry, but that's just the way it is."

My heart sinking, I sit. "I understand." I drink the water and watch her disappear down the hallway.

I've failed.

I wish someone would tell me what to do. It would be better if I were heartless. Then I would have dragged her into the portal today and dealt with the consequences. The fact is, I need her help, and making her angry wouldn't have been a good way to gain it. Still, at least she'd be in Domhan, and there would be a chance to save it.

I must have fallen asleep because I'm much more sober when I hear her breathing close by. "Are you alright, Harper?"

"I don't sleep much. You didn't get sick?" She's on the other side of the couch.

"No. I'm fine." My eyes adjust, and I see moisture on her cheeks, shining in the moonlight. "You're crying." I sit up.

She wipes her cheeks. "I would help you if I could."

"Thanks for that." I'm not certain it's true, but it's still nice of her to say. "Why are you crying?"

"Do you drink coffee?" She gets up and goes to the kitchen.

I follow. "We don't have whatever that is in my world."

She fills a basket with brown crumbs and fits it in a machine, adds water to another part, and pushes a button. "No coffee? Sounds like hell. Tea?"

"Yes, I drink tea." I'm an idiot for feeling any joy, but the fact that she's treating me like a guest makes my pulse speed.

After filling a kettle, she heats water and takes an odd white bag from a yellow box before putting it in a white mug. The second mug is blue and says *Mornings are for Coffee, not Talking*. On one side it has a drawing of a stick figure with a padlock on his lips.

"I'm going to see my mom this morning."

"May I come with you?" I hold my breath.

She stands over the stove and watches the kettle. Once it makes a horrible sound from the steam pushing through some kind of whistling device, she turns off the flame and fills the white mug. Placing it in front of me, she looks deep into my eyes. "If you want to see a dying human, I guess you can come with me. It's a sad place to visit."

Her other machine makes a beeping sound, and she pours the dark liquid called coffee, then sits silently drinking while the sun comes up. When she pours a second cup, she says, "If you want to shower, there are towels under the sink in the bathroom."

Taking the rest of my mediocre tea with me, I go to the bathroom and leave her in peace.

After a long testing period where I finally figure out how to work the shower, I get cleaned up and dressed. I borrow a comb, and Harper left a package that reads *toothbrush* on the counter for me. It's similar to what we have at home, and I'm grateful for the gesture.

In the living room, Harper waits near the door. "I like to get there early and speak with the nurses before they get too busy."

The music in the car is just loud enough to make me think she would rather not talk. The trees are beautiful here, and I watch the scenery go by, changing from the stacked homes to larger places, then a small town with a large stone university. The school's architecture reminds me of home. It's a thriving little place, even this early.

We pull off the main street and then make several turns until we arrive at a building marked *New Jersey Palliative Care.*

I follow her to the second floor of the white and gray place. It's clean, but I sense death and have to raise my walls to keep from feeling too much. Unlike the actual words I hear with Harper, I sense the pain and fear of the dying within each room.

Harper stops at a desk and speaks to a man and a woman. I look inside the door across from the desk. On a board across from the bed, it says Maggie Craig.

"Who are you?" Her voice is just a whisper. Little more than skin and bones, a woman with Harper's eyes stares at me. She has a pink cloth wrapped around her head and is hooked up to wires and tubes.

"My name is Aaran. I came with Harper to visit you." My magic opens to the wake of a dark illness growing inside her.

She raises her brows and winces. "You're not from here. What are you?"

Can she know about Domhan? It doesn't seem possible, but her nearness to the other side may give her insight.

"I came to find Harper. I need her help."

When she laughs, it's more like a wheeze. "It must have been quite a journey. Your kind don't usually come here."

"No. We stay home, but this was important." I touch her bony hand lying on top of the sheet. "She's not ready to lose you."

A tear bubbles from her. "No, but we have no control over that now. I suppose we never did."

As the eldest of my parents' children, I pride myself on unwavering self-control, but since I entered this world, that has faltered. Impulse is for my youngest brother to toy with, not me. Still, as I look at the withering form of Maggie Craig, all I can think is how her death will destroy Harper. Unable to help myself, I call my magic to pull this fog of bitter illness from her.

The heat of it burns deep into my bones, like the branding iron straight from the fire. More painful than traveling by portal, long minutes pass, and still more fire draws out of her. How she was still alive is a testament to her strength.

"Harper, make him stop. Look what it's doing to him." Maggie shakes her hand, trying to dislodge it from mine.

Harper's cool fingers touch my cheek. "Aaran, whatever you're doing, it's harming you. She wouldn't want that."

"It's the price of magic for my kind. I can take a bit more." The pain surges through my gut, up my body, and resounds inside my head like a battering ram.

The tenderness of Harper's touch keeps me grounded. Opening my eyes, I stare into hers. "One moment more." My voice is rough and weak.

"No more." Maggie's voice has the strength of a soldier.

I release the cloud of black and send it away. Stumbling back, I barely make it to the chair before my legs give out. "I will just need a few minutes."

Skin changed from gray to a nice pink, Maggie looks like a different woman. Still far too thin, but health has returned to her cheeks and eyes.

Gripping the blue-green leather on the arm of the wooden chair, I let the last of my magic rest.

Harper kneels in front of me. "What have you done?"

"What I could." Breathing is harder than I'd like, but there's enough magic left in me to restore my strength, given a bit of time.

Looking from me to her mother, Harper's eyes fill with tears. "How?" She holds up her palm. "No, don't tell me. At least, not yet." She goes to her mother, and the two women hug as if it's been years since they've seen each other.

Maggie laughs. "Is it bad that I'm craving pizza and fries?"

When they laugh together, my chest tightens. As bad as I feel, and as vulnerable as I've made myself, it was worth it to hear that sound.

Chapter Three

HARPER

Aaran healed my mother. I'm shaking and have to clasp my hands together behind mom's back to keep them still while I hug her for the hundredth time in the last hour. I'm overwhelmed with emotions I'm desperately trying to keep inside. I don't know if the magic will last, but she looks like herself. Hearing my mother's voice strong and full of wonder makes me want to shout from the rooftop.

Aaran's eyes are closed still, and he's slumped in the chair by the window. The sun streams across his golden hair. I want to help him, but have no idea how, so I concentrate on my beautiful kind mother and how her skin is pink instead of gray.

None of this is possible. It's a miracle to recover from cancer when you're so close to death. I was prepared for her to leave me. I've had a year to get ready. Now everything has changed. My mother is alive, and it's as if all the suffering and tears never happened. Except they did, and I know how precious life is. I knew before. I lost my father in an instant, but this was different. This was horrifying.

The doctors and nurses all cram into the room, looking at charts and readings. Rather than wait for someone to ask one too many questions, I tell Mom I'll be back on Sunday. She smiles and waves like it's a normal day before she got sick.

My heart is so tightly lodged in my throat that I don't know if I'll ever get a word out. I want to thank him. I want to rescue him. Instead, I focus on the path to my car and swallow tears.

As he held Mom's hand, there was a moment when I considered the idea that Aaran might harm her, but my heart told me another story. As he restored my mother's health, his bright energy faded. I send up a prayer that he'll recover. Maybe it shouldn't matter so much to me, but it does. "Should I get a doctor for you?"

Aaran's shoulders slump and his gait drags. "No. The sunshine will be enough to rebuild my strength. It will just take some time." He gets into my car and closes his eyes.

I sit beside him and start the engine. "Why did you do it, knowing it would make you so weak? You could have died." I don't know how I know this, but his sacrifice was greater than he'd like to admit.

Without lifting his head from the headrest, he turns, locking his gaze with mine. His hair falls across half of his handsome face, and the tip of his pointed ear shows between golden locks. I guess the magic he uses to hide them has faltered. His blue eyes are tired, but not as faded as before. "If you cannot help me, Harper, then my world is finished. It will fall into darkness, and everyone I love will die. I will die fighting beside them. I had nothing to lose by giving you your mother back."

My throat is tight. Rather than face my guilt, I put the car in gear and drive us back to my condo.

At an Italian restaurant and deli a block from home, I stop for food. I don't imagine there's much Italian food, if any, where Aaran comes from, but I'm hungry and buy extra in case Mom is up to eating pasta and cheese tomorrow. I pick up soup too.

When I get him inside my condo, the sun is streaming through the slider, so I open it and tell him to sit on one of my lounge chairs. "Do you want chicken soup or to try something different?"

"I want whatever that heavenly scent in the car was." His smile is a little stronger this time.

My stomach does a little butterfly dance at the sight. I wonder if everyone in his world looks like him or if all the elf women are clamoring for his attention. Once I have the ravioli on plates, I join him on the veranda. "This is called ravioli."

He takes a long sniff and grins before forking his first bite. A low moan emanates from his throat, and he closes his eyes.

Watching him eat, it's like I'm experiencing the wonder of pasta, cheese, and sauce for the first time. "You like it?"

"This is magnificent. Do you think they'd show me how to make it?" He practically inhales the rest, and his color starts returning.

Shrugging, I say, "If you ask, Paul will probably show you. He taught me last year."

Aaran freezes and looks at me as if I'm a goddess. "You make this?"

"I have made it twice to impress dates." Why that makes me blush, I have no idea. Aaran is not a date. "But since Paul's is just down the block, I usually let him do the Italian cooking."

"I would like to make this for my family when I go home." He takes his plate and mine and goes to the kitchen where he washes the dishes and leaves them in the drying rack. When he returns, his shoulders aren't so slumped. "Your mother is well liked at that place."

I nod. "I know you say you saved her because you have nothing to lose, but if you'd sped up her dying instead, wouldn't that negate my reason for turning you down?"

His full lips pull into a deep frown. "I'm not a monster. Killing your mother would not have gained me what I need, and even if it would, I would have to live with that decision."

"Maybe you healed her thinking that if my mother was not sick, I would be free to help you." The sun glistens on the surface of the lake.

"You need her. I care about you more than I should and about her as an extension of that. Why are you looking for some wrongdoing in my actions?"

"Good question." I close my eyes, and the fireflies behind my lids from staring at reflected light is like fireworks.

"What is the answer?"

"I don't trust people. In my experience, the ones you can trust die, and the rest use you until they get what they want." I have no idea why I admitted that to him.

His beautiful mouth pulls down at the corners, and sorrow fills his eyes. He sits forward, his elbows on his knees, and watches me with those big blue eyes, now full of pity. "What about Ashley and Greg? There were a lot of folks at the pub last night who seemed to genuinely care about you."

"Ashley is a good friend. Greg is okay. He and I dated in high school, but we stayed friends, and he's come and fixed things in my house when I need a handyman." I get up. "I didn't sleep well last night, and it's been a big day. I'm going to take a nap and have a good cry. Thank you for what you did. I'll help you if you give me a few days to get Mom settled."

I have no idea why I'm so emotional, but I barely get the words out before the tears come, so I make a dash for my bedroom and shut the door. I mean, maybe I do know why. My mother was just miraculously snatched from the brink of death and given back her health. That's worth a few tears. I cry into my pillow to muffle the sobs.

The door opens, and a moment later, strong arms wrap around me. "I didn't heal Maggie to manipulate you, Harper." His warm breath tickles the back of my ear. "I need you. My people need you. If I were a stronger man, I'd leave you here to have a full life without danger. I'm not that strong. My destiny is to find the first of three and bring her to the Watchers' Gate. My entire reason for being is completing this task. Can you forgive me?"

It's been so long since someone held me, I'd forgotten how good it is to be cared for. Between giving my mother back her health and this embrace, I would risk everything for him. I cover his hand with mine on my abdomen. "Let me rest like this, and we'll call it even."

He pulls me tight to his chest, my head resting on his

biceps. His voice is like a dream. "Sleep, Harper. Nothing will harm you while I watch."

It sounded like a vow made to a princess. My eyelids grow heavy. Lying like this is perfection. I feel safe and cared for, and can't remember ever feeling this way before.

"Mom, are you sure you're going to be alright here?" In the week since she was released from the hospice, she's put on a pound or two, which makes me so happy.

"I'm fine. You need to help Aaran. Your grandmother always said there was a special purpose for a child who came as such a miracle." My mother was almost forty when she finally got pregnant. All the doctors said she couldn't conceive, but then I came along when no one was expecting it.

"I remember, but I don't think this is what Grandma had in mind. I mean, I'm going to Canada because an elf says that's where we can open a portal into another world." The more I say it, the more nuts it sounds.

Mom's laugh is like the best music. It feels like a decade since I heard that sound. "My mother was wise in the ways of magic. Maybe if I'd paid more attention, and been less resistant, you would have learned more from her."

"You were just trying to protect me." I look around the condo. "Are you sure you'll be alright here all alone?"

"I'm hardly alone. Josephine is a mile away, and Wanda is only two. They're going to stop in daily and check on me, whether I want them to or not." My mom's two oldest friends have been there for us through everything, dad's death and cancer. Of course, they'll take care of Mom while I take an extended leave of absence for personal reasons.

Those were the words I said to my boss when I told him I'd be gone for a while and would let him know when I could return. If I return. My nerves kick in big time. "What do I know about saving worlds? Less than nothing."

"You'll be exactly what you're meant to be, my sweet girl." Mom cups my cheeks like she did when I was a kid. She kisses my forehead, and the soft smell of her perfume reminds me of simpler times.

The door opens wide, and Aaran walks in with my mom's best friends.

"Look at the hunk we found in the parking lot," Wanda says bawdily. She's five-foot-nothing and wears her silver hair in a bob that looks a little like an old-time football helmet. She has warm tanned skin and shining brown eyes that see more than they let on, and she has Aaran in her clutches.

Josephine is more demure on the outside but just as fun-loving inside. She grips Aaran's other arm. "Now we know why you're running away from home. If this was my prize, I'd be taking him far away from here too." She gives her wedge hairstyle a flip.

It took a full day for Aaran to recover from what he did for Mom, but he's been strong and helpful ever since. Grinning at the two women, he pats Josephine's hand. "I'll take good care of Harper, and you see that Maggie is well."

They both let go of Aaran and rush to Mom's side. Wanda grabs me around the waist and kisses my cheek. "Maggie is a miracle, just like our Harper.

Mom takes my hand and pulls me aside. She digs in her pocket. "I had this resized for you." She slides a simple gold band over the middle finger of my right hand.

I stare at the plain ring. "Was this Dad's?"

Dashing a tear away, she hugs me. "I've held on to it for too long. You should have a part of him, of us. Remember we love you."

"When did you have time to do this?" I spin the ring around my finger. It's heavy and thick, but the size is perfect.

"I think it suits you." She smiles, and the light catches her eyes.

Somehow I know she's going to be alright. I feel it deep inside me. Life radiates from her, where weeks ago, we were waiting for the end. No one has ever given me a greater gift and no one ever could. "Thank you. I love it."

After another round of hugs and kisses, I manage to keep from crying and get out the front door. It took me two weeks to talk to my boss, Ashley, and a few other people about running off with Aaran. I had no idea settling one's affairs was such a big job. I put Mom's name on all my accounts, so she'll be well taken care of if I don't make it back. She tried to refuse, but I insisted. Cash and my credit card will get us to St. John's. After that, I'll have to rely on Aaran. If there even is an after that. This entire thing is madness.

"You are screaming your thoughts." Aaran holds his ears.

Nothing surprises me anymore. I'm traveling with an elf, so... "You're reading my thoughts again? That seems very rude."

"It would be rude if you didn't scream them. Though, I can understand why you think this crazy." He bought himself a backpack and is inspecting all the zippers where he's tucked away a hoard of survival supplies. The man loves Walmart. I thought I would never get him out of the camping section.

Maybe it should bother me to have him hear some of what's in my head, but I find it comforting. Yet another thing about the last two weeks to confirm I've lost all good sense. "What will happen when we get to the island? Explain to me again why we couldn't fly there?"

He pulls a very long knife out of his pack. It's in a leather sheath, but even so, it's quite menacing. His sword is in the trunk under a blanket. "You said no weapons on a plane. We need weapons."

I suppose he knows what he's doing, but weapons are not my thing. I save the worms that crawl up on the concrete when it rains. "And you're certain I'm the right woman for this job? Because I've never wielded a weapon or harmed another living thing in my life."

His smile could melt any woman's heart—and other parts, too. "I'm sure."

"Two days of driving it is then." I head for Route 95 North with a full tank of gas and no idea what I'm getting myself into. "How do we get you across the border into Canada without any identification?"

"It won't be a problem." He taps the side of his head as if that should mean something to me.

It does fill me with joy and makes me chuckle, so that's something.

Aaran's gaze is intense as he looks from window to window.

"Will someone try to keep us from reaching Newfoundland? Why are you suddenly on guard?" I force my hands to relax on the wheel.

"I don't know for sure, but we're on the move now and that will cause a ripple in what the witch queen sees. If she's looking, and I think she is."

"You think, or you know, Aaran?" My knuckles get white again, even though I have no idea what the witch queen is or what she can do. Not really.

"I feel...unsettled." His admission makes my stomach tighten.

I asked, and he promised never to lie to me. Be careful what you wish for, Gram always used to say. I have to deepen my breathing as my pulse speeds. "Maybe it was stupid of me, but I didn't think we'd be in danger until we went to your world."

"You couldn't have known. I should have told you more about my world and the witch queen's reign, but you were working so hard to get things arranged for your mother, it never seemed like the right time." The muscle in his jaw ticks.

"Tell me now." The highway is slow with traffic. Might as well spend the time wisely.

"Are you sure you want such distraction while you drive?" He clearly doesn't want to tell me.

I give him a quick look that I hope conveys I'm not falling for any crap. "I'm not weak. I don't know how to fight, but I'm strong in a lot of ways, and I can run fast." There is no good reason for me making a case for myself.

Keeping my eyes on the road, I feel him watching me.

"You're more than strong enough, Harper. You don't even know your full strength yet and have endured more than most could handle. I'm not doubting your abilities. I'll never do that." He lets out a long breath. "The witch queen was born in the same province as my family. Her name is Vanora Braddish, though she's long been known as the witch queen. She was a very good student of magic."

"Does everyone learn magic in Domhan?" I picture every book and movie about wizards I've ever seen. It conjures up the image of Aaran in a pointed hat with black robes and a wand, which I have to banish from my mind.

There's a long pause and I can't look because I'm trying to weave into another lane. There are emergency lights ahead on the right.

Aaran says, "Magic is in all elves, and humans too, though most of you never notice your gifts. Elves learn to control it. Vanora was gifted with strong magic and the ability to wield it better than most. My father told me that when she was sixteen suns, she started toying with black magic, and when she mastered many spells, she left school and disappeared. At that time, a few villagers went missing as well. They were never found."

"Never? What do you think happened to them?" The notion of never being found to be mourned by loved ones breaks my heart.

Aaran's voice drops out of his strong storytelling baritone, and he whispers, "I think they were the first of her shadow army."

We pass the three-car fender bender that caused traffic to slow and finally get up to speed. Fear is something I'm familiar with. I feared losing my mother because I know what it feels like to lose a parent. I've never experienced my own life being in danger until the day I met Aaran. Even though he wasn't going to hurt me, I thought it was the end. That adrenaline roars through me again. "Shadow army?"

Hesitating, he lets out a sigh. "I wish I could tell you this was nothing to worry about, but I can't. Vanora turns elves and other creatures into shadow demons. They are remnants of their former selves, with only the obscurity of where the light once lived. She enslaves them with the promise of release and rest."

"That's horrible." Part of me thinks this is all made up, and I wish I could believe that part.

"There are far worse words to describe the witch queen, Harper. If I could spare you this journey, I would."

"Who are the other two women?" The notion that I'm not alone in this gives me some assurance. I hope, whoever they are, they're braver and stronger than me.

"I don't know." He clutches his backpack, then relaxes and puts it on the floor between his legs.

"Your brothers didn't tell you where they were going? That seems unsafe. What if you had to gather a second one of us? What if I refused, and one of them was needed to convince me?" I hate what I'm saying, but understanding this process is important.

Shaking his head, he frowns. "No. The oracle sent for my brothers and me. We met with them individually. I don't know what Raith and Liam were told."

"What did she tell you?"

His jaw ticks, and his hand tightens around the strap of his backpack. "The oracle gave me the magic to create a portal to you, along with your name. The oracle is a group of elves who used strong light magic that I can't begin to explain to find you. They..." He shakes his head.

"What?" His hesitation makes my heart speed up. In the past couple of weeks, I've gotten used to his directness and assuredness. Whatever he's about to say can't be good.

"They gave me the song of your soul so I could find you. It is a way to sense a person and learn what's in their heart."

"What the fuck?" I look in the rearview mirror and make my way to the shoulder, turn on my flashers, and put the car in park. "What do you mean, she gave you the song of my soul?"

Because I'm not even sure I have a soul or I believe people have souls, I don't know quite how to accept the fact that he has part of mine. Even so, I don't like that he's listening to some inner part of me. Whatever he took, no one asked my permission. What else can he do with the magic he uses to hear my soul? Am I in control of my own decisions? I'm ready to toss him from my car right here on this busy highway, where he'd have to walk a mile to get to a town. I'm breathing so hard that hyperventilation is not out of the question. It would be another first, but I'm not ruling it out. Cars pass at high speeds as I turn to face him. Rage, confusion, and hurt are at war inside me. This seems like something he should have told me while I was preparing my life to save *his* world.

He swivels his head in all directions, looking for either an escape or danger. When he focuses on me, his shoulders slump. "I should have explained before now."

"Damn skippy."

The twitch of those pretty lips is almost a distraction from my anger. Almost.

Holding up a palm in a way that might calm or show contrition, he says, "Each person in any world has an essence that makes them unique. The three who come from this world and are in the prophecy were found by the oracle through the songs of your souls. The oracle found the right song and placed its melody inside me so I could find you."

"And manipulate me?" I want to hit him, but I keep my hands fisted in my lap.

He shakes his head. "No. Just find you and ask, beg, if necessary, to get you to come and help us. If I hadn't had that song inside me, I might have come through anywhere in your world and never found you."

Letting out the breath I've been holding, I want to believe him. "Is it still inside you, this part of my soul?"

"Yes," he admits without any shame and stares into my eyes boldly, as if he's never giving up some prize.

"Why? You found me. You should give it back." Do I want to take it back? Do I even believe I have a song of my soul? Every moment with Aaran challenges what I know or don't know.

"You say that as if I've taken something away from you. I can assure you that's not the case." He looks out the rear window, then beyond, to the trees that line the road. "I have the song so I can find you if you're lost. It's still inside you, clear and strong, Harper."

"Why don't I hear it?"

"Because it's always been there and you have become so used to it, you don't notice. It's been a part of you since the moment you were conceived. I imagine that people who live near this road stop noticing the sound of the traffic." He shrugs.

"Do you hear your song?"

Why must his smile stir my insides so thoroughly?

"When I listen, yes."

"Fine." At least for now. I'm not done with this conversation, but sitting here in the open is making him nervous. I put the car in gear and find room to ease back into traffic.

"You are extraordinary." He returns to his watchfulness and his grip on his backpack.

"I'm average."

He chuckles.

Chapter Four

AARAN

When it gets dark, Harper is struggling to keep going. I wish we had cars in Domhan so I could assist in our travels, but we don't. We travel by horse. Long ago, there were dragons, but they left when the witch queen gained power and captured one of them.

In Portland, Maine, we stop for the night. The busy area, with so much activity, will keep us hidden. Harper parks the car in front of a tall white building with lots of windows and a large glass door. There are three other similar buildings close by and smaller ones that have signs boasting the kind of food they serve. She calls it a hotel and says we can stay the night. I've never heard the word before, but I assume it's similar to the travelers' inns at home.

At the desk, the clerk smiles. He's tall and big, with thick glasses and an easy way about him. "How can I help you?"

In a common area, a lady sits with two men at a small

table. All three have computers in front of them, and they're clicking away without regard to anything around them. This was a new word to me also, but Harper showed me hers and called it a laptop. It was amazing to see how she could look up our destination with a few clicks on the keys.

A second clerk is also typing on a computer.

Harper clears her throat. "Do you want your own room?"

I may be able to hear the soft sweet music of her soul, but I can't tell if she wants me to say yes or no. I held her each night until her mother moved into her home, then I was back on the couch. "I want to keep you safe, but you can decide."

Biting her bottom lip, she turns to the clerk. "We need a room for tonight. We'll be leaving in the morning."

My body reacts, but I know better than to hope for more than comfort. She deserves respect, and as much as I desire her, that decision will have to be hers.

The blue rug and white and red walls are a vast contrast to the muted tones of Harper's home. "Is it typical for these places to be so colorful?"

She adjusts her backpack on her shoulder and looks around. "It depends, but often they are. Fancy hotels less so."

Taking her pack from her shoulder, I add it to mine, and we get in the elevator. The doors open one floor up, and I follow Harper to door 206 where she waves a card over a panel and is rewarded with a click and a green light.

The room has two beds and beige paper on the walls. The art is geometric and pleasant, but nothing to catch the eye or warrant exploration.

She flops on one of the beds. "I'm too tired to eat."

"You will regret it if you don't." I drop our bags on a small bench.

Shrugging, she closes her eyes.

Outside, wolves howl.

Harper sits up. "I can't believe there are wolves in town, or even in Maine. I remember reading about how they were all pushed west by people and settlements."

Looking down from our window, I see a large canine run through the parking lot. "I don't think those are normal wolves."

Standing beside me, she gasps. "How is this possible? You said the witch queen turned elves into shadow demons. Those are actual wolves. Really big ones."

"I'm not sure, but I'm going to ward the hotel so you can get some sleep." I sit cross-legged in the middle of the other bed, close my eyes, and call my magic.

The other bed's springs squeak.

It's not easy to push aside the knowledge that Harper is watching me. Breathing and letting go of all that is material, I call the magic to life and ask for protection. The hotel forms in my mind. The white building with a blue and green illuminated sign is clear behind my eyes. Magic slips around it like a white bolt of lightning.

The whimpering of the wolves spins a web of satisfaction.

"They're leaving." Harper's voice cuts through my concentration.

Opening my eyes, I find her standing at the window.

"I can see a glow around everything," she says.

"Can you?"

"Won't people notice?" She cocks her head, and her hair falls across her back.

"Most people in this world will not see magic. My ward

is not visible to them. Those who do see it will write it off as something logical, like lights shining on the building." I rise and dig in my pack until I find one of the protein bars I packed. "Eat this and get some rest."

Making a face, she eats the bar, then grabs her pack and goes into the bathroom. When she comes back, she's in a t-shirt and gray pants that hug her shapely legs and ass.

Once she's under the covers, I turn off the lights, lie beside her, and hold her.

"Why don't you ever get under the blankets, Aaran?"

The question seems to hold within it more than my geography. My cock is more than interested in my reasons. "I've already asked too much of you, Harper. My needs are not important."

"What if I needed you?" Her voice is small and shaky.

I kiss her soft hair and breathe in the floral fragrance of shampoo. "When you say that with confidence and certainty, I'll be more than happy to make love with you."

"Okay." The soft word is almost lost in her yawn.

The sun will rise soon, and I've checked outside the window a dozen times during the night. After studying the instructions on the phone, I called the front desk and learned that breakfast would begin at six o'clock.

After a quick shower, I crouch next to the bed and brush Harper's hair from her eyes. "We need to get up and fed so we can get on the road again. The daylight should keep those wolves away for a while." I hope that's true, but I had no idea that the witch queen could manipulate beasts in this world. The idea that she's unlocked new magic sends a shiver through me.

With a soft sigh and a long stretch, Harper opens her eyes. "Good morning."

"Good morning." I step away.

She cannot possibly know how her breasts pushing against the thin white material of her top drives me wild with desire. If she did, she'd hide under the covers. Or maybe she wouldn't. Within that hope rests so much danger. I can't protect her if she's a distraction. I need to stay focused.

"I'm going to shower and dress." She stumbles to the bathroom.

"Gods preserve me," I mumble to the empty room and wish I could jump in a cold lake before she returns.

In my bag, I check the knives I bought with money my parents kept from their time in this world. I also have several types of protein bars, a canteen, and some flares. I'm not sure why I would need them, but the man in the store seemed very keen on my having them in case I need to call for help. I told him I was going on a long hike in Canada, so he was trying to be helpful. Once I'm sure everything is in place, I pull out the small notebook I placed in the front pouch and write down my thoughts about all I've seen and done in the last day. Before I put it away, I pray that one day I'll be able to reflect on this time, or that someone in the light will.

The water stops, and a few moments later, the hair dryer comes on. I know the sound from the one Harper used at her home. I made her explain all the tools and devices in her everyday life that were foreign to me.

Something crashes, and Harper screams.

I'm in the bathroom in an instant. Expecting to find blood, I'm relieved when she's alive and well and wrapped in a white towel. "What's wrong?"

She points to the mirror, her face as white as the towel.

Trying to ignore how little of her is covered, I turn toward the mirror, and it takes everything in me not to gasp at her reflection glowing in a rainbow of colors.

"What is happening to me?" Skin rosy from the hot shower, she glows anyway. This aura visible in the glass is something else. She's something else. The colors and light move and shift over her skin in soft waves of yellow, blue, green, red, and purple. A shift to white for a moment leads to the room brightening before the colors return.

I touch her shoulder, and my hand is enfolded in the warmth of both Harper and magic, unlike anything I've ever felt before. "I don't know, but it feels..."

"Feels what?" She jerks her elbow into my ribs.

With an *oof*, I close my mouth. "Amazing. Full of light. I guess this has never happened before?"

"No. I don't generally glow when I dry my hair." The fire is back in her voice, and it makes me smile.

"If it's any help, it's only your reflection. I didn't see anything different when I first walked in. Well, except that you're nearly naked."

She grabs the knot at the top of her breasts. "I'm not sick or evil?"

"No." I back toward the door. "Can I ask what you were thinking about when this started?" Sometimes magic is triggered by an intense thought. At least with elves, that's sometimes how it works.

"I prayed that I wouldn't be turned into a shadow." She blushes, which is beautiful beyond words.

I have to continue to back away or I'll drag her into my arms. "I won't ever let that happen, Harper. Maybe your aura is an answer to your prayer."

She cocks her head. "What the hell does that mean?"

Needing a bit of time, I step out of the room and speak through the safety of the closed door. "Get ready and let me stew on it. You must be starving. I know I am."

HARPER

I'm freaked out about glowing, and as we get in the car, I can feel the eyes of those wolves watching us. I search, but I can't see them. "This is creepy."

"Yes, it is." Aaran buckles his seatbelt. "We should get moving."

At least my stomach is full, and I got a good night's sleep. "They must know where we're going, Aaran. How do we get to this portal?"

"We just do." He stares out the window, looking as if he could wrestle a wolf pack on his own with his bare hands.

Pulling onto the highway, I keep my attention on the road and let Aaran worry about monsters. "Tell me something that will make me think this journey won't end in disaster."

"I don't think you can be turned to darkness." His lips lift into the most infuriatingly hot smile.

"Why?" I mean, that's nice, but I'm no angel. "I have all the same good and bad thoughts as anyone else."

"You told me that you prayed you wouldn't be turned into a shadow and the result was the most spectacular aura I've ever seen. You glow so bright with light magic that it's no wonder the oracle found you, and not surprising the witch queen has located us as well." He searches the trees on the side of the road. "I think that was the way your prayer was answered. It was to show you that darkness cannot invade your soul. She can't turn you into one of her minions, Harper. Though, she probably doesn't know that."

My heart settles for a moment, but then races again. "How do we hide my whatever-you-call-it so she can't track us?"

"Good question."

"I doubt those wolves can chase us at this speed. Will she find another resource for our next stop?" My phone GPS tells me to stay left and continue north. Maine is beautiful. I wish I had time to explore. As it is, we speed past trees and signs for parks, and I hope one day I'll get to come back.

Following a long silence, it's startling when Aaran speaks. "We should stop at the next opportunity. I've been thinking about how to hide the light in you, or at least dim it."

At a rest stop, I pull off and park. "What do you have in mind?"

"You showed your colors, so to speak, by using prayer. Prayer and spellcasting are quite similar. I used a spell to protect the hotel last night. To draw my magic, I asked the old gods to shape my magic into a protection spell. In my mind, I saw the building and formed my magic to surround it."

My life has become a comic book. "So, if I pray to be hidden from witchy, my psychedelic aura will fade?"

He shrugs. "That's my theory."

"Since I don't have a better idea, I'd say it's our best bet." I close my eyes and pray to be invisible to the witch queen and all her minions. My heartbeat slows, the hair on my arms stands on end, and warmth spreads through me, starting at my toes and rising, like pulling the blanket up from the bottom of the bed. When I open my eyes, Aaran is staring.

"That was amazing."

"You can tell?" I mean, I think it worked, but this is my first magic trick. At least the first intentional one.

"I can tell." He smiles. "Look in the mirror." He points to the rearview mirror.

Hesitating for a long moment, I finally dare to peek. I look like me; the aura is still there, but the colors lack the vibrancy they had earlier. I touch my cheek. "I did it."

Grinning at me proudly, he says, "We'd better get going if we're to find a boat to take us to the coast of Labrador today."

We make it to the Canadian border without any interference. "How are you going to cross?"

The line is long, and each car has to stop at the booths to present their passports. The officers look as intimidating as those wolves last night. My nerves are reaching their limit. I don't know if I can do this.

"Just drive up and hand the man your papers. Act as if I'm not here. If they ask, you're traveling alone to vacation at Prince Edward Island." He closes his eyes.

"They have dogs." I watch the German shepherd sniffing around the cars up ahead. "Won't they smell you?"

He lets out a long breath. "Not if I do this right."

At the booth, I say hello to the young woman who looks in my car while a man with a dog walks around it.

She takes my passport. "What's your reason for visiting Canada?"

"I've always wanted to see PEI, and I had some time off. It's just a short vacation." I force a smile.

She nods and goes into her little booth. A minute later, she returns. "Have a nice trip, Miss Craig. PEI is beautiful."

And just like that, I cross into Canada as if I'm alone, and all I can think is that I just smuggled a human being across the border into another country, and that's probably a federal offense. Except he's not human. He's an elf. Elves don't exist. So really, I've done nothing wrong. I'm totally fucking losing my mind.

We are well down the road before Aaran opens his eyes. His smile fades. "Are you okay?"

"No. No, I'm not. I'm a felon for dragging an illegal across a pretty major frontier. I'm being chased by a fucking witch and wolves and shadows and who knows what else. I glow like a damn rainbow. Nothing is normal. You saved my mother's life, and I'll be forever grateful, but I'm not this person. I'm nobody's hero. What I do is sit behind a desk and make sure containers get from point A to point B. I'm not exciting or interesting." I swerve to the side of the road, flip on my flashers, and rest my forehead on the steering wheel.

Sweat drips down my back and at my temples. I'm deep in a full-on panic attack, like the ones I had when I was a kid. I take a deep breath, but it's not full or refreshing. It shakes and stutters as I let it out, so I try again.

Aaran rubs my back and then my neck.

His touch feels so damn good, and my breathing gets steadier. "There are human women who can climb ropes and shoot guns. We have female soldiers who would be much better suited to this kind of thing. I'm no warrior." I rock my head to the side so I can see his disappointment. I brace myself for it.

His eyes are bright and clear blue like the Caribbean Sea. I see sympathy but no regret in the set of his jaw and the straight line of those perfect lips. "I don't know why you have the gifts needed to save my world, Harper. You're wrong though. You are a warrior. Maybe not in the sense that you've been trained to kill or defend with weapons. Not everyone could have cared for your mother, held a job, been a friend to an old flame, and been kind to all the other people at that pub who clearly care about you. If you want to go back, leave me here, and I'll find my way home. No one would blame you. This is a lot to ask."

What do I do? This man saved my mother from certain death. He needs my help to save his world. As crazy as that sounds, I believe him. Sitting up, I touch his cheek across the console that separates the front bucket seats of my car. "Is everyone in your world so beautiful?"

His hair is so soft, and I love the way it tucks behind his ears when he's not using it to hide those points. He says, "You can find out for yourself."

"Why not tell me?"

Covering my hand with his, he kisses my palm.

His lips send a rush of heat through me, and if we weren't on the side of a road in Canada, I'd be hard-pressed not to give in to my attraction to him.

"If I say that the elven people are fair to look at, you might not look at me the way you do. Right now, I'm unique in your eyes. By tomorrow, I'll just be one of many." He drags my palm to press over his heart.

"That seems unlikely." Gathering my wits and my hand, I pull back onto the road and head for PEI.

Chapter Five

HARPER

We arrive at Montague, population 1,961. It's a quaint town with a waterfront full of boats. "How are you going to find someone willing to take us to St. John's?"

"I think we start there." Aaran points to a place called Moe's Bar.

I have my doubts, but follow anyway. The bar is dim and smells of stale beer and other things I don't want to think about. It's early, but four men and a woman sit talking and laughing at the far end of the bar.

Aaran strides over with no preamble. "Would any of you be a boat captain?"

They stop laughing and stare at him.

A stocky man with tattoos on his arms and a touch of gray in his dark beard, says, "Are you from Scotland Yard?"

The five of them bust out laughing.

Aaran laughs too, though I doubt he has any idea what Scotland Yard is.

The man says, "You here to arrest us?"

"I just need a boat and captain to take me and my friend to St. John's tonight. Well, not exactly to St. John's. It's a place on the coast near there. Can any of you accommodate us?" Aaran's smile is warm and easy.

I lean against the bar near the door, sure that at any minute, this group of locals is going to laugh us right out of here.

"What's there that can't wait until the ferry crossing tomorrow?" The woman is tall and has blond hair also, touched with gray. Her skin has seen many years of too much sun. Her brown eyes are curious and kind.

"We have an appointment of sorts, and the longer we wait, the more dangerous it gets for us." It's easy to be impressed by the way he tells them the truth without giving anything away.

The woman's eyes narrow. She whispers, "Domhan?"

Aaran nods. "You know where we need to go?"

Frowning, she touches her ear. "Aye, I know."

"Nancy?" The bearded man is standing now too.

"What's going on?" one of the other men asks. He has red hair and a scruffy beard. "Do you want me to toss him from the bar, Nancy?"

She shakes her head. "No, Bill. It's fine. I just realized I knew this young man's parents. He and his lady need to get to the coast near St. John's tonight." She looks at the bearded man. "Will you take them, Bert?"

I walk closer.

"You know my parents?" Aaran asks.

"I came here with them more than ten years ago. I stayed." She squeezes Bert's hand.

"You're Nainsi. I remember you, though I was young when you lived with us." Aaran grips her arm.

Emotion welling in Nancy's eyes, she draws a long shaky breath. "We'll get you where you need to go."

Bert clears his throat. "I'll take them, love."

Gripping Aaran's shoulder, Nancy looks him in the eyes. "The prophecy was found?"

He nods.

The hint of an accent like Aaran's creeps into her voice. "Tell your mother that Nainsi sends her love. Tell her I've thought of them often and regretted nothing. My life has been very fine here with Bert." She gives Aaran a quick hug. "Luck to you."

We follow Bert to the dock and onto a white-and-gray fishing boat. As soon as I step on the boat, something in the ocean shifts. It darkens, and the soft waves grow angrier.

Bert frowns and looks at me. "You're like my Nancy?"

"No. I'm from New Jersey. I'm going to help Nancy's people." I grip the metal railing. "This is my first time out of the bay."

"You may get sick, but this is a good boat. She'll get us there." He starts untying lines and checking over things I don't understand. We start to drift away from the dock.

"Wait!" Nancy calls from the shore. She's running to where we were moored, with a large pack slung over her back.

Rushing to the wheelhouse, Bert starts the engine and reverses toward the dock. "What's wrong, love?"

"I'm going with you. I'll see them off, and we'll overnight

in St. John's. I'll not be left behind." As soon as we're close enough, she jumps on board with the agility of a much younger woman.

Shaking his head, Bert smiles and takes us away from civilization. Once we're clear of running into anything, he pulls her into his arms and kisses her. "I wasn't going to run off."

"No. I know." They stand watching the ocean together, and she rests her head on his shoulder.

He kisses her head. "You can spell me when I rest, and I'm sure happy to have your company. This is a long go with several stops for fuel."

She nods.

The farther out to sea we get, the rougher the ocean. My stomach is rolling, and I'm distracted from anything else by the notion that soon Aaran is going to see me hurl over the side of this fishing boat. Sitting on the long bench that runs along the side of the vessel, I clutch the rail.

Aaran touches my shoulder and sits next to me, pulling me to his side. He wraps his arms around me. "Try to think about something else, Harper."

"Something besides my nausea? That's a lot to ask." I try to laugh, but it comes out more like a groan.

Pressing both of his hands to my abdomen and with his cheek resting against the side of my head, he says something I don't understand.

My seasickness disappears in an instant. I turn to look at him. "What did you do?"

Bert turns us to the right, and I tumble back into Aaran's arms. If I'm smart, I would pull away, but I love how it feels to be held by him. He's strong yet gentle, and somehow regal. I'm in so much trouble.

He kisses my forehead. "I eased your illness."

"Won't that use up magic you'll need?"

His lips are more magic than the spell he used to calm my churning gut. I rest my cheek on his chest and wrap my arms around him. It should be awkward, but it just feels right.

"It's not much to help your seasickness. Nothing like curing an illness. I'll be fine to open the gate. Besides, I think this journey will take some time, and we can't have you weak and sick from the sea. You'll need your strength when we get to Domhan." He runs his hand over my hair as if he cherishes me as more than a key to saving his world.

Of course, that's just the lie I'm telling myself, but it's a very pretty lie.

We port at the easternmost point of Nova Scotia, and Bert gets fuel.

Aaran helps him, and I sit. The wide ocean between us and Newfoundland is gray with whitecaps ready to pull me under. Dark clouds gather, and it's hard to tell from what direction the weather is coming. I've never seen clouds pull together from more than one direction, and I know nothing about storms at sea, but it frightens me. "I don't know if I can do this."

Sitting beside me, Nancy sighs. "No one truly knows what they're capable of until they're tested in the real world."

"Is this the real world? I was beginning to think I got lost in a dream slash nightmare." I watch the people work on the docks.

Bert and Aaran have disappeared into a small gray building with white trim. These docks are filled with boats in slips, along with men and women with thick biceps to lift coils of two-inch rope and bins filled with fish. "I'm not strong or brave."

"I used to say that about myself, and then Aaran's mother, Elspeth Riordan, picked me to come to the human world and search for the answers that would save Domhan. She thought I would bring something special to the search. I met Bert and stayed when she and the others returned home. Perhaps my staying was really about waiting for the two of you to come through and need passage to the portal." Her eyes smile as Bert's laughter carries from the doorway of the building. "It's been a good life here." She dashes a newly shed tear.

"Do you regret staying?" It's none of my business, but her emotions have me curious, and it's a good distraction from my worries.

Shaking her head, she smiles. "Not for one moment. I've loved living here, and Bert and I have been very happy."

I like the idea of a love that survives with all the differences they must have faced. "Is it rude of me to ask why your ears aren't pointed?"

Her laugh is full and light. "Not at all. I use a glamor spell to hide my ears and the difference in aging. I noticed Aaran is keeping his ears round for the viewing of humans."

"Really. Doesn't that take a lot of effort to keep up all the time?" I'm still confused about how magic works. I mean, who wouldn't be? "Aaran nearly used all his energy when he healed my mother in hospice."

"Did he?" She frowns and her bright eyes dim. "Is that how he convinced you to go on this journey?"

"No. Though, it was easier to say yes, knowing my mother was safe. He said that if the witch queen wins and turns your world dark, it will only be the beginning, and that eventually, she would come here and destroy our world as well." I'm distracted by Aaran and Bert returning to the boat. Both carry five-gallon gas cans. The red-and-black tanks make Aaran's arms bulge as he lifts them over the side of the boat. They use thick bungee cords to strap them to the sides of the rear deck.

"If your mother was in a way near to death, he could have died trying to heal her. If you'd already told him no, he probably had little to live for. If you are part of the key to the survival of Domhan and defeating the witch queen, then everything Aaran knows will be gone. Saving your mother may have been his gift to you. The fact that the effort didn't kill him must mean something." Nancy's watching Aaran work on coiling a rope as if she's seeing him in a new light.

"What does it mean?" I don't know what I would have done if Aaran had died to save my mom. The thought creates such an ache in my chest that I have to clutch it and breathe through.

Nancy shakes her head. "I don't know. I'm no oracle. But that kind of magic is a special gift from the old gods." When she smiles, there's something new in her eyes and I think it's hope.

After a long night and then a rest in one of the ports along the southern coast of Newfoundland, Bert slumps. The rain is coming down harder now. "This last bit will be tricky."

"Why?" All the coastline and ocean look the same to me. As I stare ahead, it's the same foreboding view as I saw behind.

He points to the landmass ahead. "We have to go around this point, then we can head northwest to the cove where Nancy came from." He clears his throat. "I suppose I always knew she'd go back one day."

I turn to Nancy, where she's leaning against the wall of the bridge. "Are you coming with us?"

Nancy stands straight. "I can't stay here safe and sound while my people fight for their lives and Domhan."

"I know." His jaw ticks. "And I can't watch you leave me. I suppose that means I'm going to Domhan too."

Pretty sure whatever is about to be said is private, I back toward the door and excuse myself.

Aaran stands at the side rail, staring out at the sea. His eyes narrow.

Searching in the same direction, I don't see anything but clouds and waves. "Is there something there?"

He shakes his head. "I thought there was, but now I don't see anything."

The ocean rolls and crashes as if it wants us to go back. Saltwater sprays over the rails, and I hold on with both hands. Normal rain rages until it's pouring down in cold sheets, and wind whips my hair into my face.

"We should get inside the bridge." Aaran's voice barely

reaches me over the booming thunder, rain pounding the deck, and crashing ocean.

The boat's rocking hurls me halfway across the deck, and I struggle to stay on my feet.

Aaran wraps his arm around my waist. "Hang on."

Loving the feel of his arm banding around me, I smile up at him, but my pleasure is short-lived.

Behind him, a dark mass moves across the sky, blending in with the storm clouds. For a moment, I think it's part of the weather, but it moves too purposefully to be nature. "Aaran?"

He follows my gaze. "Shadow demon!" Shoving me behind him, he raises his hands in defense. A golden wave pushes from his fingers, stopping the descent of the demon and sending it careening to the right.

Bert screams from the window, "Hang on!"

A wave crashes over the port side.

I'm swallowed by salt water and fall on my ass as I'm hurled across the deck. Only the rail keeps me from plunging into the ocean, the cold metal bruising my shoulder. Coughing up seawater, I search the sky, but it's dark, and all I see is the driving rain in the wheelhouse lights.

Water flows out the drains at the sides of the swamped deck, nearly taking me with it.

Grabbing my upper arm, Aaran helps me to my feet, then crouches, ready for the next attack.

Nancy rushes down the steps, and her glamor disappears. Long blond hair and a youthful face replace the middle-aged woman, while pointed ears push through, leaving no doubt of her elven nature. "There!" She points at the darkness, and a shard of silver shoots from her fingers, illuminating the shadow within the clouds.

The demon screams and changes direction to avoid the missile. It shoots straight up into the sky.

Bert screams, "What should I do?"

"Keep going!" Aaran commands and waves his hand toward the front of the boat.

The screeching of the demon returns.

Another wave floods the deck, but I'm holding tight to the rail and stay upright.

I've barely caught my breath and spit the salt from my mouth when the demon is spinning like a top and shooting straight for me. Lifting my hands, I pray for some kind of strength. A bright white light shoots out of my fingers. It pushes the demon into the sea.

Barely able to breathe, I stare at my hands as if I've never seen them before. How can this be possible?

The demon pops out of the sea and hovers at the rail. There's almost a human face in the black emptiness where a head should be. It stares at me, then turns to Aaran and flies forward like an arrow. With a deafening screech, it wraps itself around his throat.

Hitting the deck hard, Aaran's head bounces against the wood. His eyes roll back, and his face turns red. Then his color drains away.

Fury fills me from someplace deep inside and mixes with the terror of losing Aaran. He may be new in my life, but I'm not letting him die for me or because of me. Power surges through me, it balls up in the center of my chest, and I grab the shadow demon with both hands.

Blinding light pours from my hands, fills the demon, and explodes.

I hit the deck hard enough to jar my teeth.

Ash floats down in black smudges and is washed away by the driving rain.

Aaran gasps for air.

Crawling across the wooden deck, I make my way to him. Cupping his cheeks, I stare into his eyes. The soot on my fingers marks his pale face. "Talk to me!"

He blinks several times before focusing on me. "I'm okay. What did you do?" He touches the ash.

Nancy reaches for us. "Let's get you both inside." She helps Aaran up.

My hands shake, and my teeth chatter. Suddenly freezing, I make my way up the steps and into the wheelhouse.

The rain lightens as it hits the windows, and the boat's rocking eases.

Colored light outlines everything and everyone. Nancy is bathed in blue, and Bert in green. Aaran shines golden like a Greek statue. My hands glow the colors of the rainbow, then flash white before the lights fade. Unable to keep my knees from buckling, I sit shivering on a storage box behind the captain's chair. "It's cold."

Bert leaps to his feet. "Nancy, take the wheel. She's going into shock."

Everything gets a bit fuzzy as Bert eases me to my back. He puts something under my feet to raise them and covers me with blankets. "Take deep breaths, Harper. You're alright. Just breathe."

"I killed that thing?" My mind returns to the bright light and the ash.

"You were magnificent," Nancy says. "I've never seen magic like that."

Aaran caresses my cheek and combs my hair from my face. "You're fine, *mo chroi*. I've got you."

My heart slows, and it's easier to breathe. Things slowly come back into focus. "It was a person once, and I killed it. I did kill it, didn't I?"

"You did." Aaran kisses my forehead. "You saved my life."

"It's better off now, Harper." Nancy dries her hair with a blue towel. "They're living in a kind of hell as shadow demons. You did it a favor."

Bert says, "Take her down to the galley. Her pack is under the bench. Get her into some dry clothes."

"I'm sorry. I don't know what happened." I clutch Aaran's shoulders as he helps me down the narrow steps.

"Nothing to apologize for. You just used magic more powerful than any I've ever seen. It was bound to have some effect." I sit on the chair by the table while Aaran lifts the cushion on the bench and pulls out my small duffel bag. "Do you need help changing?"

I can't decide if he's blushing because he'd like to help or he wouldn't. My joints ache and my shoulder hurts, but I get to my feet and wrap my hand around the strap. Teeth still chattering, I attempt a smile. "Maybe you can undress me under better circumstances. I can manage."

Grabbing his backpack, he rewards me with a smile that almost makes me change my mind about the timing. He leans on the counter and cocks his gorgeous head. "I'd be happy to do that, Harper Craig."

The only parts of me that are warm are my cheeks,

which I'm sure are bright red. I rush into the tiny bunk room. Hands shaking, I manage to get myself out of my wet clothes and into dry ones. Glad to have packed an extra pair of sneakers, I pull them on. When I walk back into the galley, I stop short as Aaran pulls his black t-shirt over his broad back. Even though I've just experienced the impossible, my skin tingles with desire. This is one of the most emotional days I've ever lived through, and that's saying something. "Will there be more shadow demons?"

Aaran pulls his shirt down and turns toward me. "It must have taken extraordinary magic to get that one into this world. I wouldn't think she'd waste more magic to send a second. Even if she knows it failed, she'll wait for us to come to Domhan."

"Because magic has a price even for the witch queen?" I lay my wet clothes over a bar that runs along the wall. It's probably to keep the crew upright in rough seas, but it will work as a drying rack for now.

"Yes. Even she has to live within the reality of magical limitations." He places his wet clothes next to mine, then stares at me. "Thank you, Harper."

A tear rolls down my cheek. I nearly lost him.

He pulls me into his arms and holds me tight. "I'm sorry to have put you in danger."

"We both knew it would be like this." Speaking against his chest muffles my voice, but his nod against the crown of my head tells me he heard me.

"We should try to sleep. We have a few hours before we reach the portal."

Chapter Six

HARPER

Being in a tiny bed with Aaran is how I want to sleep every night for the rest of my life. It's not realistic, but it's a good dream.

Nancy's voice cuts through the perfect moment. "You two should come upstairs. We're pulling into the cove."

Aaran sighs. "I wish we could stay like this, *mo chroí*. You fit in my arms like you were made to be here."

"You say nice things." I push myself to sit and put on my sneakers. It shouldn't ache so much to move away from him. Wanting to take in one more deep breath and fill my senses with his woodsy essence is not a reasonable desire. Yet, it's there gnawing at me. Rolling my shoulders makes me wince.

"It's a nasty bruise. I can see it through that shirt. Let me heal it." He runs his hand along my neck and pushes my long-sleeve sleep shirt down, exposing my shoulder.

His touch burns through me like wildfire in summer. The tingle of his magic gives me goose bumps.

The pain ebbs, and I roll my shoulder again. If I stay like this much longer, I'm going to throw myself at him. "Thanks." I get up. "That's much better."

Without daring to look at him, I step into the galley. Gathering my damp clothes, I wish Aaran was a human man I met at the DMV and went to coffee with. I wish he and I were ordinary people getting to know each other. With a sigh, I fill my duffel. Nothing about us is normal, not how we met or who we are. For sure this journey isn't average.

Before I think too much, I climb the steep stairs to the bridge. Bright sunlight streams in, and the sea is as still as I've ever seen it. "It's like none of it ever happened."

"A new day." Bert stands at the helm and studies the water and land outside the windows as he slows the engines. He maneuvers his boat through a narrow break in what looks like a cliff and calls out to Nancy to throw the anchor.

As he cuts the motor, the anchor catches on the bottom and there's a slight jerk.

I lose my balance, but Aaran's arm wraps around my waist, steadying me. Heat flushes my cheeks, and he pulls away. Being near him is all I want and also too distracting. If I'm going to be part of saving his world, it should be for the right reasons. After the battle with the shadow demon, there's no doubt I'm meant to be here.

The sheer cliff rises beside the boat. I step onto the deck. "How will we reach the top?"

Nancy studies me for a long moment. Perhaps she's making sure I've recovered from my episode after killing the demon. She points to the cliff. "There are steps carved into the wall."

I follow her finger and see the steep stairs. "How did anyone manage that?"

"Magic." She shrugs. For her, such things are simple.

For me, I'm in a state of constant amazement.

Bert steps out, followed by Aaran. "It's a long climb."

Hugging him, Nancy says, "I'll come back when I can. You know I have to go."

The way Bert smiles at her, his dark eyes full of love, makes me yearn for what they have. He cups her cheek. "You don't think I'm letting you go without me, my Nancy?"

She shakes her head. "It's dangerous. You could be killed in a war that's not yours."

"I told you last night, your war is my war. We go together, or not at all." There's grit in Bert's voice that wasn't there before.

With a nod, Nancy kisses him hard on the lips. "Together then. What about the boat?"

"I called Bill while you slept and told him we'd be away a while. He'll come and fetch her." He gives the boat one more look, grabs a duffel from inside, and heads for the port side closest to the steps.

Dashing a tear from her cheek, Nancy follows. "Did you tell him to look after Moe's for us as well?"

"I did. I suppose we can call you Nainsi again, love."

Her laughter floats down the cliff.

I accept Aaran's steadying hand, and he holds mine, keeping me on the boat. "Thank you, Harper."

"You already thanked me for killing the demon."

Holding his hand, alone on the boat, if only for a moment, feels intimate.

"I appreciate you saving me, but you know we'll face far worse where we're going." His bright blue eyes shine with warning.

"I know." I'm not sure what his world holds for me, but war is dangerous, and I have no doubt I'm heading into a war with magical beings.

Leaning in, he kisses my cheek. "You are the bravest woman I've ever met. I will do all in my power to keep you safe and get you back to your mother."

I pull him in and press my lips to his. Sparks of what might have been under *normal* circumstances flash between us. His lips are strong and soft, and once I taste them, I don't want to stop.

"You're coming up or staying below?" Nainsi calls from halfway up the cliff, which ends our kiss.

Cheeks burning, I press my forehead to Aaran's chest.

He kisses the top of my head. "We'd better get going, *mo chroi.*"

The steps are uneven but well carved. Still, the sheerness of the view to my right makes me dizzy. I grip the rock and keep climbing.

"Don't look down." Aaran chuckles from a few steps below me.

"Why do people always say that when it only makes someone want to look?" Still, I take the advice and keep my eyes on the steps in front of me. My legs and ass are on fire when we reach the top, but then the view is spectacular.

The ocean and green land are like something out of a Gothic novel. Even with the heat of the sun, the wind is cool and steady. My hair flies into my eyes. We cross a flat area to three standing stones.

Nainsi grips Bert's hand. "Last chance to change your mind, my love."

"I go where you go," he says. There's no wavering in his tone. He'd run through fire for her.

My parents had a love like that, and I'd always dreamed I would find the same. After almost ten years of dating, I've fallen into doubt.

Standing in front of the stones, Aaran says words I don't understand and raises his hands. As he lowers them in an arc, a hole opens. It's black inside, and the wind whips erratically as it did the day I first met him.

Without a word, Nainsi and Bert step through and disappear.

Aaran looks back at me and offers his hand.

Swallowing down the lump of fear in my throat, I place my hand in his and step into the swirling wind. Inside the portal, it's as if I'm falling and flying at the same time. Stars zip past me at lightning speed and in every direction. There are colors and pitch darkness. My stomach roils, and I can't catch my breath. It feels as if my flesh is being ripped from my bones. I'm dying. There's no doubt in my mind. All of this, and I die with this portal chopping me to bits.

Then it all stops and Aaran grips my elbows to keep my knees from buckling. "We're here. Can you stand?"

"What the fuck was that?" Testing my legs, I lift one foot, then the other. "I think so."

"That was a portal. It's not pleasant." Sympathy fills those beautiful eyes.

"So when you came through the wall, it felt like you were being ripped to pieces."

He gave one little wince. I feel like my face will permanently show the agony of that horrible thing.

"That portal was made with oracle magic. It's not as bad."

"Why didn't it bring us to the mound near the old city?" Nainsi helps Bert stand and shakes off the effects.

Easing his hands away, Aaran makes sure I can keep my feet. "My mother altered the exit point so that it would always bring those in the light to a safe place. Every time a portal or the surrounding area is touch by dark magic, the spell alters the exit point. So, we don't always know where we'll land. The old city is never safe anymore. The witch queen has ruined it and much of the eastern continent with dark magic. This is better. At least we won't need another portal to bring us across the ocean."

Another sea, which is the darkest navy with a purple sheen, spreads as far as I can see. Above, three planets or moons shine in the pale blue sky.

My mouth is open, and I force it closed. "This is Domhan?"

Taking my hand, Aaran leads me away from the sea. "Part of it anyway. This is Clandunna in the south. It's not where I left from, nor where I expected us to arrive. I'd hoped we'd be closer to home." He points to a river flowing in the distance. "There's a village near the river. We should be able to get a meal and rest there We can get home via the river."

He says home as if I'm part of the place where his people are. My home is so far away now, I may never see it again. I release him and stare back at the flow of the foreign sea. It's beautiful, but the air rings with danger and death. The shadow demon I killed screams in my head, and I shake the memory away. That is what this place will become if I don't at least try. My heart aches for my world, for my mother. Soon I'll meet the people here and add them to my worries. *Harper, you made your decision. Pull up your big girl panties and see this through.*

Wrapping me in his arms from behind, he whispers, "Do you see the planets?"

I nod and shift my gaze from the ocean to the sky. It would probably be better if I didn't let him hold me, but I'm not strong enough to forgo his touch as well as my life in the human world. Aaran is the only thing about this journey that feels right.

"The larger orb is Eridan. The shadow of that world colors our sea. The smallest is her moon."

Everything is different. I have no idea what direction I'm facing in this new world. "What about the third?" I lean into his chest.

"That is Arcania. The Queen has taken that world and breeds her demons." Disgust roils through him, and I feel it through my senses more acutely than I've ever sensed anyone's feelings.

"Were there other people there that she destroyed?" I already know the answer, but I need to hear him say it.

"They were an elf-like race, though not as far along in their evolution as us. They were peaceful, and now they are oppressed and bespelled." He steps back.

"Is there no way to save them from her magic?" It seems unfair to give up on them.

His jaw ticks, and his shoulders are rigid. "None that we have found. All the light is gone from those who are turned."

"Where does the light go?" The suffering of Arcania flows across space and time, filling me with regret. If I had known sooner, could I have saved them?

Aaran shrugs. "Away." He reaches for my hand. "We should go to the village and rest. The journey from here to my home in Tús Nua will be difficult."

With a last look at the glowing sea and the celestial scenery of Domhan, I put aside light and dark thoughts and walk across the green grass between jutting rocks toward a valley where homes look like dollhouses from this distance.

Nainsi and Bert are far ahead, walking side by side.

At the edge of town, Nainsi speaks to a tall elven couple who nod slowly at whatever she's saying.

They turn to look in our direction, and I hesitate.

Aaran squeezes my hand. "It's fine, Harper. These are good people."

Like Nainsi and Aaran, the elves of Clandunna are tall and beautiful. They look as if they're perhaps thirty, but Aaran looks far younger than his age, so these new elves might be much older.

As we approach, the woman smiles at Aaran. "You are well, my friend Riordan?" She takes both of his hands in hers and kisses his cheek.

"Well enough, but not where I expected to be. As nice as it is to see you, Selina, I thought I'd be closer to home." He turns to the man and gives the same greeting. "Jax."

Jax bows his head smoothly. "Aaran Riordan, you are welcome, as are those who travel with you. Clandunna is honored to have you here with your long-awaited friend."

Though he calls me friend, he looks at me warily at best. His lips are pulled in a tight line, his eyes sharp with concern.

"Thank you. May I introduce Harper Craig of the human world? She has agreed to help us in our hour of need." He draws me closer with a hand at the small of my back.

Unsure how to greet these elves, I smile and wait.

Aaran says, "Harper, this is Selina and Dax of the Clandunna. They are the caretakers of this place. In your world, a mayor of sorts."

I offer my hands. "Caretaker sounds far nicer. It's a pleasure to meet you."

Taking my hands, Selina smiles, making her even more beautiful. "We're happy you're here, Harper. We've waited many suns."

Once they both kiss me on the cheek, we walk into the village. Dozens of stone houses are organized in groupings that I imagine are families as they expand and grow. It's organic and makes sense at the same time.

A group of little boys play in a nearby field. No girls. Only beautiful male children. Even if by some miracle we defeat the witch queen, break the curse, and save this world, it will take a generation to regain what they've lost. So many questions roll around in my head, but I'm being introduced to every elf we pass as we make our way to the center of town, where we sit at a large table.

"Your father was here when the moons were full," Selina tells Aaran. "It was kind of him to come all this way to check on us."

"He and my mother are worried for all of Domhan."

Jax brings a large pitcher and glasses and pours enough

for everyone before he sits. "Your mother bid him come to tell us about the portals, and I think to make sure we were still here and had not fallen to darkness."

The drink is a cider, definitely alcoholic, and the fruit is similar to an apple, but different. I can't remember when I ate last, so I sip slowly. "Does the witch queen come or send shadow demons?"

Jax's eyes darken, and his knuckles whiten on the glass. "Her minions are getting closer, but our magic is strong. Nothing without light can enter our domain. Selina has seen to it with the oracle's help." He looks at her with loving eyes.

"I pray the magic will hold long enough." Selina's lips pull into a frown. "Your father didn't have news of you or your brothers. I hope they too have found a human woman willing to help."

The Jersey Girl in me has her doubts. I mean, it's one thing to convince one human woman to risk her life for an alien world, quite another to convince three. I may have come all this way for nothing, and with the portals out of whack, the chances of my getting home are even smaller.

Despite all there is to see and hear, my eyelids start to droop.

Selina gasps. "You're exhausted. I'm sorry. We shall show you where you can rest, and have a fine feast tonight to celebrate your coming."

The gray stone house is cool and comfortable, with three bedrooms joined by a large living area. Two couches and a chair are covered in moss-green cloth, and a braided rug in the center of the room reminds me of the one in my grand-mother's house when I was little.

My head feels fuzzy, and I'm not sure if it's the cider,

exhaustion, or that I'm going mad from so much information so quickly.

An elf with brown hair and green eyes shows me to my room. "My name is Baily, Miss Craig, and should you need anything, I live in the house to the right. There's cider and wine in the cold box, as well as bread and butter in the larder if you're hungry."

"Thank you. I think, for now, I just need to rest. You can call me Harper." Through the open door, the white fluffy bed almost screams out for me. I drift in its direction.

"Harper it is, then. I'll let you rest. We're all very glad you've come." Her voice is filled with hope.

My heart clenches. At the bedroom door, I turn back toward her. "I'm glad to be here, but I'm just a woman. I'm no warrior, Baily. I have no idea how to stop a witch or break a curse. I came because Aaran asked, and he saved my mother's life. I came because I don't want this world to die because I was too afraid to try."

What I admitted should terrify Baily, but she grins wide. "Maybe that you care about a race of people you knew nothing of is a kind of magic too, Harper. You're part of the prophecy, and nowhere in it did it say go to the human world and find warrior women. It said to find the right women. I believe Aaran did that tenfold when he found you."

I'm going to cry if I stay here another moment. "Thank you." I back into the bedroom and close the door.

I have no idea how long I've slept when Aaran's arms slip around me. "Is it time to get up?"

"No, *mo chroi*. Sleep. I just wanted to…"

My body responds as if he said make love, even though he didn't. I roll toward him. "To what?"

A sliver of sunlight slips through the curtains and shines across his bright blue eyes, but there's fear there too. "Know that you're safe, you're real, you're here in Domhan."

Somehow his fear makes me feel better. I'd hate to think I was the only one. I smooth his hair away from his forehead. "I'm real enough." I touch his lips and press my hips forward.

He eases his knee between my thighs. "Why, Harper?"

"Does there have to be a reason?" Threading my fingers through his hair, I kiss his throat.

His cock is thick and hard against my hip as he leans in and grips the back of my head. Close enough to kiss me, he holds back. "There's always a reason. I want you. You must know that. I've wanted you almost from the first moment I saw you."

"Then why are we talking?" I kiss his chin then suck his bottom lip into my mouth.

Warm and welcoming, his mouth caresses mine, drawing low moans from us both. He breaks the kiss. "If you're giving yourself to me out of fear, I'd rather wait for another emotion. Desperation, fear, and loss are the emotions I feel flowing from you, Harper, and I understand them. You're far from home and everything you know. I want to comfort you. I want to be what you need. But sex should be more between us."

"So elves only have sex for morally suitable reasons?"

His laugh is sexy as hell. "No, we have sex for all the

reasons, including fun and lust." The look in his eyes is intense as he stares into mine. I hear his voice in my head. *"I just want it to be more between us."*

"You're in my head? I heard you." My pulse speeds.

"What did you hear?"

Maybe I have lost my mind. "You said you wanted there to be more between us. But you didn't say it out loud."

He kisses my cheek, my nose, and my lips. "That's something new. Hearing entire sentences isn't even something I've ever been able to do. Mostly I just sense feelings and the occasional 'I'm going to hit him with a bat.'"

That seems like so long ago. "I would hate to die and never to have known what it was like to be with you."

Aaran leans in and rolls his hips just enough to add fire to the spark between my legs.

An enormous crash jerks us both upright and breaks the moment.

"Hell!" Bert's voice carries from the living room.

After kissing my nose, Aaran gets out of bed. "I suppose that was a sign of sorts."

I swing my legs over the side of the bed. "It must be."

We step out of the bedroom, and Bert is in the kitchen with glass and cider on the floor and blood seeping from the bottom of his bare feet. His dark hair is sticking out in the worst bedhead I've ever seen, and he's wearing his boxers and nothing else. "I wanted a piece of bread and knocked over the pitcher."

Nainsi rubs her eyes and joins us. "Well, you've got yourself in a fine pickle, Bertram Donaldson."

"Yes, well when the lot of you are done gaping, maybe you could help a fellow out."

Chapter Seven

AARAN

The cut on the bottom of Bert's foot is deep, but after a good tongue lashing, Nainsi heals it.

I am sorry for the interruption, but perhaps it's for the best. I'll need more than a quick tumble with Harper, and there isn't time for more than that.

A crowd is gathering in the center of the village, and the guest house is only a few steps away from all the commotion.

Late summer brings cooler nights and is reason enough for a large fire to set a party around. Harper's arrival has lifted the spirits of these people. They see hope where before there were only visions of the end of our lives, our way of life.

Watching her dance with one of the boys, I wish I could spare her all of this. If I had let her mother die, she might have been safe in the human world. An impossible choice, but I still don't know if it was the right one. Though at the time, it felt obvious to save Maggie and spare Harper the loss of another parent. For my own selfish reasons, I want her back in her strange little connected home, safe from what's to come.

Her laugh is like music on the breeze.

If I had left her there, she would not lie in my arms as we rest or look at me as if I'm all she sees. Perhaps that need for her attention is even more selfish.

Maybe she hears my thoughts. She turns to me, and her warm smile draws me in. Her hair shines in the firelight with streaks of red and blond in a rare moment when it's loose about her shoulders. Selina sent Harper a flowing green dress that sparkles with silver threads and hugs her curves.

Like a fish on her hook, I'm reeled in until I'm standing inches from her. "You look very beautiful."

Her cheeks turn the most delicious peach color. "I'm glad you think so." She smooths her hands down the soft silk of the dress, accentuating the way it fits along the sides of her breasts and narrows at her waist. "I've never worn anything so elegant."

Three elves with a fiddle, lute, and drum are our entertainment for the evening. They play a slower, softer tune than the jig Harper danced with the boy.

I wrap an arm around her waist and take her hand. "I'm sorry to have dragged you into this. Maybe I shouldn't say that, or even think it, but I would take you home to safety if I could."

Her lips are full, and knowing how soft they are, it's hard to concentrate on the steps of the dance. She cocks her head, and her waves of luscious hair tumble along her long neck. "You have no choice, Aaran. If your oracle is right, all of these people will die without me and the other two human women. Do you think I want that to happen? I'm afraid, terrified actually, but I said I would do this, and I will if I can."

How had she become this brave soul? Her gaze shifts to the group of young boys playing near the edge of the party, and then to the large group eating at the long tables laden with every kind of food. Everyone is happy and hopeful, while I'm wishing she were home safe with her mother.

Fear and worry reflect in her green eyes before she closes them and presses her cheek to my shoulder. "Let's just enjoy the night. Tomorrow we can think about shadows and light."

"Wise as well as beautiful." I wrap her tightly in my arms. "How will I do without you when you return to your world?"

She sighs against me. "I imagine you'll go on with your life here. From what I understand, your mother is an important person. You'll likely have many duties to fulfill. You'll have no time to think about the human woman you once knew for a short time."

"I hope you know that's not true." Unable to resist, I comb my fingers through her silken hair. "I imagine I will think of you every day of my life, Harper Craig, and elves live a long time."

"You always say nice things." Another sigh and then the music ends.

Nainsi grabs Harper's hand. "Come and eat something. You have never had a true elven feast, and there are many lovely things to try."

There's no choice but to release her, though I want to hold her for a lifetime or more.

"She is lovely." Selina offers me a cup of cider. "I have never seen a human before. I expected them to look more like Nainsi's mate." She nods toward the burly dark-haired fisherman.

"Humans are even more diverse than elves, Selina." I keep an eye on Harper as she tries the fish pie.

"Are they all as brave and noble as the two here tonight?" Selina drinks, and as Jax joins us, she wraps her arm through his.

"I was only there for a few weeks, but I would say they are some brave and some cowardly, some noble and some ignoble. They are as varied as the snowflakes in winter." I love the way Harper's nose wrinkles when she doesn't like the sour wine an elder gives her to try.

"And evil? Are there those who are evil among them?" Jax looks toward the woods that border the land to the east.

I search where he's looking but see nothing. When I was at Harper's home, I watched her television each day. It was full of news of such things. "I didn't meet anyone who felt dark, but I heard stories of murder and chaos in the human world. Not dissimilar to Domhan."

Jax's eyes are sharp, and his jaw ticks. "But here we have elves like me who sense the evil in another."

Patting his arm, Selina soothes, but says, "And yet, with all our abilities, we didn't stop Vanora from becoming a monster, or the people who followed her from being turned into shadow demons. Do not judge the human world, Jax. We know little of it other than they lack magic."

Not swayed, Jax continues, "Yet I feel the magic in this woman Aaran brought. It is strong."

"She is in the light." I shouldn't have to defend Harper. Even if I did, it shouldn't feel so ferocious.

Selina steps in front of her husband and presses a hand to his chest. "Do not insult our guests."

Jax nods once in acceptance.

Turning toward me, Selina's eyes are bright and sympathetic. "Harper is neither light nor dark. I feel her magic as keenly as Jax does. You would too if you would allow yourself to see."

"I was sent to find her and bring her here. I've seen her magic as she used it to save my life and kill a shadow demon. She is in the light." I force my hands to relax so I'm not threatening the leader of an elven community. My heart is pounding, and I take a step back as well.

With a soft smile, Selina shows why she is the leader here. "No one is accusing this chosen one of anything, Aaran. We are only noting that she could be turned to darkness, as it too lives within her. I find her charming and true, but her magic is a rainbow of light with all the colors showing. Surely you have seen that."

Remembering the first time Harper's aura appeared in the hotel mirror, I can't deny that there were dark hues as well as light. "I have seen."

"Then we must pray that her character is as strong as her magic." Jax's stance has relaxed, and he wraps an arm around Selina's waist.

"I believe in Harper Craig. I have staked my life on it." My heart tightens as I watch her close her eyes in rapture over a sweet bite of dessert.

HARPER

The party is still going on late into the night. The bonfire has been fed, and sparks roar into the darkness.

The planets and moon appear smaller and sit higher in the sky. Another has risen, and I'm told that's another moon. It looks similar to Earth's moon, and I can't help admiring other similarities between my world and Aaran's. This place and these people have burrowed under my skin and into my heart in such a short time that I can hardly breathe from the responsibility of their lives.

Suddenly the party feels too crowded, too close.

Walking out of the circle of firelight, I head for the trees and some peace. I need to think. The orbiting celestial bodies and stars give plenty of light, and soon I'm sitting alone on a boulder with only the trees for company.

What if I'm the weakest link in this impossible chain? What if it's my fault these people die, or worse, are turned into shadow demons? I'm clumsy and a devout procrastinator. My closets are a mess, and I rarely fold my clothes before I stuff them in a drawer. How am I the savior for these people?

My breath is coming harder and faster, and my head gets light. Leaning forward, I put my head between my knees. "Breathe, Harper. Don't pass out alone in the woods of a strange world."

"It would make things easier if you did, as you say, pass out." A woman's stern voice cuts the silence.

I stand and put my hands up as if I have some kind of weapon.

A portal with no swirl or wind is open in the trees, and in front of it is a woman with raven hair and large hazel eyes. "You look very ordinary to be a prophecy."

"Who are you?" I step back, but my calves hit the boulder.

"I can end all your worries, chosen one." She's beautiful, but something about her makes my stomach churn. "I am Vanora Braddish. You should be honored I came for you personally. I wouldn't make the journey for just anyone."

"The witch queen," I mutter.

Her smile reveals straight white teeth, but even they look wrong. "I am all-seeing, all-knowing. You wish to be released from this unfair burden these elves have placed on you. I can give you that. Come with me, and I'll spare your world when the time comes."

"I don't believe you."

Her eyes flash with rage, and for a second, she's not beautiful. Her eyes are sunken black holes in a rutted face and her hair is wiry and thin. Then she's again stunning. "You doubt my word?"

It's a glamor. This is what she looked like before she gave in to the darkness growing inside her. I don't even need to touch her to feel the putrefaction of her soul. "Everything about you is a lie, Vanora Braddish."

She lifts her hand, and dark fire shoots from her palms.

I duck and cover my head while holding my hands up and praying for strength.

The dark magic bounces off me and hits a tall tree behind me. The tree explodes, and raindrop-size shards of wood and bits of leaves rain down.

Screams sound from the village, and soon the sound of running feet reaches us.

Vanora narrows her gaze on me. "What are you?"

"Nothing. I'm a woman." I have no idea what she means or what I'm meant to say. I don't know why her magic bounced off me, and if I'm honest, I have no business defending anyone against this creature.

"And you accuse me of lying. No one and nothing can stop my magic."

Aaran, Nainsi, Bert, Jax, and Selina rush into the woods, followed by hundreds of armed elves. Aaran has his sword out and his other hand raised for magic. They stop short at the sight of Vanora.

The way she shattered that tree, I fear for them. Standing between the witch queen and the people of Clandunna, I realize she could kill them with another blast, and maybe I could save a few, but not all. "What do you want from me, witch?"

Aaran steps forward.

Shooting magic at another tree, Vanora backs him off and shatters the arbor to tiny bits. "Stay back, eldest of the Riordan. I will kill them all. This is between me and your chosen human. Let her decide how this evening of celebration will end." She looks at me. "Come with me now, chosen one." She practically spits out the title. "Or I will see this village razed to the ground. I will kill every living thing within the stench of this place. It will be nothing but death for as far as your feeble eyes can see. Choose."

Aaran watches, his face stricken with pain and worry. *Can he know my choices are untenable? He must know. Watch all these people I came here to save die, or go to my death with this evil monster.* I focus my thoughts on his. *I will hold on as long as I can. Keep them safe.*

In return, I hear Aaran's voice clear and true in my mind. *I will come for you, mo chroi.*

Gripping my hands together so she can't see how they shake, I turn my back on the elves and walk into the shadowy portal with the witch queen.

AARAN

Jax and Selina have been arguing for ten minutes over the value of saving Harper, or if it's even possible. Their four children, all boys, sit on the steps of the cottage, their blond heads turning as they look at their mother and then their father as if they're at a sporting match.

Nainsi is attempting reason with a compelling speech about the fact that we'll all die eventually if we don't save Harper.

Bert remains silent but stays by my side. I have the feeling, despite his lack of magic, he knows what I'm planning.

It's nice to have someone's full support.

I'm only half listening. How can I get to the old city quickly and without being detected? Once I get there, how do I reach Harper without being turned into a shadow demon? No elf has ever returned from the old city since Vanora and her followers overthrew my mother's government.

Selina turns toward me. "I assume you're going no matter what is decided here?"

"Do you have the means to speak to my mother?" My magic is not going to be enough. I have questions only my mother can answer.

After studying me for a long moment, she says, "I can call to her through the scrying bowl."

Jax shakes his head. "We don't know if the witch can intercept those messages."

"We don't know that she can't either, and I suspect she's a bit busy with other matters at this moment." Selina opens a cupboard under the stairs and pulls a glass bowl nearly two feet in diameter from the shelf. Bringing it to the table, she says, "Broc, fetch some water."

The eldest boy jumps from the steps and runs to the kitchen. A few moments later, he returns with a pitcher of water.

Taking it from him, Selina smooths his hair. She pours the water into the scrying bowl until the vessel is nearly full, then backs away. "Do you know the magic, or do you need me to begin?"

I stand over the bowl. "I know the magic." Closing my eyes, I focus my thoughts, pushing the strain and worry over Harper to the back of my mind. It takes all my training to move her out of the forefront, and the image of her stepping through the dark portal is the last thing to budge.

Calling the magic, I open my eyes and think of my mother. The water in the bowl wavers as if someone spilled a drop at the center. My mother's blue eyes and the feather made of gold that she wears in her hair are the first things I see. Her image is murky but becomes clearer until she's smiling up at me, as comforting and beautiful as ever.

"Aaran, you are well?" The relief in her voice warms me.

My father's face slides in next to hers. "We're happy to see you. Where are you? Did you find her?"

"It's more than good to see you both too. I'm fine. We came through with Nainsi and her man Bert." My burden feels a bit easier seeing my parents and knowing they're well. "We're in Clandunna. Have Raith or Liam come home?"

Mother shakes her head. "We've not heard from either of your brothers yet."

"Did the human woman come back with you?" My father is all business, even though I know he's glad I'm alive and well.

"That's why I'm scrying for you. Mother, Vanora took her. She threatened the village to get Harper to go with her. I have to go after her, but I don't know the magic to get me to the old city without being detected." The hint of desperation in my voice isn't something I'm proud of, but there's no help for it. I feel as if my heart has been torn in half.

Sorrow shines in Mother's eyes. "That poor woman. Vanora will try to change her."

"She may already be a shadow demon." My father curses.

Nainsi says, "No. I don't think it's that simple to change the chosen one, Brion. If she could have, she'd have done it while we were all watching. That would have ended all our hopes. If should could have made us think Harper ran off, she'd have taken the girl without any fuss. Instead, a tree exploded. One of the very old ones, as if it was giving its last to send out a warning. I think Vanora attacked Harper and somehow the tree was the casualty. Whatever magic is in that girl, and I've seen the beginnings of it, it may be stronger than the witch queen's."

That gets Father's attention. "You can use the ancient gates. Vanora can't control the magic of the old gods. I'll warn you, the ride is pretty rough, but you can land less than a mile to the west of the old city. It's on a hillside, and there will be some cover, but not much."

Mother nods. "From Clandunna, the nearest gate is twenty miles east. There you'll find an old stone gate hidden in a stand of trees. Use caution, Aaran. Your magic has to be pure and full of light if you're to get to her without losing yourself. If Selina can part with a few good soldiers, take a small party."

"I will give you what you need," Selina says.

Father's frown says it all. He knows trying to gain access to the old city and the castle is near to suicide. Once it was our capital, and we called it Priomn Bhail; now it is Tobhtá, ruin. I was born there but feel few ties to the place. The valley where my mother and father hold the peace is my home.

Father says, "Without the chosen ones, we are doomed, son."

"I promised her I would come for her and protect her. I'll not waver on that promise."

Mother cocks her head as if she's looking inside my soul. Her smile is soft and knowing. "I know you will always do what is right. We don't doubt you, Aaran. We are parents who fear losing our oldest child."

I swallow down the knot in my throat. "I'll see you soon." As I let the magic go, the water dims, and the images disappear.

Nainsi slaps me on the back. "I thought for a moment you would let her go."

"No." I grip the hilt of my sword.

"I didn't hear you make her any promises in the woods." Jax slips his sword into the sheath at his side.

"We can speak without words." It seems personal, but if I'm going to gain a few warriors from Clandunna, I'll have to be as honest as I can.

Selina steps close and cups my cheeks. Looking deeply into my eyes, she examines me as if I'm new to her. "You have a bond with Harper?"

I nod. "Though I didn't know such a thing was possible without other intimacies." Most people only gain such a bond after sex on the night of their promise.

Cocking her head, Selina says, "No. Nor did I. I must stay here and protect the people. Jax will go with you, and he will choose four more of our best warriors. I don't imagine you will want too large a group."

I bow. "Thank you, Selina. The eight of us will be more than enough and small enough to slip through unnoticed."

Jax grips Bert's shoulder. "The old portals are not meant for your kind. Are you certain you wish to go on this mission, Bert Donaldson?"

"Will it kill me?" There's no fear in Bert's question.

Jax smiles wildly. "No, but it may make you wish you were dead for a moment or two."

"I can live with that." Bert is a strong man who earned his muscles through hard work at sea.

"Let's get you a weapon. Do you think you can handle a sword?" Jax starts toward the door with Nainsi and Bert.

"I'm better with throwing knives, but a good dagger might do."

I watch them go, and I stare at the closed door long after they're gone. Closing my eyes, I lean my palms on the table. "I should have protected her better. I never saw her leave the party."

Selina sits and slowly spins the scrying bowl. "You will find her and get her out of there. I do not doubt you or Harper Craig. She is true, and I think her heart leans toward good."

Selina's four sons sit with their sweet faces between the spindles on the stairs. I want to save them. Four pairs of blue eyes blink back at me. I pray that my brothers and I will succeed and help save them and the world for them to grow up in. "Even though Jax doubts her?"

Looking at her boys, she smiles. "I long for a daughter for them to dote on. Jax is cautious about things he doesn't understand. The world of humans is wrought with tales of dishonor, and that is what worries him."

"There are many stories that tell the opposite. But I understand his concern. We all fear what we don't know. I thought I would walk into the human world, tell Harper to come with me, and be back at the Watchers' Gate in five minutes." I laugh at my arrogance.

"Harper is not a woman to be bullied." Selina grins.

"No. Nor is she a woman who does anything without reason. She saved this village tonight. Vanora knew she couldn't destroy Harper with the magic at her disposal. She needs something more for that, but she could have killed these people. Harper has known you for only a few hours, yet she traded her life for yours." I wish I could have talked her out of it, but at the same time, I'm so proud of her.

"She is more than we expected." Selina dashes a tear away. "My people will migrate toward the new city in the valley. We will join your mother for the battles to come. We have hidden in the safety of my magic for too long. And tonight, it failed. Vanora found a way through." She sighs and looks at the wide eyes of her children. "Regardless of the promises made tonight, she will kill or take who she can. I have no faith in her word."

I admire Selina's reasoning and pity her task of moving her home, family, and people. "My mother will be honored by your coming."

With a final bow, I go back to the guest house and gather mine and Harper's things.

Chapter Eight

HARPER

In the unlikely event that I live through the witch queen's torture, I search the long throne room for anything that might help. Faded gold and white arches reach to a high ceiling. It was probably a beautiful hall where parties were held. Now it's a black and gray tomb with shadow demons hovering around the perimeter. Soot darkens the dozen tall windows, and barely any sunlight comes through. It's like a long-forgotten Gothic cathedral, but nothing holy could exist here.

Darkness and shadows.

I thought I would be brave in the face of whatever Vanora did to me, but my screams echo off the towering, singed stone walls. Black lightning shoots from her fingers and rips into my body. It feels like my blood is on fire, and my bones are being crushed. I collapse to the rough blood-stained stone floor. I will die soon. Blood, my blood, marks everything. I should be dead already. This horrible magic is far worse than the portal.

Vanora screams in frustration. "Why won't she turn? What magic does this puny human have that can thwart my spells?" She strides down the steps of the dais and approaches, but stops a few feet away. "What is the source of your magic?"

"I have no magic." I try to focus on her face, but my vision is blurry as every part of me wants to fall into oblivion and make this agony stop.

"Lies!" she screeches. "I am the most powerful elf that has ever lived. I am the witch queen. None can resist my magic. You will become part of my shadow demon army. You will be my shining warning to all who would act against me. None will dare come to aid them once one of their prophesized humans is mine."

Still not breaching some invisible line between us, she shoots her magic at me, and I career across the bone-breaking floor. My skin tears and scrapes in a dozen places. Pain beyond measure fills my soul.

Where Aaran's magic had been easy and cool, like grass in a spring breeze, Vanora's magic hurts, even when not directed at me. It's like a nail digging a path through a steel pipe or the stripping of a metal screw where everyone around cringes.

"There are no old trees to protect her here. Why won't she die? Why won't she be taken?" Panic tinges Vanora's voice.

She's afraid of me. There's power in that.

"She will fall, my queen. They all will. We will find the

right magic to break these human interlopers." The masculine voice sounds calm and confident.

Vanora storms past me, still keeping her distance, and another set of feet follow her.

As my gaze clears, I keep my movements slow and slight, hoping they won't notice me watching. Knowledge is my only power now. A few feet from me, on a dais, Vanora is slouched on an ornate throne. The wood is dark green and gold with inset jewels that have been polished to a shine. It's the only clean spot in the room.

Strange she would make one spot clean. Why not keep the entire castle alive for her use. I don't know much about magic, but it seems a small thing to clean or make someone else do it. Unless what looks like charring is something darker. Maybe her evil has permeated the walls. So why not the throne? Too many questions without answers.

With her elbow on the padded arm, Vanora leans on her hand. She's even paler than she was in the woods. Perhaps trying to kill me has weakened her.

Aaran said that even Vanora had to deal with the limitations of magic and its costs.

"I want her to feel the emptiness of shadow." Her voice bites with rage.

A tall, slim man stands at her right hand. "I will help you find the magic that will destroy her and those like her. We will make the humans from the prophecy wish they'd never been born, and when we are done with Domhan, we will take the human world for our own." With hair as white as snow, he has a face as young and fair as all the elves. His eyes are black as night, and his lips rosy, like a child's. He is a hideous amalgamation of contrast. Once, he might have been handsome; now evil emanates from his every pore.

With eyes filled with adoration, she looks up at him. "Do you promise, Ciaran? I'm tired and need to rest. Will you go through the old scrolls and find the magic to destroy that?" She waves a hand in my general direction.

I close my eyes and hold my breath. Going unnoticed for a time is my best hope. I don't think I can survive more torture.

Ciaran commands, "Take it away. Put it in the dungeon."

Footsteps pad across the stone, and two sets of dirty bare feet approach me. I'm lifted gently and removed from the hall. A tall, sallow-faced elf with his head covered by a brown hood is my transport. He follows a smaller elf with a similar hood.

Rather than being handled like baggage as I expect, I'm reverently held like a child, carried down several passages and staircases, and placed on the floor of a cell.

"Who are you?" My voice is rough and scrapes painfully against my raw throat.

"Dorian." He gestures to the female elf. "Cara."

"I am Harper. Why are you here?" Why are these beautiful creatures filthy and living in this evil place?

Dorian cocks his head. "She took everyone from our village, bound our magic, and brought us here to serve her. She turns those who oppose her into shadow demons." He points out the barred window high on the wall where dark wisps of evil troll the sky.

"I'm sorry." I try to sit up, but every molecule in my body hurts, so I rest my cheek on the cold stone floor.

Removing his hooded cloak, Dorian says, "Our enslavement was not your doing." He lays it on the ground, and then lifts me onto it. "You must be important and powerful to have resisted her magic and made her so angry."

"I'm supposed to help two others defeat her." Even shrugging hurts. I ball up the hood and rest my cheek on the rough fabric. "Thank you, Dorian."

He nods gravely. "Cara will return with food, and if we can find some medicine, we will bring it. Her voice was removed with magic, and she cannot speak. The witch queen needed Cara's healing magic, so she wasn't completely bound like the rest of us. Many other forms of magic require spoken spells, but she can still heal and help you as healing magic is through touch."

My chest tightens thinking of what these elves have suffered under the thumb of a tyrant.

They turn, walk out of my cell and close the door.

A moment later, the lock clicks into place, though I see no jailer.

Maybe this is where I'll die. My heart knows Aaran will come for me. I don't know how or when, but he will do whatever it takes to free me. All I have to do is stay alive long enough to be rescued.

The portal could have taken me a day or weeks away, so it's impossible to know how long before Aaran, Bert, and Nainsi will come to help me. The idea of weeks of the torture I just endured makes me ache in my soul. My body hurts too much to sob the way I need to, but the tears come and dampen Dorian's cloak.

Outside, demons screech as they circle the castle. The window has no glass, and the sound grates on the inside of my skull and grows louder until my cell rings with their horror. My skin prickles with their pain, as if I've touched someone deeply troubled and can't get away.

This is its own kind of suffering. I cover my ears with my hands, but their pain bleeds through, and I'm riddled with the pain of the demons' purgatory. I want to save them, but they are hers and beyond help from me or anyone else. I think about Dorian and Cara and wonder how many other elves are held here as slaves. At least they might be rescued. Trying to focus on what can be done eases the flow of shadow demon pain, but doesn't remove it.

Unable to sleep, I shake and have no control to reel in the emotions or the effects.

It might be hours or minutes that passed before Cara returns. Silently, she places a tray on the stone floor and kneels beside me. Placing her hand on my cheek, she somehow dims the onslaught of the shadow demons' torment. Her touch is feather-like, and her fingers cool. Without a word, she conveys that I must build a wall in my mind to keep them out.

I pray for the strength to build that wall, and the screeching leaves my head. Though they can still be heard outside.

"Thank you, Cara." I struggle to sit.

Offering her hand, she silently helps me, but will not meet my gaze.

I take the cup of water, and with shaking hands, I drink. After one bite of the hard biscuit, I put it down. The effort is too great.

Cara takes a packet from inside her cloak. The beautiful green dress I borrowed from Selina is ripped along my side and the silver has lost its sheen. Cara pulls the fabric aside.

She smooths something cool on my skin along my battered ribs.

I jerk away from the touch. "Sorry. It hurts." I keep my voice low so I don't scare her off.

Cara's eyes are soft blue and full of sympathy. She continues to tend my cuts and bruises. The light buzz of her magic eases my pain enough that I can take a full breath.

Vanora made me bleed. No. It was the stone floor that cut me when I fell. "Why doesn't she use a sword or knife?"

The hint of a smile plays on Cara's lips.

I don't expect a reply, but I like that she smiles. At least I know she can hear me, even if she can't speak. "She could shoot an arrow through my heart and kill me. I'm only flesh and blood. Is it pride or something else?"

As Cara smooths the salve along my shoulder blade, it hurts so much I wince. Her hand stills for a moment, and then she continues. When she finishes, she looks at me and presses her hands together as if in prayer.

I don't know if she means to say that she'll pray for me or that I should pray. I can promise her that I'm praying. Instead of saying that, I give the same gesture. My father's ring no longer sits on my finger. It must have fallen off. "Thank you. You are very kind."

The thought of my treasure in the hands of that horrible witch is somehow worse than torture. It's completely stupid considering my situation, but I wait for Cara to leave before I let the tears fall. I shouldn't cry over a ring. I'm alive, and I should be thankful for that. Still, that ring felt like the last link to my world.

Somehow, I have to live. This world may not survive if I die. That horrible man said they'd go to Earth next. I can't let either world suffer if I can stop it. "Why doesn't Vanora stab me through the heart?"

With my eyes closed, I float in a space between asleep and awake. The liminal state is soft, and the pain of my flesh ebbs away. This is how I imagine death will feel.

"You are not dead, Harper Craig." The voice is strong and feminine.

I open my eyes, and rather than the cold cell of my prison, I'm in a field where a breeze moves the grass. But I don't feel the wind or the grass. "This isn't real."

An elven woman with long blond hair and bright blue eyes walks out of a cloud and stands in front of me. "It's not false either, daughter of the human world. You are here with me in your mind. I hoped you might relax enough that I could speak to you."

There's something familiar about her. Her gaze is direct with command and kind with concern. "You're Aaran's mother?" She barely looks older than him, but I know I'm right just the same.

She smiles and dips her chin in the slightest nod. "Elspeth Riordan. He blames himself for you being in danger."

"Is he coming for me?" I've never had a dream so real, yet I know this is more reality than vision.

"He will do what he can, but it will be up to you to survive." She steps closer and puts a hand on my cheek.

I can't feel her touch, but I sense the mothering it conveys. "He saved my mother's life. Even though I told him I wouldn't come and help him, he saved her life. It nearly killed him. You should be very proud of him."

Staring at me, she cocks her head. "He is a fine man. You

have changed him. I only saw him in the scrying pool, but I could see the change." She shakes the thought away, and her expression grows serious. "Listen to me now. There isn't much time. Vanora will try to turn you, kill you, and even make you a demon. You must hold on. You're not elven or of a world she's learned the magic of. It will take her time to learn enough to do you real harm."

"Why doesn't she use a blade?"

Elspeth tightens her jaw in the same way Aaran does when he's considering something. "She doesn't wish to get too close to you. It's wise not to touch unknown magic."

"She could shoot an arrow or throw a spear. There are so many ways to kill a human. Why does she only use magic?" It feels like this is important.

"I will ask the oracle. In the meantime, we shall count it a blessing. Stay alive, Harper. Help is coming." Elspeth fades away as a cloud blows in and covers her.

Lying on the stone and Dorian's cloak, I shiver, even in my sleep.

AARAN

Twenty miles doesn't seem like much, but when you factor in rough terrain and no roads, it takes longer than I'd like, even on the fine horses meant to make the journey easier. The entire way, I'm near panic thinking about what Harper might be enduring.

She's still alive. I can't quite explain how I know, but I feel her inside me, as if her heart beats alongside mine. There's comfort in that, but it's not enough. I want to tear a hole in the world to get to her, but I have to settle for an ancient portal created by the old gods.

When we reach the stand of trees marked by a jagged stone jutting from the ground, we dismount.

Jax hands his reins to his son. "You'll take the horses and meet your mother on the road." He ruffles his hair.

Once the animals are tethered, Broc mounts, and with one last look at his father, he rides down the mountain toward the road where Selina's people will migrate toward the new city.

I step past the stone and through the edge of the forest. Blinking until my eyes adjust to the shade of the woods, I focus on two large pillars capped by a black stone to form an arch. Like the trees near Clandunna, these trees are old. They sway and creak, and a wiser elf might know what warning they give. I have neither the time nor the skill to listen to their message.

Lifting my hands, I bring the portal magic.

"Speak one word, boy, and I'll flay open your elven gut." The gruff voice comes from behind the tree just left of the portal.

"Show yourself." I draw my sword, as does the rest of the party.

Bert narrows his eyes and holds a small throwing knife near his ear.

A man perhaps four feet tall, but wide with muscle, steps into view. His eyes are dark brown, and his hair is of similar color and wildly tangled with his beard. His leather armor and knee-high boots leave no doubt this is a dwarven warrior. "You have no business here. This gate is held by my father's father."

"Dwarves have no place this far south," Jax bites out with his sword ready to battle. "Go back to your mountains and greedy ways."

"The old gods gifted this to my family. I am the honored one to guard it against the likes of you." The dwarf holds a two-handed sword high.

With a sigh, I lower my weapon and make a formal bow. "Good dwarf, we have urgent need of this portal."

He scoffs, but his eyes are intelligent, and he lowers his sword. "What need could you have that would interest me, elf?"

Think Aaran. Don't be rash just because Jax looks ready to lop off the dwarf's head.

I motion my crew to lower their weapons. Nainsi and Bert instantly stand down, and after a tense moment, Jax and the others do as well. The warriors look to Jax for what to do next. Four men, all well trained and ready to kill this dwarf with whom they have no issue, but solely based on bad blood between the races from before any of them were born.

In a formal tone, I say, "I am Aaran, son of Elspeth Riordan."

The dwarf pulls his shoulders back and holds his sword in front of him with the point facing down. "I am Fancor, son of Fan."

I bow again. "Are you forbidden to let anyone through the portal, Fancor, or is the use at your discretion?"

His chest puffs up. "The portal of the old gods is for urgency, not to get a pup home to his mother."

The way he growls makes me smile, but I hold my amusement. "I can assure you our need is far greater than seeing my honored mother, though that would be a valid use in my opinion, good dwarf."

Fancor laughs. "Perhaps it would, but I would be remiss in my duty if I let ye pass for that purpose."

"Perhaps so."

Jax steps forward. "Just kill him. If you won't do it, I have no qualms." He lifts his sword.

For his part, Fancor only raises an eyebrow, making me wonder if he could have killed us all before we stepped into the trees, but waited to find out our purpose.

Placing my hand on Jax's arm, I bite my tongue, not wanting to have to remind him that on this occasion, I am in command. "Wait." Keeping my voice soft and cordial despite my mounting worry over Harper, I choose reason. "Fancor, perhaps you might let me tell you why we need this gate."

He scratches his beard. "I have been here for three moons without company and am not opposed to hearing a tale. Tell your story, Aaran, son of Elspeth. But be warned, if you are agents of the witch queen, I will kill you all."

It's not often that a threat is good news, but in this case, I take Fancor's words as hopeful. I tell him a brief version of the past few weeks, beginning with the prophecy and ending with Harper trading her life for the lives of the villagers and being taken by the witch queen. "So, good dwarf, you can see why we need to reach the old city with great haste. I cannot leave Harper with that monster. Even if we didn't need her help, I could not leave her to such a fate."

Fancor runs his hands over his long beard. "I had not heard that a prophecy had been found. This human woman,

Harper, how can you be sure she's not already dead or worse?"

Rage fights its way up my chest, but I push it down. "She lives and is whole."

He cocks his head. "You sound very certain."

"If it were a simple thing to destroy Harper, then Vanora would have done it with all of us as an audience." I give Nainsi a nod. "She couldn't destroy her with the magic she knows. That's not to say she can't hurt and ruin someone so pure of heart as Harper. Nor is it assurance that the witch won't learn new magic and try again and again." My heart is pounding, and I have to still my shaking hands. I have to get to Harper.

With a curt nod, Fancor sheaths his sword at his back. "I will go with you. If this human holds the fate of our world within her, my sword will be hers."

Jax growls. "You have no need to spy on us, dwarf."

Hands perched on his hips, Fancor faces the much taller elf. "Don't I, elf? It was your kind who raised the witch queen, and then when she turned to dark, you allowed her to prosper. If the elves had stopped her all those years ago, you would have female babies. Your doom is counting down, is it not? Do not forget that it was your soft belief in reasoning with a witch that is the peril of all of Domhan. Dwarves have seen only sons all these years. We lost the dragons, who hide from this cursed place. I know the fairies, who keep to their own, have also been damaged by the incompetencies of elves to manage their own."

"She is evil, but that is not our fault." Jax's conviction wavers, and his tone eases. He shakes his head. "We never believed she would go so far, and when she did, it was too late. All elves bear the shame of Vanora's betrayal."

"Either I go with you, or none shall pass." Fancor reaches for his sword.

Hoping for peace, I hold up my hand palm out. All this arguing and placing blame is taking up time. I need to get to the old city. "Your generous offer to assist is welcome, Fancor. Will you open the gate, or shall I?"

"This magic isn't for the faint of heart, Aaran Riordan. Are you certain your heart is pure enough to wield such a spell?" Fancor's voice is full of gruff warning.

"Perhaps that is the true test, friend." Without waiting for more, I lift my hands and call the magic, all the while considering my mother's words of warning. My magic must be pure. I know from my studies that the gates of the old gods can transport anywhere another gate is present. No one knows how many of these exist in Domhan and beyond, so I keep my focus on the old city.

In the center of my mind, the image of Harper alone, beaten and crying forms. Her pain echoes through me. She is my only goal, the source of my most powerful magic, and where my loyalties lie. I see nothing but her. I hear only her voice and sorrow. Within her, I feel hope and her belief that I will come for her.

"That's quite good." Fancor laughs and slaps me on the back. "For an elf."

In the center of the arch, rainbow colors swirl, throwing wind toward us.

"This is going to hurt." Bert grips Nainsi's hand, and the two walk in before I can, planning to protect me from whatever might be on the other side.

Worried about whatever that might be, I jump through the portal. It pulls me in every direction at once. Light and dark come in waves. Images flash through my mind in random succession, first of my mother, and then of the witch queen. Harper glows with dark magic and screams in pain. Slashing with his battle sword and throwing magic, Fancor bullies his way past a crowd of dark elves. Bert ducks, a dagger barely missing him.

I can't tell what's real, or if any of it is. The images are disjointed. My stomach roils, as if I'm rolling down a steep hill in an out-of-control cart. Landing with a hard slam against the ground, I instinctively shield my face as thorns bite my skin.

"We've got you." Bert grips my arm and yanks me from the briars.

Nainsi pulls back the tangled bramble, but not before Fancor tumbles through, effectively flattening out most of the thorn bush.

"What in the demons' dark is all this?" He rips a thorn from his biceps. "I've not been through here before. I never wanted to get this close to that witch."

"I'd say no one has been through in quite some time." I help Nainsi pull the rest of the bush back just in time to save the warriors the pain. They still come through hard and grunt as they impact the limestone ground.

The portal took us across the Beò Ocean to the eastern continent of Ear Talamh. Night falls earlier here. In the distance comes the shadow demons' wails. The castle spire and battlement in the old city peek over the ridge. My gut twists. Harper is in that terrible place. I am to blame, but those thoughts will not help her. It's more important to get her out of there, and then beat myself up later when I beg her forgiveness.

Bert slaps my back, and I wonder if he's thinking the same thing.

Fancor takes his place beside Bert, who guards Nainsi's back as we march toward probable death. "You are neither elf nor dwarf." He narrows his eyes. "What manner of being are you then?"

Always easy in manner, Bert grins. "I'm a human, like the woman we go to save."

Fancor gapes. "Are you now? You're the first I've met. So, if I understand such things, you have no magic in you? How do you live?"

Bert shrugs. "We don't miss what we never had. Until I met Nainsi, I didn't even know such things were possible. Humans managed quite nicely without what you call magic. We have an occasional miracle, and we're happy with it. Besides, where you have magic, we have electricity."

With the rocky path getting steeper and the ground less forgiving, we're forced to climb in single file. As the sun dips below the horizon, the shadow demons' wails grow louder.

Fancor says, "I'd like to hear more about your world and its miracles, sir."

Nodding, Bert grips a rock to keep steady. "I'll be happy to tell you as soon as we have Harper safe, friend."

My gut twists. She's alive, I tell myself. Clutching my chest, I feel her there. Closing my eyes, I listen for the song of her soul, and it whispers weakly to me. Steadying my breathing, I pull myself together and focus on the job before us. Get to the old city, find Harper, and get her out alive. It's hard to ignore my affection for her, but I have a duty that supersedes my desires.

As we crest the next rise, a clearer view of the second tower and shadow demons swirling around the old castle further darkens my mood. Attacking the tower at night when the demons are more active is suicide. "Stay low, but keep moving."

Jax steps beside me. "We'll have to wait for daylight."

"I know." But I don't like it.

Chapter Nine

HARPER

Another elf comes and takes me by the arm. "Come."

How long have I slept, hours or days? I have no idea. I'm stiff and sore from lying on the hard stones and the torture.

"Where are you taking me?" Maybe I can talk him into going elsewhere.

"She calls for you." His voice is strong but not aggressive.

I stumble at the cell door, and he grips me tighter to keep me upright. His attempt to save me from a fall is as painful as the fall might have been. I grunt and suck air in through my teeth.

He stops, gentles his grip, and bows his head. "I apologize. I only meant to keep you from injuring yourself."

Once the sharpest of the pain subsides, I attempt a smile. "I know. I'm alright. What is your name?"

"I am Beran." His commanding voice makes me think he

was a soldier before being enslaved. He whispers, "Are you one of the humans who is prophesied?

I shrug. "That's what they tell me, but I hardly think I can save anyone. I'm surprised you know about me. I mean, being here, like this."

Once again taking my arm, he leads me down a long corridor. "She's afraid of you. She laments your existence to that traitorous pig, Ciaran."

"I'm sorry I failed you. I came to this world to help, but I wasn't good enough." Pain and guilt and hopelessness well up inside me, and I hate that I can't manage them any more than I can control my situation.

"Stay alive, human." He pulls his lips into a line, and his jaw tightens.

It seems to me a sign that he's done talking, which is pretty annoying since he's probably the last person with whom I'll ever have a conversation. Pulling my arm free, I lift my chin and walk on my own. Every step is agony, but I refuse to let him or anyone else see how dangerously close I am to a complete meltdown. This Jersey Girl will not be terrorized by anyone or anything. They may kill me, but they won't break me.

In the hall where I was abused and where I'll likely die, pillars rise fifty feet to the ceiling, are large enough to hide two men, and I wonder what evil lurks behind them. Though they are stained sooty black like the rest of the hall, a hint of gold shines through at the top of each beveled ridge. The broken and rough floor, which I thought was gray stone, has a pattern beneath the grime, like marble. "I guess she spoils everything she touches."

Beran takes my arm again and draws me to the center of

the hall. With a gentle squeeze, he releases me to continue toward the dais alone, then backs away until I no longer hear his footsteps.

Terrible and familiar, the witch queen steps in front of the throne, dressed in black leggings and a tunic. On the belt at her hip hangs a dagger with a golden stone on the hilt. As if for some effect, she's wearing a black cape that nearly reaches the ground. It seems completely impractical, but what do I know of elf witches?

She takes out her dagger and buries the tip deep in the arm of the throne. "Your world is puzzling to me."

Twenty feet from the dais, I stop. She plans to kill me or make me a shadow demon. I'm not giving this aberration any information. Who knows what she'll do if she can reach Earth. Not that I know anything about magic. Until a few weeks ago, I thought magic wasn't real.

"My spies tell me humans wield no magic. Why don't you use the magic available to you?" She narrows her gaze.

Something pokes my back and shoves me forward, bruising just under my right shoulder blade. I stumble, but keep on my feet.

Ciaran, also dressed in black, but minus the cape, circles me. A sword hangs from his belt, and his cuffs are adorned with red lace. Like some demonic drum major, he twirls a pale wooden rod painted with black markings. He strikes behind my legs, forcing my knees to smack the hard ground.

I cry out, but bite my lip, stilling any other sounds.

"Answer, or I will beat you with this until you beg for the chance to speak." He smacks the back of my head with the rod.

Grabbing the already swelling lump, I say, "I don't know

the answer. We know nothing of magic. Maybe we've forgotten over the years."

"Useless," Vanora says. "You are of no value, human." She spreads her fingers and thrusts her arms forward.

Jagged black bolts streak toward me from her fingertips, and when they strike, pain rips through my center, burning cold, and I pray for death to end the unbearable pain. It rises from my gut up to my chest, neck, and head. My screams fill the hall in a never-ending cry. I can't stop myself, nor can I move any muscle. Hovering above the floor, racked with agony, I force my mind to detach.

Aaran is coming for me. His mother's words come back, telling me that I have to survive. If Vanora breaks my mind, I'm done for. I can't let her inside me.

"She thinks someone will rescue her," Ciaran singsongs, as if he's amused. "Stupid little human. So helpless. Once my queen finds the key to your world's magic, we shall spend less than a day conquering your people and making them all slaves."

A shadow demon swoops past my face.

How had Ciaran known I was thinking about rescue?

He taps his temple. Smooth skin, long silken hair, and blue eyes, he could be from a fairy tale. Of course, some of those are pretty dark. Maybe there's more truth in them than I ever considered.

I have to keep him out of my mind. All I have to do is what Elspeth said. *Stay alive*—and the song from that old seventies movie that my mom loves filters through like a crazy earworm. I repeat the lyrics over and over in my mind and float in a haze where my body and mind are disconnected.

"The shadow demon felt the magic in her world; so did the wolves. They drew from it, even though it was altered. I just need to open the human up and find her magic. Killing her now gets me no closer to using her magic to take her world." Vanora's voice grates on the inside of my skull. The lightning she shoots comes faster and stronger.

The agony persists. My screams ring in my head. Still, I'm alive. I only need to survive long enough for someone to come for me and hope this witch queen can be distracted long enough for me to get away. It's too much to hope for, so I just keep singing that song in my head, not all of it, just the chorus, in time to the catchy beat.

Ciaran holds the side of his head. "What is that?"

Pointing her finger at me, Vanora says, "It's her. She thinks a little mind game will keep me from flaying her open and gathering her essence. She's foolish enough to believe she can stop me."

There's denial and concern in her voice. Maybe I'm wrong, but it seems to me that my repeatedly singing the same few bars is effectively bothering Ciaran. For that alone, it's worth it.

Hope spreads from the center of my chest. It's only the three of us in the throne room now. I worry that those the witch has imprisoned might be hurt when Aaran comes for me. At the edge of my mind, I feel him getting closer. Still, I sing on. I can't allow Vanora or Ciaran to read more of my thoughts about rescue. Just the words to the old song. I'll give them nothing else.

When Ciaran grabs my shoulders and lifts me from the ground, there's no beauty in him. The vile person inside his pleasing exterior shines through. His skin, which sags with age, is marked and pocked. His bright eyes are black, dull, dim and wanting. His shoulders slump with the weight of keeping Vanora happy. She's a demanding master, and he has suffered for his betrayal. Not the least sorry for him, I filter his true reflection back to him.

His eyes widen, and he cries loud enough for the rough sound to bounce off the walls. He lets me go, and I plummet to my ass.

As he staggers backward, Vanora stops her torture and runs to him.

Keeping the image of his true likeness in my mind, I pray that he sees nothing else.

"What is it?"

He screams and covers his eyes as his back comes up against a pillar. Even the gold thread on his shirt dims in my sight. The skin of his throat sags, and his veins show black through papery flesh. His hands are gnarled with swollen knuckles.

As Vanora pushes his hair back from his face, instead of silken white strands, I see gray, stringy and matted.

His true visage is so clear in my head that I send it to him again and again. This is what he gets for invading my thoughts.

"Make her stop, my queen. She's killing me." He clutches his face and hair, looking for proof that what I'm showing him is a lie.

Only it's not a lie. It's what I see. Maybe it's what he knows lurks inside himself. Ugly is as ugly does, my grand-mother used to say.

"Stop her!" With a shaking hand, he points one long black fingernail at me.

Vanora turns. Her black cape billowing behind her, she stalks toward me. "Stop this, you miserable animal."

Leaning on my hands, I stare at them both. "I'm not doing anything but showing him the truth. There's no getting away from what's inside your rotting body. Show what you want to the world, but I see you." I have no idea where this new strength has come from, but I'm just so angry. I can't stop using the one weapon I have to defend myself against their magic.

"Stop!" Vanora charges forward, putting herself between me and Ciaran.

I pray the image he sees degrades further and shows him the unmarked grave where his fetid body will lie when his master abandons him for someone new.

"No!" His wails echo through the room, hurting my ears.

As Vanora draws closer, I try to back away like a crab, but my arms give out. Even if my mind remains strong, my muscles scream with agony.

She slaps my face, then screams in pain and holds her hand tight to her chest.

Warm blood runs down my cheek. My focus slips for a moment, but I gather myself and show him the beautiful new elven man of perhaps twenty, who sits beside Vanora on her black throne. "You mean nothing to her. Once she's used you up, she'll discard you like she has so many before." I'm making a guess, but it hits home, and his eyes dart toward her.

"She lies." Vanora reaches for me with both hands as if she might strangle me.

The moment she grips my throat, she pulls her smoking

fingers back and screams. Her flesh bubbles, and the burn spreads.

Stunned, I falter, releasing my attack on Ciaran. Had I burned her? Is that why she can't touch me?

He straightens, and despite what I've shown him, he runs to her aid.

A thunderous cracking of wood and stone overshadows her agonized shrieking.

The castle is collapsing. I'm prepared to be buried alive. It can't be worse than what I've already suffered. Instead of falling stone and eternal darkness, daylight shines through, blinding me to the room as Aaran's face flashes in my mind. Courage wells up inside me. I stagger to my feet and launch myself at Vanora with my hands outstretched toward her face.

My index finger makes contact with her left cheek and leaves a nasty burn just as Ciaran bats me away.

I crash to the ground and slide until my shoulder hits a pillar.

Dust and rubble fly in every direction. Booted feet on the marble floor and battle cries hurt my ears. Total chaos surrounds me, but someone lifts me from the floor and carries me out of the way. Aaran, Nainsi, Jax, and several others raise their swords to attack Ciaran, who also lifts his weapon.

A short stocky man screams, "I get the witch!"

The hall fills with shadow demons, all screeching like banshees as they surround Vanora and Ciaran before my rescuers reach her. Gray shadows lift them and crash through one of the windows to carry them away.

The silence that follows is bliss.

Bert's concerned face comes into focus. "I've got you, Harper." Even though his voice is calm, he's on his guard.

"I burned her." I stare at my fingers. My blood, and maybe hers, mark my skin. The pain of a hundred cuts and bruises lances through me as the threat subsides. The room spins, Bert's face blurs, and everything goes black.

AARAN

I drop my sword and rush to the side wall where Bert is holding an unconscious Harper. Her dress is in tatters. Blood, dried and fresh, covers her, but still she breathes. My heart is pounding so hard I can't catch my breath.

Charging into the great hall, I focused on battle. Now, it's hard to hold my composure in the face of what Harper must have suffered. I cup her face where blood still drips from three long cuts along her cheek. "Harper?" My instinct is to shake her awake. I need to know she's alive and that her mind is still sound. "I should never have made you come here."

While Bert holds her as if she were his child, he shakes his head. "She came because she wanted to. It was her choice. It was the right thing to do, and our Harper is a person who always does right. Don't diminish her choice by taking it away from her."

He's right, but I want her well, whole. Whatever she

suffered in the hours it took us to arrive, I cannot imagine. Is my Harper still inside her?

Nainsi puts her hand on my shoulder. "Let's get her out of this tainted place. She needs healing."

Again, someone else is more rational than me. Again, my emotions have clouded my judgment. I slip my arm under her knees and around her back.

"Be gentle with her. She's beaten up, and even passed out, probably hurts." Bert stands as I lift Harper from his embrace.

Turning, I'm stunned to see dozens of elves walking out doors and the shadows of pillars. Wearing rags, they're emaciated and approach with heads bowed.

For an instant, I pull Harper closer to protect her, but these elves are not a danger.

Jax speaks to one of them, then approaches me. "They were taken from the northern city of Fioseil and kept as slaves. Their magic is bound. That's how she kept them."

I nod, but my priority is getting Harper out of this oppressive castle's dark magic. Still, the shuffle of many feet following behind me adds the weight of each one's safety heavy on my shoulders.

"The witch won't stay away," Fancor says. "She only ran because she was injured. I'm guessing your woman did the wounding. This human must be stronger than she looks." He strides ahead toward an area just outside the wall, where tattered tents circle a stone well.

More elves, some sickly, step out of their makeshift homes.

There are so many. How will I get them all to safety and get Harper to Tús Nua under my mother's protection? "Jax, can you and your soldiers see what these people need and how bad their condition is?"

Fancor drops the bucket and hauls up water. He tastes it. "Not bad. Not poisoned." He carries the bucket to the partially crumbling wall I'm sitting on with Harper in my lap.

Bert leans my sword against the wall beside me.

Nainsi kneels, and without touching Harper, she runs her hands from head to toe. "It was her magic Vanora was after. She vibrates with defenses I don't understand, as if something surrounded the part of her under attack."

A female elf with haunted eyes drops to her knees and places her hands on top of Nainsi's. Together, they press their palms to Harper's abdomen. Magic glows around them and through Harper.

It vibrates along my spine as healing flows through this woman I pledged to keep safe. I failed. She might have been killed, and she'll never again be the sweet unsullied person I found getting her driver's license. Her injuries may be healed, but everything leaves a scar. The blame lies with me.

Blinking her eyes open, Harper draws a deep breath. She stares at me. "You came."

Fancor kneels beside her and holds a cup of water. "Drink, girl."

With a long look at Fancor, she tries to sit, but winces. "Have we met?"

"Drink." He puts the cup to her lips.

Glancing at me, she waits for my nod before complying. "Thank you."

"I am Fancor, son of Fan of the Great Mountains. I came

to give aid in battle in the name of my father." He makes an awkward bow.

"The water was good." Closing her eyes, Harper lays her hand over the two at her stomach. "I hope this doesn't mean I'm dying and you're easing my pain. If I'm going to die, I want to know."

Nainsi grins. "You're not dying."

The sober elf who helped with the healing stands and backs away with her head lowered.

"Thank you, Cara." Harper keeps her eyes closed. "Did Vanora leave? Are they gone?"

We are still in danger. Perhaps a hundred elves are looking to me for guidance. "She ran, but she'll be back when she's healed. We need to get out of here."

Getting to her feet, Harper stumbles and leans on Fancor for support. "You're very sturdy."

"I am, indeed. It would be my honor to be your crutch, or I'll carry you if you'd prefer." He grips her elbow and scans her, as if determining the best way to be of service. "I'm as strong as any elf or the man from your world."

"Have you been to my world?"

He huffs. "No."

Her laugh is short but sends a shred of hope to my heart. "Still, you're probably right, Mr. Fancor." Staring into my eyes, she raises her eyebrows. "Now what?"

Wrapping my arms around her, I lift her, and she puts her arms around my neck. "Now we get you out of here." I stride toward the outer gates. They used to gleam silver and gold, but now are black, as if a fungus has grown on them.

Swords drawn, the soldiers who came with me surround us.

Harper whispers, "Aaran, what about these people? Will you leave them here to be slaves to that monster?" Resting her head on my shoulder, she gazes back at the ragged group staring after us.

Part of me knows I should leave them or come back for them, but I can't do that. These are my people just as much as those inside the new city. Taking a hundred undernourished and ill elves so far will add time to our journey. "No. We won't leave them, Harper."

Nainsi smiles and points up the mountain. "If we can get over that ridge, I think we can draw enough magic to mask ourselves."

I nod despite the difficult logistics of moving a group this large. A portal would damage the sick and injured. Harper isn't strong enough. Even for me, a fourth portal this soon would be dangerous. We'll have to walk, and it's a long way, with an ocean between here and home. Putting Harper on her feet, I wait until she's stable.

Fancor rushes over to catch her if she should waver. I've never spent much time with dwarves. My people have made a habit of avoiding the Great Mountains and their inhabitants. For the first time, I question the wisdom of that.

Facing those who were slaves to the witch queen, I take a deep breath and hope this is the right thing. Two men stand with the healer at the front as I approach. "Do you think with help your people can make it over that ridge?"

Relief flickers in the taller man's blue eyes. He holds out his hand. "I am Dorian. We have enough who still have the strength to carry those who have none. If it means the possibility of freedom, we will make the journey."

"You can come with us to Tús Nua. It's possible my

mother can break the bind on your magic. If not, at least you'll be out from under the witch queen." Mist is burning off the hills, and the barren land stretches farther than I can see. "It will take many days."

Dorian nods and lifts a man who's little more than skin and bones. Beran does the same with a woman, as do other elves who still have their strength. The soldiers keep their swords drawn and lead the way as Nainsi, Bert, Fancor, and Jax each help with the weak or ill.

We leave the old city with over a hundred elves, two humans, and a dwarf.

Harper hugs my neck. "I should walk so you can carry one of them."

Gripping her tighter, I say. "No. You're healing, but not healed."

"Who are they?" She points to the soldiers flanking us.

Elves have very good hearing, and the ginger elf smiles. "I'm Brekin. I've come with Avon, Glen, and Lare to help protect you on your journey west."

She thanks him and the others. "Are we very far from the new capital?"

Avon is very tall, even for an elf. He is the oldest and keeps his long blond hair braided. "We have a long journey, my lady. You were taken across the Beò Ocean. It will take some time to bring you to safety."

She laughs. "Is there such a place here?"

Avon frowns but doesn't confirm her assumption.

There are no safe places in Domhan any longer. That's why Harper is here. I hold her tighter and shield my mind so she doesn't hear my worries.

Once the city is in the distance, Harper talks about what

was done to her, but not about the pain of it. She speaks of my mother coming to her in a vision and Cara rubbing salve on her wounds and using magic to ease her pain. She gets tears in her eyes when she tells us how Dorian gave up his cloak so she wouldn't have to lie on the cold stone dungeon floor.

I'm amazed at how while Vanora tried to rip her magic free, she kept herself sane by singing a human song. This woman is special far beyond my feelings for her. Most of those, I must keep to myself, but perhaps one day I'll be able to tell her. Stuffing that away, I ask, "She wanted your magic?"

"She doesn't know how the magic in my world works." Harper stares back at the parade of elves in rags following us. "Not that I do. I never knew I had magic before I met you. I could sometimes sense things about people, but never more than that, and most of the time I found it uncomfortable to know what fate or fortune lay in store for someone."

Fancor adjusts the woman clinging to his back. "Dwarves rarely use magic for more than healing and the portals, but the old texts say we did many cycles ago, before the dragons came to Domhan. Maybe your people are more like us."

"Maybe." She smiles. "Maybe we just forgot, and perhaps it's for the best. Many humans are better off without the ability to shoot lightning from their hands." She wiggles her fingers.

I think she meant it to be lighthearted, but Fancor winces. He must have some idea of the pain black lightning causes. Harper should not have survived. The fact that she did is a blessing, but when the witch queen recovers, she'll be even more rabid to find the answers behind the riddle of human magic.

Chapter Ten

HARPER

When we are far enough away from the hellish castle, Jax finds us a place he thinks will be safe to rest. I'm so tired I can barely see. It's embarrassing, but I let Aaran carry me the entire way. My legs feel as if they've been turned to jelly. For all I know, they have. Every cell in my body aches and some of me is in agony. Inside, I feel as if part of me was torn away. Perhaps it was my innocence that the witch queen took. Maybe I have PTSD. I feel like a worn-out dish towel, with insufficient threads left to be useful. Yet just like that rag, I linger.

As Aaran eases me to a patch of grass on the side of a hill, Bert rushes over to cushion any chance I might be jostled. "There, you go, Harper," Bert says. He lets out a long breath and goes to help build a fire at the center of the camp.

I'd like to watch the goings-on, but I'm too tired. All I see is people rushing here and there in a blur. Tears prickle my eyes, and I don't have the strength to keep them down.

Aaran kneels between me and the bustling elves. His handsome face has a streak of dirt across his cheek. His eyes are bright but narrowed. Cupping my face in his hands, he says, "I'm more sorry than I can ever atone for, *mo chroi*."

"You're sorry?" I can't fathom what he might be apologizing for.

Running his thumbs under my eyes, he wipes away my tears. "More than I can say. How will you forgive me? Of course, you can't. I made you a promise and could not keep it." There's bitterness in his tone that I can't account for.

"Are you taking the blame for my capture?" The truth of that starts to sort itself in my abused and mottled brain. "You didn't tell me to go into the woods alone. You didn't send for that hag. She is to blame, and I am to blame."

"I promised to keep you safe." He brushes my hair off my forehead.

And there it is. He made a promise, and now it haunts him.

I cover one of his hands with mine. "You came for me. That's all that matters."

"I should have been by your side at all times." Dropping his hands, he lowers his gaze from mine.

It hurts to breathe too deeply, and I wince at the attempt, then try again with better success. "Aaran, these kinds of promises are never worth crap. My father promised to spend a lifetime with my mother, but he died. It's not his fault. He meant the vow at the time. Still, he couldn't keep it. I just need some time to heal and maybe a good shrink for the rest of my life. I'll be fine."

Easing his chin up, he looks long into my eyes, and my heart pounds even though I'm too exhausted to do anything but look. He says, "Then you forgive me?"

My muscles scream as I sit up straight and try to stretch, only to have to stop my arms halfway up, and lower them. Even that is too much effort. "I don't think this was your fault, but if you need my forgiveness, then you have it."

He pulls me into his arms. "Thank you."

It is agony and ecstasy all at once. "Gently," I whisper.

"What is a shrink?"

Even laughing hurts and transforms into a groan. "A doctor to tell your problems to."

"Ah." Easing his hug, he kisses my cheek. "I'm going to get you some water. The lake isn't far. If you want to bathe, I can carry you there."

I need to wash. There's no doubt about it. "Can I rest a while?"

He nods. "I'll bring you water. I thought we'd be able to portal since you've only been through two, but you're not strong enough, and I've already been through three. I should have brought more soldiers from the village." Digging in his backpack that he bought in New Jersey, he pulls out a small blanket.

My life in my world feels like an eternity ago, but it was only a few days—or a lifetime. I tuck the rolled-up blue and green flowered throw under my head and lie on my side in the cool grass. "Thanks. I lost my father's ring."

Sorrow fills his too-blue eyes. "He's with you still."

"I know." It comes out teary and weak. I want to tell him to rest or to care for the others. I want to beg him to lie beside me and keep me company. I don't say any of it. I let my tears fall and close my eyes.

AARAN

Harper's tears break my heart. I want to wipe them away and all the memories of the witch queen with them. Later I will try to ease her pain. Now I need to help secure the encampment and be ready to ward off attacks.

Vanora was damaged, that much was obvious. She will need time to heal, but how long, I don't know. For the moment, I think we are safe.

Over a hundred souls to look after. I was supposed to bring one human woman from her world to Domhan. It should have been simple. Perhaps that's my lesson. Nothing is ever as easy as expected.

As I speak the spells that ward the area and will alert us if an attack is imminent, I pray my brothers will have had an easier path. I have more questions than answers, and that worries me.

Once food is cooking on the fire and water has been brought from the lake just west of our position, I sit a few feet from where Harper is sleeping. Someone covered her with a threadbare blanket, and several of the freed elves watch her from different places around the camp.

As the sun dips below the horizon and the two moons

rise, her sleep is fitful, and nightmares haunt her. Flashes of black lightning snap from her mind to mine.

To keep my wits, I block her thoughts. If I don't, I fear I'll run off in a rage to find and kill that bitch who harmed Harper. That is not the way to destroy Vanora. It's been tried, and those warriors were all lost to shadow. It takes a few moments to calm myself.

I'm not one to ask for help, but maybe that's a flaw in my character. I'm grateful for the extra eyes and would welcome their support if a battle comes, which it likely will.

I remove my sword and belt and rest them beside me. My hand itches to grasp the hilt and keep the first watch, but Jax has taken charge for the first few hours, and Harper may need me if she wakes.

Bert sits across from me and hands me a leg of a small bird that's been roasted. "It's slim pickings here."

Fancor slaps Bert on the back. "That foul woman has poisoned much of this land, and the game with it. We'll fare better in the mountains or across the sea. Even the fish in Mòr Lake are few now."

Nainsi sits next to Bert. "These people need care. I don't know if they'll make the journey ahead."

"They can't stay here." Fancor finishes a bite of meat. "We'll take things slow, but which way are we heading?"

Quiet as a mouse, Harper moves and sits beside me.

"You should rest," Nainsi tells her.

"I can't. What are the options for ways to go? You said it's farther to your home now than it was from the village?" She shifts uncomfortably on the hard ground. Her sweet face twists, and her lips are pulled tight.

I pull her off the dampening ground and into my lap.

She doesn't protest, just tucks her head under my chin and rests her cheek on my chest.

Pushing aside how perfect and right this feels, I say, "We are on the eastern continent of Ear Talamh. The castle where you were held was where my mother ruled before the witch queen conquered these lands. We could travel east, but the desert would be harsh on you, and many of the elves would perish in their current condition. Beyond the desert is an ocean that swallowed up miles of land centuries ago. It is shallow, but to walk on the lost land holds its own dangers. Beyond that is an ocean, but there's no port to find a ship.

"Then we go west." Fancor sounds grim.

Nainsi says, "Will you not go to your own home, Fancor? It might be better for your health to portal to the Great Mountains range and bid our plight farewell."

I can't disagree with Nainsi. The dwarf would be safer if he went home. This is not his fight. When he looks at me, I nod, hoping he knows I'd not blame him for moving on with his life. His coming this far was a gift.

Fancor's gaze softens as he settles his attention on Harper. "If you can use my sword, I'll see this through. I'll send word to my people of our quest."

"How will you do that?" Harper shifts to look at the dwarf.

Blushing, Fancor smiles. "Dwarves have a way with creatures. I'll call an eagle and ask him to carry my message to my king."

A hint of a smile pulls at Harper's lips.

"So we go west and find a boat still intact at the old port?" Nainsi shakes her head. "The journey by the Beò Ocean isn't much better than traveling east. We did it thirty years ago with well-maintained ships and trained crews, and still lost many on the way."

I know she's right. I was a child and still remember the sickness of endless days at sea. Mother and Father hid me away below when it got rough. "It will be worse now. The sailors who bring goods from the south and Great Mountains say anyone who ventures across has to go through or south of the Amadan Islands because the monsters of the north are thriving with Vanora's power growing."

"Are the islands bad?" Harper asks.

Nainsi shrugs. "Not bad. The people of the Amadan Islands are not fond of outsiders and can be a bit testy."

Bert pats his wife's knee. "West it is. Do you think we can remain a day or two and try to get these people fed and a bit stronger?" He directs his question to me.

All around the camp, the freed elves are too thin, and many are sick from lack of magic. "They need their magic restored. Staying here is dangerous. The longer we wait, the more time Vanora has to heal and return."

Fancor grunts. "A good night's rest away from the dark magic of Tobhtá will help them. They've been under the witch's thumb a long time. Tonight, they can breathe. You've done a good thing here."

My heart tells me he's right, but my gut tightens with the responsibility of all these lives.

Taking Harper in my arms, I stand and grab the straps of both of our packs brought from her world. "How about a soak in the warm lake? It might help you sleep."

Since she doesn't protest, I walk out of our circle of new friends and down the hill to the large lake that used to give sustenance to this area when the ruined castle was white and tall and called Priomh Bhaile. It is where I was born, and seeing it in ruin and black with dark magic stabbed me deep in my soul.

"You were born here?" she asks, probably hearing my thoughts.

At the shoreline, I put her on her feet and miss her arms around my neck as she hobbles to the water's edge.

"It's safe." I untie my boots and step out of them. My knife falls out of one boot, and I place it carefully where I can get it if need be.

She looks back at me with wide eyes as I pull my shirt over my head. "They took my shoes." She looks down at her bare feet. "I guess so I wouldn't try to run away."

Stepping out of my trousers, I swallow down my anger at the witch queen and her token man. "They did it to make you feel vulnerable."

"It worked," she squeaks out through tears.

"Turn around." When she does, I unbutton the dress she had looked so beautiful in at the feast. Only now it is in tatters. "I brought you a change of clothes." I toss the dress on the shore. It's hard not to cringe at the bruises marking her skin from her neck down the length of her back. Even her legs are cut and bruised. I run my hand along her spine. "I would have given myself to save you, Harper."

Facing me with her bottom lip puffed out, she shakes her head. "I wouldn't have wanted that."

"You're very beautiful." I trace the line of her jaw. Holding my desire for her apart, I lift her and walk into the warm water of Mòr Lake.

"I'm bruised and cut. I'm damaged inside and out. How

can you say I'm beautiful?" She clings to my neck and winces as the water touches various scrapes and cuts.

The sand under my feet is soft. I let her legs float down.

She stands, looking up at me with watery eyes of moss green. Those are eyes I could get lost in for a thousand years. "You will heal, *mo chroi*." I put my hands on her cheeks and cup her head with my fingers. Closing my eyes, I pull my magic forth.

She grips my hands and pulls them away. "You can't heal everything with magic, Aaran. What is broken in me cannot be wished away."

Opening my eyes, I see her strength, and it's beyond anything I have ever known. "You are very special. Most would have died in that castle. Most would have broken under the strain of torture. If you won't let me take these memories from you, will you at least let me admire you?"

A small, familiar smile pulls at her lips. "If you have soap in that bag of yours, you can do anything you want with me." She winks.

My heart expands at that hint of Harper's humor shining through. Other parts also expand, but those ideas will have to wait. "If you're not put off by magic, I can conjure a bar of soap."

She cocks her head, and it's adorable. Her hair floats in the water like lace. The swell of her breasts breaches the surface. She may not feel it at the moment, but she's the most beautiful woman I've ever seen. She looks around. "From what?"

Stepping back, I cup the water in my hands and call my magic to transform. Light surrounds my fingers and swallows up my wrists.

Harper gasps but doesn't move away. "Amazing."

A moment later, I hand her a round pat of soap.

She rolls it between her hands, and when she has a lather, she washes her face. Bubbles float across the lake. Once the dirt is gone, a dark bruise stands out along her jaw, and the underside of her eyes are shaded as well. Reaching up to wash her hair, she winces, unable to lift her arms above her shoulders.

Taking the pat from her, I ask, "May I?" Once she nods, I circle behind her and lather her tangled strands. I massage her skull gently.

"That feels so good." Her voice is barely a whisper.

This is more intimate than I planned. Once every strand is washed, I hand her the soap. "Lean back and float if you can."

When she does, the rosy peaks of her breasts make my mouth water. I must look away and concentrate on running my fingers through her hair. I scoop water to pour carefully around her face. "I think it will be difficult to get some of these knots out."

"Maybe I can borrow a brush from someone." Her voice shakes, maybe from exhaustion or fear. She runs the soap along one arm and then the other before lathering her chest and abdomen. When she reaches between her legs, I have to close my eyes. My body yearns for this woman.

Braving a look, I'm relieved when suds hide her womanly parts. "Do you want me to wash your legs and back?"

Her throat bobs as she hands me the soap.

I keep my focus on the job, and not the softness of her skin, or the way she quivers as my fingers slip along the inside of her thighs. I wash her feet before helping her stand. When her back is clean, I clear my throat and step away to take my own brief bath.

"I feel better. Thank you." She takes a few tentative steps toward the shore.

Scooping her up, I carry her to the grassy beach. Calling on wind magic, I dry us both.

When I put her on the ground, she covers herself. Even in the moonlight, her bruises stand out against her fair skin.

Gathering the clothes I brought for her, I hand them over. "I wish I had the opportunity to kill Vanora just for what she did to you." I dress and dig into the bottom of my pack for the leather shoes Selina insisted I take in case they were needed.

She pulls on her jeans and the t-shirt with a funny black mouse on the front. "I think if it was easy to kill her, she couldn't have done all she has in the last thirty years."

"You're right. I still would do anything to take this pain from you." I hand her the footwear. "Selina said you might need these."

With a wan smile, she puts them on. "Only a little big, but far better than nothing."

I rinse off her tattered dress and tear off a few pieces. "When these dry, we can stuff the toes. That should help."

Standing, she holds out her hand. "I'd like to try to walk back. Maybe if I can make it, the sick will try a little harder to recover." She shakes her head. "That's probably stupid."

Lacing our fingers together, I say, "It's brilliant, Harper. You mean more to those people than you can ever imagine. They need something to believe in and right now, that's you."

"I hope I won't disappoint them. I'm just a girl from Jersey. I'm no hero." Her breath is more shudder.

We take a few steps. "You're absolutely perfect, *mo chroi.*"

Her legs are weak, and the going is slow, but we walk into camp hand in hand, and she smiles at the elves and even says hello to a few who smile at her.

She is the definition of strength, and she doesn't even know it.

Back on the short rise in the grass, she lies with her head on the little blanket I brought from her world. With a long exhale, she closes her eyes.

Someone left a worn comb with two teeth missing. A wooden cup steams next to it with the scent of camomhail leaves wafting up. My mother made the luibhe tì whenever were sick as children. All those memories of hard times and simpler times waft through my mind.

Surrounding the camp, Jax and his men are evenly spaced, keeping watch.

Confident that we are safe for the moment, I slip in behind her, wrap my arm around her, and take her hand.

She hugs my arm close to her chest. "She will come looking for me, won't she?"

There's no point in hiding the truth from her. "After her failed attempts to understand human magic and what happened today, she'll be even more keen to capture you."

"Should we find another way, and let Jax take these people across the sea without me? They might be safer if I am far away."

I consider it, and I cannot deny her logic. Still... "No. We'll all stay together. You will be Vanora's main target, but she will want her slaves back or dead. She won't want them to reach my mother. I think she'd kill them rather than let them get to the western continent of Siar Fàilte. She'll want you alive, and staying together might keep her from destroying the others."

The fire smolders as she sighs. "I don't want anyone to die because of me."

I hold her more secure. "We would all die to save this world, and you are necessary to that end."

"Is that why you came for me?" She shakes her head and releases my hand. "Don't answer that. I'm just feeling vulnerable and sad. It was a stupid question."

Not letting her pull away, I kiss her damp hair. "I think we should try to comb your hair before you sleep."

With a long sigh, she sits up and picks up the brown comb.

I sip the tea, and deeming it made from healing herbs that grow wild, I hand it to her as I take the comb. "Drink this. It will ease your sore muscles."

Sitting with her back to me, she does as I tell her with an indignant huff that makes joy flare inside me. Hurt, sad, and a little broken, my Harper will recover. I know it because I can't bear a world where she doesn't.

One small bit at a time, I begin detangling the damp mess. When I hit a knot, I ease the strands apart as gently as possible. "I promised to keep you safe. I broke that promise, but I'll never leave you in harm's way, Harper. Domhan needs you, that's true. It would be a lie to deny that I would have had to try to find and recover you no matter what."

Her shoulders stiffen.

"That doesn't mean it didn't destroy me when Vanora

took you. The needs of this world are one thing, and my own feelings are something different. Don't you know what *mo chroi* means?"

She draws in a long breath with a shake, and her back rises then falls. "I know it means *my heart*."

"So then you know how I feel." I run the comb through the left side of her hair, which is now tangle free.

"In my world, people call each other names like sweetheart and hon all the time. Sometimes it means you like a person, and other times it's just to be nice or get someone's attention." She toys with the ends of her hair and adjusts her seat to give me better access to her right side. In the dimming firelight, her skin looks flushed and warm.

I lower my chin to whisper in her ear. "I would not use the elvish term so lightly. I call you *mo chroi* because without you, I would be empty."

She jerks away and winces before looking over her shoulder and meeting my gaze. "I'm human."

"I'm aware." I smile. "Let me finish your hair."

After a pause, she turns away again. "I will go back to my home and my mother when this is done."

Even though this is not new information, it still hurts. "When that time comes, I will have to deal with it."

"So you want me for now, and you came to save me because you want me, and when your brothers find the other two humans, you'll need us to save your world." She keeps her tone even, as if this is a business discussion.

I comb through the last knot and slip the teeth through her drying tresses again and again. "While I don't know what will happen in the course of our journey to the Great Gate or what lies beyond for us, I can promise you one thing. I will want you for all time. You are my heart, and if we survive, I would beg for the opportunity to remain with you."

She leans back against my chest, and I wrap my arms around her. "You always say the nicest things, even if they are impossible dreams, Aaran Riordan."

Part of me knows that what she says is true. I don't care. The idea of living without Harper hurts too much. "We have now."

"We have now," she whispers, taking the comb from my hand and placing it to the side. She lies on her side, eyes clear, watching the flames dim and the camp settle.

Behind her, I hold her until her breath is steady and even, and I'm glad for her to find sleep finally.

Chapter Eleven

HARPER

I wake up with the sun above the horizon and the camp bustling around me. This is our third camp, and the third morning I've struggled to wake since we left Tobhtá. My hair is a riot of waves. I should have braided it last night. With a sigh, I comb my fingers through the mess and make one plait while the elves cook in battered pots and pans they brought with them.

The pain in my gut lurks like it could escalate at any moment. I rub the space just under my sternum and take a breath, let it out, and accept that there are other people here in far worse condition.

Nainsi smiles as she walks toward me. "You look better." She sits.

"I feel as if I've been run over by a truck." I laugh. "Which is actually better than I felt yesterday."

We both chuckle, and she examines a bruise and scratch on my upper arm. "You're stronger than you look."

"Do you think so?" I take my shoes off and adjust the stuffing in the toes before putting them back on.

"I do. Humans are more than elves give them credit for." She points to Bert. He's talking to Fancor and Jax. "Look at my man and how he cares nothing for the differences in the beings around him. He sees the similarities instead." She grows serious. "Vanora destroys Domhan first because she is from here and it's easier for her. When she is done with us, she will find a way into other worlds like yours and destroy those, too."

"Why? What does she want? How much power can she need? How many slaves does she require?" Frustration boils inside me.

"I've read your history books, Harper. You have had the same kind of tyrants in your world. They might not have shot black lightning from their fingers, but they were just as evil. How much would have been enough for them? If Hitler had succeeded in dominating your world and had known of other worlds, do you think he would have been satisfied?" She picks up the comb from the ground and puts it in her leather pack.

There's no need to respond to the question. We both know the answer. "I guess we had better stop the witch queen here then."

Cara walks over and hands each of us a large leaf. On top is a small pile of fish and some kind of white vegetable.

"Thank you." Once Cara has bowed and walked away, I stare at the strange breakfast.

Nainsi eats several bites before noticing that I've not

touched mine. She says, "It's not bad. Needs some seasoning, but the fish is fresh, and the corble reminds me of my childhood."

"Corble?" I taste the fish and agree that while I'm not used to fish for breakfast, it tastes familiar.

"It's a nut that grows wild on this continent. We don't see it across the sea. Try it. It's almost like corn." She finishes her food and licks her fingers. "I'd better see if I can help Aaran so we can get these people fed and heading around the lake."

As she strides across the camp, I catch sight of Aaran helping an older man fashion a splint around his crooked leg. These people are so kind. How did Vanora go so wrong? How many more like her are there in this world, like Ciaran? I shiver at the thought of his evil mind touching mine as he looked for information.

I finish my food and agree that the corble tastes like corn.

Beran approaches with a look of either concern or embarrassment. I can't tell which. He kneels. "I found this on the ground after you were struck down in the great hall. There didn't seem a good time to return it until now." He hands me my father's wedding ring.

My throat tightens, and tears spring to my eyes. I wrap my arms around his neck. "Thank you." It's not enough. I don't know what else to say. "Thank you."

When I let him go, he's blushing. "You are welcome. I thought it might have some meaning to you." He rushes away.

I clutch the ring a moment longer before slipping it on my finger. It's just a token with no magic, but it makes me feel stronger somehow. Beran can't know how he brought my parents back to me, but I am grateful.

In the distance, there's movement in the sky, like smoke, only the shifting isn't smooth or in the same direction as the wind. It goes east and then west in a strange pattern. As it draws closer, I can make out the wings of black birds.

Jax, his men, and Nainsi all start chanting something I don't understand.

The others all lie flat on the ground and freeze like everyone in the Driver's Motor Vehicle office.

Aaran runs to me and covers me with his body. "Don't move."

A gray haze forms around us, and the metal-tinged air is still. "What are they?" I whisper.

"Blackbirds, but they are under Vanora's eye. She searches for us." As the birds fly overhead, he holds his breath.

I do the same. My lungs ache by the time he lets out his breath.

The gray haze lifts.

Aaran rises. "We have to get moving. There's no way to know if they saw us before the shield went up."

Standing slowly, I try not to show my pain as it spreads from my stomach. "Could she have healed this quickly?"

He shrugs. "Even if she's still hurt, she has other means to reach us."

Not sure what that means, I try out my legs and am pleased that while they still feel weak, they hold my weight.

The hilly terrain levels out as we leave the camp a few miles behind us. Somehow having the lake nearby feels comforting. Of course, it also reminds me of how Aaran washed my hair, back, and legs. Had I not been so battered, I would have begged him to make love to me that night. Instead, he held me while I slept, which was nearly as good.

There are tall trees in the distant north, but here the ground is dry and the trees short and gnarled. A good deal of bramble lines the hills, and the grasses have given way to thorny bushes that have seen better seasons.

It's slow going with so many people, and quite a few of them still sick or injured despite Cara's efforts each night.

Aaran steadfastly makes sure no one is left behind.

My speed lags as my legs strain to keep me upright.

"Get on my back," Aaran commands, stopping in front of me.

I'm not an outdoorsy girl. I'm used to a suburban lifestyle with an occasional camping trip where I drink beer around a campfire and sleep in a tent with an air mattress. Between Vanora's torture and sleeping on the ground, I feel like I'm eighty years old. Without an argument, I climb on his back and wrap my arms around his chest.

He grips my calves, one in each hand, and walks us to the front of the group.

Jax gives him a nod and drops back.

I'm not sure what it all means, or how such strategies are

best implemented, but I study everything. "Where would Vanora have gone to recover?"

"I do not know."

"So you don't know the other places she and her shadow army live?" This is troubling. "Is this world as big as mine?"

Nainsi answers, "Similar, but Domhan only has two continents and some islands. Much of the world is covered in sea."

"Part of which, we'll have to traverse," Fancor says gruffly. "Sailing is not my favorite thing."

Bert slaps him on the back. "Get seasick, do you?"

I swear Fancor turns a bit green even though we're on dry land.

Laughing, Bert says, "Nothing to be ashamed of. I was sick my first month at sea in the Navy. Had to be given IV fluids and kept in the sick bay for a week. You can get past it."

"Why can't Vanora get through to my world?" It's a question that's been niggling at the back of my mind.

Aaran lifts me higher. "The old gods protected your world long ago. They made the portals work only with light magic, which she can no longer wield."

"Then how did she get her wolves and shadow demons through?" Even knowing I have to fight this battle in this world, my heart wants to keep my mother and my friends safe.

Vanora has already proven she can break through the barrier. It's only a matter of time before she wages her evil war on Earth.

Aaran says, "She's learning new things. The elf who helps her is crafty. He knows old elven and reads the sacred scrolls. Eventually, she will break through all barriers."

"Is that how she came to get me on the western continent?"

Nainsi grunts. "She shouldn't have been able to. The oracle protects the west. The trees didn't know her magic wouldn't kill you. They sacrificed themselves to keep you safe."

"The trees?" What in the hell is she talking about? I close my eyes and see that old gnarled tree swaying in the breeze. The black lightning heading for me, but then the tree exploded.

"That wood is ancient, as are many. The trees have a life to them. They must have sensed her evil and protected you." Nainsi's eyes darken. "The price was that Vanora destroyed another of their kind."

"That's terrible." I want to know more about the trees, but my skin tingles, and my arms glow in myriad colors. "Aaran, it's happening again, only there's no mirror."

Everyone gasps.

What happened in the hotel when I glowed? This must mean something. "The wolves. They came at night. Aaran told me about elves being turned into shadow demons. In the morning, I prayed that I wouldn't be turned into a shadow, and I started to glow."

Before we can discuss my theory, the wolves' low growl rises above our footsteps. Six of them stalk toward us from the northwest. Larger than normal wolves, they are as beautiful as they are terrifying. Saliva drips from their bared teeth.

I get down from Aaran's back.

After drawing his knife from his boot, he hands it to me. "Don't get killed." He slips his sword from its sheath and runs toward the wolves.

All the elven warriors and Fancor rush after Aaran. Nainsi and Bert stay with me to protect the weak.

I suppose I should include myself in that group, but I grip my knife and bend my knees. I'm ready to defend myself and these elves who were so kind to me while I was in pieces.

From the back of the group, a dozen elves brandishing sticks and cookware run to help.

Nainsi says, "You're glowing like a beacon, Harper. Can you stop it?"

I wish the glow would go away to keep us safe. As I keep that thought in my head, my arms fade to a normal color. It's a warning. I tuck that knowledge away to talk to Aaran about when we're all safe.

"That's better." Nainsi raises her sword and stands with her legs spread.

I take up a similar stance with the knife.

Bert doesn't lift his knives. He holds one in each hand and keeps them by his side. "Harper, keep out of harm's way. You're not strong enough to fight yet."

He's right, but I stand my ground.

Ahead, a wolf charges at Aaran and leaps, its long canines gleaming in the sunshine.

Aaran continues forward at a run, slides as if he's stealing a base, and slices the underbelly of the beast.

The wolf's eyes dim, and it falls in a heap to the ground.

Two of the warrior elves shoot arrows, killing another wolf.

Jax slices the air while a wolf dodges his strikes. Taking a step back, Jax pulls a small blade from his thigh sheath and throws, hitting the wolf in the eye.

It collapses.

A wolf has one of the elves in its mouth, shaking him like a toy.

"No!" I can't stop the scream from getting out.

Fancor turns to see why I'm yelling. He runs from the wolf he's fighting, leaving Avon to continue, raises his broad sword and lops off the wolf's head.

Aaran is fighting one wolf, but the last comes directly toward me.

Dorian and Beran rush to shield me.

Nainsi and Bert close in so there are no gaps in the line between me and the beast.

Fear and rage war inside me. My legs wobble with the strain of keeping upright.

Cara and three elves I don't know stand beside and behind me. More elves surround me.

The wolf howls a deafening sound.

I can barely see it now through the crush of elves determined to protect me, a human they don't know but who they believe will save their world. A vision of my mother sick and dying flashes through my mind. Another of her walking out of the hospice healthy. I can practically feel her arms around me in our last embrace. I'm not dying here or letting them drag me to wherever Vanora is holed up.

Turning the knife so that it points down, I'm ready to stab anything with fur that comes through the line. If I thought I could get past these elves, I would rather be injured than let them endure any more of Vanora's evil.

It's all too much. I inhale deeply and let out a roaring scream as the wolf reaches Dorian with its gaping maw ready to bite. My scream fills the air, reverberating off the ground, shimmering over the lake.

Stopping, the wolf whines, and its ears lower. Eyes wide, it stares through the crowd at me. It backs up several steps and scans the bodies of its dead packmates. Unbelievably, it turns and runs north, tearing up the ground as it goes.

The crowd around me separates.

Nainsi blinks and stares at me. "What was that?"

"I don't know. I got angry." My cheeks heat, and the pain in my middle grows sharper.

Cara smiles, and it may be the first time she has in many years. It seems to surprise her, and she touches her lips. She pats my cheek before walking to where the bitten elf, Lare, lies motionless on the ground.

Dorian grins then bows to me, as does Beran.

As Aaran comes closer, the elves part. As he looks me up and down, his breath is shaking. "You're not hurt."

"No. I'm fine. It never even got close to me." I hand him the knife.

He slips it inside his boot. Without warning, he lifts me into a hug, hard and quick. Stepping back, he says, "We need to get you a weapon and train you to use it."

I'd hoped for something more touching, but I can't argue with him. If I'm to be attacked at every turn, I should know how to defend myself. A voice in my head is yelling that I should demand a portal back to my own world where the worst danger I've ever been in was a fender bender on Route 1 in rush hour traffic.

Nainsi and Aaran rush over to the two injured elves. Nainsi heals their wounds and sets a broken arm.

Cara has her hands on Lare. After a few minutes, she stands and shakes her head.

My feet give out, but Bert wraps an arm around me to keep me upright. "Hold on, Harper. I've got you."

"I didn't want anyone to die protecting me." My tears come quietly and rain down.

Bert sighs. "He died doing what soldiers do. He died protecting his people. It wasn't about you. None of this is. This is about saving Domhan from a tyrant."

Throat tight, I nod. He's right. It's selfish and arrogant to think it's about me. I'm needed to keep these people safe.

"I'm sorry to say, he's not the first, and likely won't be the last. He fought bravely, which is all a good soldier wants from his service." Bert lifts me off my feet, carries me to an outcropping of rocks, and settles my back against them. "Rest. I'm sure we'll move on as soon as possible."

The roar exhausted me. I rest my head back on the rock and close my eyes. I just need a minute or two to recover.

It seems like only a minute later when Aaran is kneeling in front of me, gently shaking my shoulder. "Harper, we're ready to send Lare off."

"Lare?" The sun is high, and I have to blink to focus.

"The one who fell." He helps me to my feet.

I was in such a deep sleep that I almost forgot where I was and what happened. We walk together to the edge of the lake where they stacked wood and bramble high. Lare's body, wrapped in cloth, is placed on top.

Jax steps to the edge of the burial pyre holding a torch. He speaks in a language I've only heard in muttered spells, but his voice is loud and clear.

Aaran whispers in my ear. "He says Lare was a good soldier and son of Pallera. He goes now, with honor, to be with his father and his father's father. He goes with our blessing and thanks for the sacrifice he made to save others. It was his duty, and he is fulfilled."

Jax lowers the flame to the bottom of the wood. The dry tinder catches immediately, and Jax backs away as the fire engulfs Lare.

We watch for a few minutes. Several elves kneel and pray.

Lowering to his knee with his back to me, Aaran says, "We have to get moving."

I climb on piggyback style and lay my head on his shoulder. "I guess I didn't think this through well before I agreed to come with you."

His back stretches beneath me as he takes a deep breath. "Would you have chosen differently if you had known what the last few days have been?" Before I can answer, he says, "Of course you would have. I can't blame you. I would send you home if I could, *mo chroi*. I would see you safe and in your mother's embrace."

"Aaran, we are in this together. I would have come even knowing what I know now, because along with what Vanora did and seeing what I saw today, I have met your people. I have seen their suffering and their kindness. If it is within me to save your world, I have to try." My throat is tight by the time I get it all out. I wish there weren't so many people all around us so we could stop and I could see his face.

His hold on my calves tightens. "You are..." He shakes his head and jogs forward.

The entire party speeds up as we round the lake's north side. Many are still being carried, but the defeat of the wolves and the loss of Lare seems to have renewed the strength of the elves and their desire to live.

The sun crosses the sky, and clouds roll in, bringing a drizzle as we trudge on.

Aaran slows and looks around the plains that spread out in all directions. Mountains rise to the northeast, and a forest lies far to the north. "We'll have to stop for the night soon. I don't like the lack of cover or place to hide you and the injured."

"Do you think she would attack again so soon? I thought magic took a toll. She sent the blackbirds and the wolves. Doesn't that require magical expenditure?" In the distance, if I squint, I can barely see the sea. The plains roll downward to the east.

He nods. "It would require magic to send the beasts."

"Then we should be safe for now. It took her almost four days to recover from my touch. You recovered your strength with the help of the sun in my world. Is it the same for her? Will the sun heal her?"

His cheek pulls back as he smiles. "Very good, Harper. You would make an excellent student."

It's best if I keep my barely-getting-by grades to myself. He already knows I was lazy about my driver's license, no need to tell him I was lazy in school as well.

"Vanora's magic is dark, though it wasn't always. She

has embraced evil and so her resources come from else-where. She can draw magic to heal herself from deep inside this world where fire burns and demons prevail." He shivers. "It's pure evil she feeds on, and there is much to gather."

"Is it hell, like in the bible?" I'd never given the idea of heaven and hell much thought. At least not since I was a child.

"I don't know that word, but Coire is another world within this one, and it is the place where dark magic gets its power." He shivers again, as if speaking of the place gives him the willies.

Fancor carries a woman who looks young but must be over thirty. Skin and bones, she hugs his neck as if holding on for her life. He says, "My people call it Ifreann, but it references the same place."

"I've heard that name too." Aaran lifts me a bit higher.

The jerking motion sends a shock of pain through me that radiates from my center. I try not to wince, but a soft hiss escapes nonetheless. "Sorry."

He steps to the side and lowers me to the ground. "You're still in pain? Why didn't you say something?"

"It seemed like there were other fish to fry. Also, it got worse after I screamed, or whatever that was." I hold my upper abdomen. "It's a duller version of the pain from the black lightning."

The entire group stops and hovers around me.

Aaran kneels beside me and places his hand just under my breasts.

I'd like to be the kind of woman who doesn't blush when being touched by a man in full view of a hundred people.

However, my cheeks are on fire, and I lower my face, hoping it goes unnoticed.

The tingle that I've learned to associate with magic warms me as Aaran searches for whatever is wrong with me.

His frown deepens. "She's left some bit of her darkness inside you, Harper." His eyes open, and their bright blue irises are filled with concern. "I'm going to try to remove it."

I look at the sun low on the horizon and put my hand over his. "Wait. You said your magic is restored by the sun. There will be none soon. You should wait until morning at least. What if whatever it is kills you?"

Nainsi puts her hand on Aaran's shoulder. "She's right. You shouldn't attempt this without knowing more about the magic."

His lips tighten to a thin line. "We can't leave this inside her to fester."

Stepping to the front, Cara eases him aside and places her hands on my stomach. Her magic is cool and vibrates faster but softer than Aaran's. Without words to know her by, Cara is a mystery, but as her magic strengthens, the pain ebbs.

I don't want anyone to be injured in an effort to heal me. I can manage the painful reminder of my time in the presence of the witch queen and her horrible consort.

After a few minutes, Cara's cheeks pale. Before I can put a hand on her to stop her, she backs away. She nods to Aaran and gestures to me, indicating he should try again.

Still sitting beside me, he leans in. His hands warm me. His magic draws away more evil or heals the wound. The ache lessens. After two minutes, Cara pulls Aaran away and waves at Nainsi to treat me.

I keep my questions to myself. What are they doing? Are they healing or absorbing evil? Can Vanora's magic harm them as they treat me?

Jax lends his magic next. His hands are cold, and he glares at me, as if I am the cause of his problems. Perhaps it is how he looks all the time. Though, in Clandunna he was tender with Selina and his children. He is yet another person in this insane world who I can't figure out.

Fancor kneels beside me. His round cheeks turn bright red. "My people are not natural healers, dear girl, but I shall lend what help I can."

"Thank you."

His magic is bright and forceful at the same time. It's strange how each person's magic feels so different, like a fingerprint. Fancor's hands are rough, and it's as if heat radiates from the dwarf. Somehow, he feels more human than the elves. He and Bert are not dissimilar.

Bert is taller, but both men are broad and muscular. Both speak directly without anything to hide.

The bright red dims only slightly at the apple of his cheeks and he pulls back. "I sense nothing dark anymore. How do you feel?" His dark eyes stare intently into mine.

I draw a long deep breath, and indeed the hurt that was deep inside me is gone. Searching for it, I continue to draw in air and stretch. "I feel better."

Chapter Twelve

AARAN

Fancor grins wide, as if Harper were his child and had achieved some great honor or passed a vital test. Backing away, he puts his thick hands on his hips and nods approval to the group who healed her. The dwarf seems to have taken on the role of elder brother to all of us in a very short time.

I surprise myself with my fondness for Fancor. He didn't have to come with us through the portal or raise his sword in battle, but he did so twice to benefit our cause. He certainly had no responsibility to journey across land and sea. Yet, here he is, lending his magic to us to save a human he's known for only a few days.

Perhaps it's time to rethink everything I've been told about dwarves.

My own joy is more tentative. I want to believe what Vanora did was temporary, but this lingering dark within

Harper worries me. It's unusual for light or dark to linger unless the spell is placed with intent, but the magic felt unfocused and hazy.

My mother would not approve of my affection for Harper, and as I will someday take her place as leader, I shouldn't entertain feelings, yet I won't ignore them. It's far too late for that. "Are you certain you're alright?" I go back to her side and put my hands just under her breasts. The gray fog that lurked within her has lifted. *I don't think Vanora knew she left that with you.* It's the first time I've opened my mind to her since taking her to the lake.

"I'm still sore in many places, but the ache in my center is gone." Her eyes are soft green as she stares at me. So many questions roll through her mind that I can't keep up.

Rather than try, I touch her cheek. "Later." Pulling my hand away, I reject the idea of ignoring my desire. We would both know it was a lie, and a hurtful one. Unless Harper feels nothing for me, and I sense that's not the case.

Despite my terror at the idea of losing her, for many more reasons other than the needs of Domhan, I step away. I am responsible for all of these people. Looking out over the worried faces of the ragtag elven party, I say, "It's getting dark. We'll have to make camp here. Tomorrow we must make our way toward the sea and find a ship worthy enough to get us to Siar Fàilte. Those who are injured, come forward before the sun goes down. We may not be able to restore your magic at this time, but we can ease any hurts so that you might travel easier."

A surge of pride from Harper hits me like a warm bath.

It's a little terrifying how much I crave her approval. My entire world and the existence of my species, not to mention the danger of death to everyone I know, should be my highest priority. However, Harper is above everything else. She is the double moons, the sun, and all the worlds. The rest is responsibility; she is air and the beating of my heart.

When the healing is done and the camp made, the entire party eats around a fire big enough to have cooked several large deer hunted in the tall grass to the east.

Harper doesn't eat much. She's thin, and her cheeks are hollow. Since the darkness has been lifted, I can only guess what ails her is emotional. Still, she doesn't want to be sent home. She wants to fight.

Putting her food on the leaf, she asks, "Are there other species of people in Domhan besides elves and dwarves?"

Jax nods and talks around a mouthful of food. "The fairy folk live on an island in the south. They keep to themselves, and all the better for it. They care nothing about the concerns of the world."

I wonder if that's true. We thought the same of the dwarf race before Fancor came into our company.

Jax continues, "Centaurs live on both continents and keep to the southern forests. Selina thinks they were once one people, but were separated long ago. Elves and centaurs have been allies in war, as well as fought each other over the centuries.

"Some say banshees haunt the sacred forest and sea to the north. We steer clear of those vile beasts. Then there are the mysteries of the sea, mermaids, mermen, and monsters whose names we don't know or won't say.

"The lesser elves once lived on a large island far south, but it's believed they are all taken by evil now."

Harper asks, "Lesser elves?"

Sighing, I pick up her leaf and give it to her in an attempt to get her to eat more. "They are similar to us, but not as far along the evolutionary ladder. Crude language and use of tools. Kind people, but Jax is right. Those on Domhan and those on Arcania are no longer free. Most were turned into shadow demons, others into beasts of burden." My gut clenches. "My mother tried to help them, but we had never built trust between the races, so they would not listen."

Wide-eyed, Harper nibbles a bit of meat and listens.

Fancor grunts. "Then there are the giants, but they keep to themselves. The dragons are lost because of the witch."

"There are dragons?"

It's too terrible a tale for me to tell. I nod to Fancor.

A dreamy smile pulls Fancor's lips. His eyes brighten. "Once the sky was alive with dragons in all seven colors: blue, red, green, gold, silver, black, and white. It was glorious. They had their nesting on the mountaintop and"—he nods in Jax's direction—"some elves joined with dragons and kept watch on Domhan. As a boy, I dreamed of being the first of my kind to ride a dragon. In my dreams, she was pearly white, and I could survey the land through her sharp eyes." Gaze drifting to the stars, he seems lost in the magic of his memories.

"What happened to them?" Harper finishes her last bite of meat and puts the leaf aside. Gripping her hands together under her chin, she looks young and innocent.

Guilt for putting her in danger rushes up, nearly choking me. The fact that there was no other option doesn't make it easier, nor do I feel less guilty.

With another long sigh, Fancor says, "Before Vanora took the great tower and the Priomh Bhaile, she dabbled in all manner of black magic. She learned how to turn elves to shadow demons, or bánánach as my people call them. She built an army, small at first, but it grew. The elves did what they could, but she was too clever and moved from place to place, eluding them. She took consorts and fed off their power. You met her latest lover, Ciaran." He spits on the ground. "He was a high lord's son before he was lured to Vanora's side. He, like the others before him, has great magic. Not enough to sustain her venomous appetite though. She'll drain him, and he'll die. His dried husk will be left behind for no one to mourn."

Thinking about Lord and Lady Sevelline, I add, "His parents have already mourned their son."

"They say he's a changeling. He can become a bear," Jax adds.

I don't bother to tell them that he can change into other animals as well. "Finish the story about the dragons, Fancor, if you will."

He gives a brisk shake of his head, as if he'd lost his train of thought. "Before Vanora became the witch queen, she thought to turn the dragons to her favor. She knew that if she could conquer the dragons and put her lesser elves on their backs, she could wage her war from the sky without ever having to leave her hiding place."

Fancor stands and tosses a few sticks and leaves into the fire. All gazes are locked on the leather-armored dwarf as he combs his fingers over his beard. His gold family crest shines in the firelight. "She went across the sea to the high mountain where the dragons nest. It's a forbidden place unless you have leave to go there. No one knows how she got through without the dragons turning her to ash or sending her back in time." Pacing, he shakes his head and fists his hands. "She stole an egg and meant to bargain for the life of the unborn dragon. She expected to cast her spell and ensnare them all."

Harper gasps. "She took a baby?"

"Held the black egg hostage knowing dragons will do anything to keep their young safe." Fancor looks around the fire at the wide eyes of the elves.

Some nod, knowing the story. Others are just enraptured by his tale.

"How did they save the egg?" Harper's voice is full of hope and prayer.

Looking at her, Fancor sniffs. "Ah lass, they didn't save that poor egg, nor the babe inside. Their leader, Trocar, knew what Vanora was about. Trocar was the bravest dragon. Songs have been written about his beauty and his skill. A black dragon, and so large, his head spans the length of three men, and eyes of shining gold." He says the last with a slight tune of the old bards.

Someone in the crowd hums the tune as well.

Continuing, Fancor sighs. "He tricked Vanora by bowing down to her. It was enough time to smash the poor little unborn's egg and give the other dragons time to escape the spell. Only Trocor was caught in Vanora's plan, and only Trocor has been seen in these skies since. Though now, rather than admire him, all who see him hide in fear."

Elven voices softly sing the song of Trocor.

Harper's arms are tightly wrapped around her bent knees. A tear runs down her soft cheek. "Where did the others go?"

"We think they are locked in time." I take her hand and pull her into my lap. "The elders believe that Trocor's mate, Delana, cast the spell that sent all the dragons into a place where time does not exist."

"Aye," Fancor agrees. "It is said that they will stay locked in time with no way out until the balance of magic is returned to Domhan. Though others say they are gone forever." Shaking his head, he steps out of the circle and drags his bed roll off to the side.

The rest of the party follow his lead and find their places just outside the fire's light.

The elves sing "The Lament of Delana." It's a sorrowful ballad recounting the sacrifice of Trocar and the loss of dragons in our world.

Lifting Harper, I carry her to the place near a rock outcropping where I've already laid out blankets. It's a bit outside the ring, but I need her to myself. "Why are you crying? Is it for the lost egg?"

She rests next to me and curls against my body. "No. That is sad though."

"Why then?" I wrap my arms around her and breathe in her scent, which is more earth and grass now than the flowers she carried in her world.

"For Delana. She is trapped in time and can't mourn her mate. I wonder if she knows the passage of time here or will have to weep for his loss when she returns. Will he die in the battle ahead? Can he be saved? Sometimes love doesn't prevail. Life is not always fair." She wipes her face with her fingers. "I wonder if all of this is a dream, and soon I will wake up in my own house in New Jersey."

"If you do, what will you think? Will you be relieved that your life is unchanged, and no danger exists?" Now that I have asked, I wonder if I want to hear the answer.

Silence hangs between us. Her voice is soft, and she threads her fingers through mine where our hands rest on her abdomen. "I would miss you."

Nothing could have prepared me for those words. No declarations about doing the right thing or saving worlds from evil. She would miss me. More joy than I deserve, and certainly more than I've ever before felt, scorches through me. "I would send you back if I could. To keep you safe."

"Safety is an illusion. No one is ever really safe. I could go back to my world and be hit by a truck while crossing the street. Those wolves might follow and drag me back here. I miss my mother and sleeping in a bed, but I know this is where I belong. At least, for now." She closes her eyes, turns toward me, and kisses my chin.

Cupping her jaw, I wait until she opens her eyes. "I don't want to hurt you, but I want you, *mo chroi*."

"You're not worried about making love for the wrong reasons?" Her smile glints in her green eyes.

Combing her hair away from her face, I lower my lips to just above hers. "I'm worried about so many things. If I had lost you, I don't know if I could have survived."

"Because the prophecy says you need me to beat Vanora." Turning away, she bites her bottom lip.

Firming my grip, I ease her gaze back to mine. "Because I'm not sure who I am without you anymore. Because my heart would have broken into a million pieces. I know we're from different worlds, and the future is beyond our control. I know you will leave me behind like a forgotten dream when this is over." My chest aches, but I have to tell her the truth. "Harper Craig, I love you. In this time, in this place, and for all time, in all places, my heart is yours."

Her drawn breath quivers. "You love me? I never thought. But somehow, I knew." Eyes lowered, she's talking to herself. When she looks at me again, unshed tears shimmer in the moss green of her eyes. Pushing me to my back, she lies on me and brushes my hair out of my face. "I think I've always loved you, even when you were a dream."

Full of joy and desire, my cock presses between us. "I'd understand if you wanted to wait for a proper bed or at least more privacy." The moon and planet Arcania shine behind her head, and she looks like a mystical spirit complete with a halo.

Looking at the fire and the elves bedded down twenty yards away, she giggles. "Can we sneak away?"

"I did see an old fairy glen when I went hunting with the soldiers earlier. They can be dangerous for those not fully in the light, but it will be safe for us."

"What is a fairy glen?" she whispers.

"Fairy glens, even after the fairy folk abandoned them and went to live away from elf kind, are blessed and hidden from Vanora's evil. It's a short walk over those hills. Do you think you can make it?" Reluctantly, I roll us to standing and take her hand. In the other, I grab the blanket. When she nods, I say, "Come."

I can't help noticing Fancor watching us leave the camp. He doesn't rise, but he sits up on his makeshift bed. He's a good soldier. In time, I feel he'll be a good friend. "Centuries ago, when the old gods still roamed the land, the fairy folk lived all over Domhan. They blessed certain places with light magic. Even now, those places cannot be harmed or even seen by dark magic. Someone like Vanora wouldn't even see the glen. It's likely some of the group didn't see it either, though I noticed Jax and his men all looking in that direction."

We make our way through the tall grass and over a slightly larger hill to a small stand of trees that form a canopy over a little green glen. Mushrooms grow in a stark white circle inside the tree line, and soft moss grows along the ground like a well-worn feather mattress. A small stream bubbles through a carved path across the middle before disappearing into an underground spring.

Harper releases my hand and turns in a circle. Her unbound hair spins in a wide arch. "This is magical."

Laying the blanket on the moss, I leave it to take her around her waist. "You are magical."

A soft smile on her beautiful lips, she rises to her toes and kisses me. "Are there a lot of places like this in Domhan?"

I run my thumb under a bruise that still mars her cheek and slip the fingers of my other hand under the bottom of her shirt. The skin of her back is smooth and soft in contrast to the denim pants she wears. "There are not that many. This is only the second one I've ever found."

"Should we take it as a good sign that this one was here, and you stumbled across it?" Resting her cheek on my chest, she sighs, rocking to a tune only she hears, and with her, I hear it too.

Wondering if perhaps she changed her mind about why

we came here, I hold her close and caress her soft skin but make no attempt to seduce her. She's been through so much. I want her to be in control.

Just when I think this will remain a lovely dance in the glen, she tugs my shirt from my trousers and skims her fingers along my back. "Can you take this off?"

My cock jumps to full attention. Backing up half a step, I pull the fabric over my head and toss it to the ground. I'm watching and trying to keep my breath steady, and my heart pounds as she steps out of her shoes and wiggles her bare toes in the moss.

Her smile is like the first light of the sunshine. My insides turn soft at the sight of her happiness. The firstborn son of the rightful queen or not, I'm nothing without this small, kind human.

I'm becoming a poet, and that's more like my soldier middle brother than me. I'm supposed to be the sensible one, well trained, smart, steady. That's what I was born to. Since I met Harper, my world has been upside down.

She strips out of her shirt and pants and stands naked only a foot away. She covers a long, red, but healing gash across her ribs. "I'm a little beat up."

I drop my trousers and kneel at her feet. Moving her hand aside, I kiss the place where she was wounded, I continue to other bruises and marks. Each one of them is my fault. I will never forget that. "You're perfect, Harper. Never hide from me. Everything about you is beautiful."

Pressing her hands to my shoulders, she sways with each touch of my lips. "I think I should warn you that it's been some time since I had sex, and I'm already close to coming just from your little kisses."

Her skin is pink, as if the admission cost her some embarrassment, though I can't imagine why. "Then let me help you."

Pressing my lips lower, I grip her ass in both hands, avoiding a bruise on her hip. I slip my tongue between her folds. She's sweet and wet. Her musky essence is like a love spell.

Without demanding, I nudge her legs wider, and she cries my name as I find the pearl-like button at the top of her sex. I suck and lick and hold her shaking legs while reveling in how sensitive she is.

True to her word, she contracts with her orgasm, and her fingers dig into my shoulders. "Oh god. Aaran, that's so fucking good. You have to stop."

I lap up every drop of her sweet juices, ignoring her demand that I stop. When she steps back, I rise and lift her in my arms.

"I can walk now." She trails er fingers along my cheek.

It would be a mistake to tell her I long to take care of her. "I know you can." I lay her on the blanket and follow her down. "I know parts of you are still tender. Tell me if anything is uncomfortable. I never wish to cause you harm."

Covering her lips with mine, I draw her tongue into a dance. Her tiny moan vibrates in her throat, and I long for more sounds and pleasures. Greedily, I want all her pleasures to be shared with me.

Threading her fingers through my hair, she grips my scalp with more strength than expected. Though, I should know by now that everything about Harper is surprising.

Chapter Thirteen

HARPER

Uncomfortable? Is he mad? I feel no pain, yet I'm uncomfortable with desire like nothing I've ever experienced. Anything I know from my life before has nothing on being held in Aaran's arms or feeling his lips on mine. His mouth between my legs was the ultimate pleasure, but only took the edge off. I need more of him, all of him. If I could crawl inside his skin, it wouldn't be close enough.

His back muscles ripple under my fingers. A dark bruise marks his shoulder. It must have happened fighting the wolves. A series of scratches mar his neck and the edge of his hairline just above his temple. These imperfections only heighten his good looks. He's the most beautiful being I've ever seen. The other elves are also attractive, but Aaran is spectacular. How am I going to live without him when I return to New Jersey?

I quash the thought. *Enjoy the moment*, I scream inside my head.

Maybe he heard me. He breaks the kiss and stares into my eyes for a long, intense moment. In the light of this strange world's night, his blue eyes are as dark as the deepest sea. Lowering his head, he takes my nipple into his warm wet mouth and sucks.

Pleasure shoots directly to my clit, which pulses and aches. I wrap my leg around his and press upward, searching for relief. "I need you, Aaran."

His deep growl is feral and vibrates against my skin. He licks my other nipple and runs his tongue around it before sucking and letting his teeth worry the tight bud.

It takes all my will to stifle the scream building inside me because not far from here are elves with acute hearing. It wouldn't take much imagination to figure out what we were doing if I screamed his name here in the little green fairy glen.

Thick and hard, his cock presses against my thigh. I reach between us and slide my hand along the turgid flesh. A bead of cum wets the tip, and I spread it over the head.

"Harper, you don't know what you do to me."

"I think I do." I grip a handful of his thick hair and pull his face level with mine. Tilting, I cover his lips and plunge my tongue inside. He's warm and soft while hard and strong all over. This man, this elf, is perfect.

With his knees, he nudges my thighs apart. Holding his weight off of me, the muscles bulge as he notches himself at my pussy.

What is he waiting for? I lift my hips and take in the tip of his shaft. A soft moan escapes, and I repeat, pushing higher to take a little more. I long to ease the ache of desire torturing me most exquisitely.

With a low animalistic growl, he presses inside me, inch by maddening inch. Stretching me, filling me, becoming one with me.

Pleasure explodes inside me, and my body sucks and pulses around his cock. My nails dig into his shoulders. I scream into his mouth while my orgasm sends a shock wave to every cell in my body. I break the kiss to catch my breath. I had no idea I was capable of so much rapture in so short a time. "Oh. Why is it so much? That's..."

Holding above me, buried deep within me, he asks, "Are you alright?"

Is he insane? "Move. Please move."

Releasing his breath, he combs my hair away from my eyes and pulls back. Gaze locked with mine, he presses deep again. Again and again, he fills me, making love to me slowly. Stare intense, he never looks away and somehow, it's more intimate than anything I've ever experienced.

It's perfection, and I may go insane all at once. I rock my hips to meet every thrust. Another orgasm builds within. "Faster. God, Aaran, I'm going to come again."

He covers my lips in a deep kiss. His tongue and cock thrusting and retreating synchronously. Hard and fast, and needing more, needing everything, I meet every move.

I try to hold back and wait for him, but there's no chance. My pussy tightens as bliss takes me over the edge. I pull away from his kiss and press my teeth against his muscular shoulder.

Holding his weight on one elbow, he cups the back of my head while my body quakes with wave after wave of the most spectacular orgasm of my life. Nothing can compare to this moment.

On a sound that's more animal than man, he thrusts hard once, and again, before pulling free and coming between us.

A small part of me wishes he'd come inside me. I want to feel his warm seed, and I yearn for the possibility of his beautiful child to grow within me. It's completely insane. I've never even considered children, never felt motherly. A logical and sensible woman knows it is considerate and smart not to risk a pregnancy, if our species are even compatible. Clearly, he believes we are. Still, we're at war, and I live in another world, and have a life there. Not to mention the curse. Though a boy child that looked like Aaran wouldn't be a bad thing. I quash the notion before my longing for him becomes too intense.

His kisses soften, and he peppers them along my cheek and my forehead. "Harper," he says on a breath. Rolling to his back, he holds me against his chest.

The aches and pains of my torture find their voice again, but I close my eyes and let the pleasure of the moment be my focus. "That was wonderful."

"I hurt you?" He caresses my bruised back.

"No. Vanora, Ciaran, and dark magic hurt me. You made me forget for a while." My muscles feel like jelly. "Aaran?"

"Hmm?"

"Can I hear the song of your soul?" It's strange the thought came into my head now. It's the first peace we've had since shortly after coming to this world. I long for more of him, all of him.

Brushing my hair from my face, he smiles. "Close your eyes."

I do and his fingers slide around my neck as I relax my cheek against his chest. Then the soft hum filters into my consciousness. It's soft, full of highs and lows. If there is a melody, the verse is too long to find the start and finish. As if music were made by wind through leaves and the swaying of ancient tree trunks, that is the song of Aaran's soul. And it speaks to mine.

A soft sigh escapes me, and I nuzzle against him. "So beautiful. Can we sleep here?"

Kissing the top of my head, he says. "For a while, *mo chroi*. Sleep. I will wake you when it's time to return to camp."

I want to stay awake and talk, then make love again. I want all my days and nights to be about pleasure and forget about the troubles of the world. Longing for a romance that is born of passion rather than drama won't make it so or keep my exhaustion at bay.

The steady rise and fall of Aaran's chest lulls me until my dreams take me back to Vanora's clutches and turn into nightmares.

Cool water on my stomach pulls me awake.

With a torn piece of cloth, Aaran kneels next to me. He washes the proof of our lovemaking from my abdomen, then presses the cold cloth between my legs and cleans me there too.

I bend my knee, opening for him. A soft sigh escapes. "That's nice."

With a naughty grin, he presses a kiss just above my slit. "I wish we had time for more, but the sun will be up soon." With a long exhale, he hands me my clothes.

I'm unable to take my eyes off his strong, wide back as he walks to the edge of the stream and dips his rag to clean himself. Despite denying us both more pleasure, his cock is at the ready while he drags the cloth over it.

"You're not making this easier with the thoughts going through that wonderful mind of yours." It's a scolding, but the passion in his eyes when he looks back at me shows that he wishes there was more time too.

I shrug without apology and pull my jeans on. It's strange, but I feel remarkably good. The healing wound on my stomach is several shades lighter, and the bruises have gone away. I'm pulling on my t-shirt when Aaran runs his hand along my shoulder blade.

"This was much darker yesterday." He caresses my skin with the softest touch until I pull the cotton down.

I run my hand over his shoulder, and his bruise is only a faint yellow mark now. "I'm feeling better." I step into my elven shoes and tie the laces.

He dresses and rolls the blanket, letting his hand linger on the moss. "The fairy magic favors us."

"Is that good?" I go to the stream, cup the cold water, and drink. The water is sweet and clean. Since arriving in Domhan nothing is familiar. In New Jersey, I never drank water straight from a source. Even when we camped when I was a kid, we brought bottled water for drinking and washed in the showers provided by the campgrounds. Everything since I left home is new for me.

Offering me his hand, he nods. "Fairy magic can be

mischievous, but if you feel better, then the remnants of those who made this place feel you are worthy of healing."

"And you?"

He rolls his shoulders. "I feel better too."

Once we're hand in hand, I look back at the little haven that kept us safe and allowed us to make a memory. The water shimmers in the light of the planet I can't remember the name of. The lush blanket of moss reminds me of how welcoming this place was for lovers. I take a mental picture to savor for the rest of my life. "I don't ever want to forget this place."

"No. We won't forget the hospitality of the fairies." He squeezes my hand, and we step out of the fairy glen and into the high grass.

Someone clears his throat.

Aaran freezes and puts himself between me and the noise.

Fancor's gruff voice cuts through the predawn. "I beg your pardon. Just keeping watch over you and the lady, Riordan."

My face is on fire. Has he been hiding here all night?

Shaking his head, Aaran tucks my hand in his. "Is that Jax I hear stomping along to the north?"

"Oh, aye. He took a shift as well." He falls in step beside us. "It's a good sign having a fairy glen in our path."

"Why?" I ask, despite my embarrassment that the entire camp likely knows we sneaked off to have sex.

"They are rare and full of magic. Most people consider them good luck." Fancor has the courtesy not to ask about our luck within the glen, for which I'm grateful.

Jax is not as courteous. "At least some of our party was

lucky." With a snort, he storms into the camp where Cara and Dorian are already awake, stoking the fire back to life.

I'm sure my face is bright red, but I don't bother to hide. It's not my fault that I'm here, and my grandma always said you can't choose who you love. I can't be sorry for a few hours of passion with Aaran. It was beautiful, and nothing Jax says will sully the glen for me.

With a soft smile, Aaran kisses my cheek and goes to help wake the elves and ready them to travel.

I toss what little we have into the pack, then braid my hair before joining Cara.

She's pulling the spines out of some leaves and feeding them into a pot on the fire. It reminds me of cooking chard or cabbage. Pulling some toward me, I watch, learn, and help. She smiles.

I have so many questions about Vanora, but I suppose those answers will come in time. "Cara, did you have to heal the witch queen often?"

Dorian pours more water into the pot from a jug. "The witch queen required healing for herself, her whore, and those followers who are not shadows. The war of good and evil takes its toll and Vanora threatened the lives of the slaves to gain Cara's help. Much of the payment for the use of her healing was to be tormented by those who are shadow demons. She has endured much."

She gives him a sharp look.

"You're right. We have all suffered at the hands of the witch queen," Dorian says.

From the way he touches her face and the love in his eyes, I realize they are mates. I suppose I should have seen it before. "Perhaps Aaran's mother can restore your voice."

Cara smiles at Dorian.

"She says that as long as I can hear her, that is enough." He nods and kisses her forehead. "Even so, I miss your voice." He gives me a wink. "Even when she was scolding me."

They share a look that perhaps isn't meant for my eyes before he moves off to help pack up the camp.

The sun is above the horizon when we're finally all moving west. I don't allow Aaran to carry me. Between all the healing and the effects of the glen, I feel much better.

Walking next to him, I can't help but ask, "Why didn't we bring all the injured elves into the glen for healing?"

Hiking his pack higher, he scans the land between us and the sea. "The fairy's magic is not guaranteed. They favored us, but that doesn't mean they would the others. In fact, the magic can resent the asking. To try would be foolish and waste time we don't have. Vanora will heal. She will hunt us herself or with her armies."

"How do we fight armies of those shadow demons?" The idea of it makes my gut tighten. Their energy is so horrid it's like having all the joy ripped from you. I shudder. The longer I am in this world, the more I think this is an impossible task we will never survive.

His fingers gently touching the back of my neck shakes me from my negative thoughts. He speaks softly for my ears only. "I thought we would have a few moments this morning before we reached camp. It didn't occur to me that there were guards in the meadow."

I blush, though I don't really feel embarrassed. It's more the warm memories of our bodies entwined that heat my cheeks. "What did you want to say?"

He looks around as if making sure no one is too close. "That being with you was the greatest gift I have ever received and to thank you for the honor."

"My end of the bargain was just as valuable. No need to thank me." It comes out more annoyed than I intended. In my experience, men thank you for sex when they leave the bed before the sun comes up and don't expect to call you for another date.

Shaking his head, he takes my hand. "This is coming out wrong. I only meant to say that the time in the glen with you was important to me. Not a moment, or a whim, but a vital part of my life that I will always cherish."

In the center of my chest, a knot forms. My heart doesn't know if it's full or about to break. "If we survive this, which honestly, seems unlikely, I will go back to my world."

"Yes. I know." He squeezes my fingers before releasing them. "I still stand by my feelings. Whatever happens, we will have those memories. They will carry me."

What does that mean? Carry him where? To the end of his life? Is that what I want, for him to never know a lasting love? "Aaran, when I go, you'll marry a nice elf and make elf babies. Girls, who have your hair and eyes."

Nainsi steps beside me. "I can see the ocean's shine in the distance. Maybe a day and a half from here."

Bert squints. "Then we'll need to find a seaworthy ship

from there. Ships need upkeep, and who knows what that witch has done over the years."

Where Aaran's mind had been a soft hum inside me, he closes that door now. I didn't actually hear his thoughts, though I think, if I had tried, I could have. It was a sense of his well-being. Now there is nothing, and I miss it.

His jaw ticks. "We just have to see what we find. I'm glad you decided to join us, Bert. Not sure if anyone else knows how to sail across an ocean with any skill."

Bert huffs. "That's a good question. I'll make a round through the group and see if there are any sailors among us."

Nainsi slaps his bottom. "I can sail, captain."

Grinning wide, Bert says, "You're a fine first mate, my love."

They take different directions and begin their inquiries. "Aaran?"

He shifts his gaze to me. His handsome face is tight, and worry creases his brow.

"We can worry about whatever is between us if we live. I will happily take whatever moments you spare for me while this madness ensues. Please don't add my feelings to your list of troubles." It's the best I can do. I don't have all the pretty words that he does. I've never needed them or wanted them until now.

The tightness around his eyes eases even as sorrow creeps into his gaze. "I want to promise you everything."

"If you could promise to survive, that would be more than enough for me." It's a half-truth, but he's still closed off, so he can't know.

Rather than tell me a lie to give me false hope, he takes

my fingers in his and kisses the back, then turns my hand over and presses his lips to my palm.

The warmth of his love spreads from where his lips touch.

Without a word more, we walk across the open plain exposed to whatever evil Vanora has planned, with our army of freed slaves beside us.

A day and a half totally exposed. If the witch has a dragon, she could wipe us all out in a heartbeat.

Chapter Fourteen

AARAN

Thirty yards from the shipyard, we've been silently waiting for an hour. A dune meant to prevent rising seas from flooding the nearby villages keeps us hidden. The houses behind us are long abandoned. Lesser elves who look as if they haven't eaten for days, maybe weeks, guard the ship. Dawn hasn't yet broken. So, it's better to wait for the darkest hour to attack. Then we can set sail in daylight.

When my mother led our people across the sea, we abandoned this port. Those who stayed were either conscripted by Vanora or turned into her shadow demons. Moored to the stone bulkhead with thick ropes, two ships float at the wooden docks. Buildings that used to be for storage and port offices stand against the moonlit sky.

The acridness of sea and rotting fish fills the air, along with the undertone of putrefaction. Nothing is as it should be. None of this should have happened. My family failed this continent.

Far too late for blame, I banish the thoughts and keep my attention on the larger of the ships and the movement aboard.

"Why didn't she kill me?" Harper whispers from where we lie watching.

"Can we talk about this later?"

She blinks. "We may be dead later."

"Then it probably won't matter." At least not to us.

Jax has taken half of our numbers and gone to the northern end of the port. Splitting our forces may give us an advantage. I can barely make out the silhouette of them hiding behind the old port master's house.

Narrowing her eyes at me, she changes the subject. "Those people on the ship are what you call lesser elves?"

"Yes."

"And you're going to kill them?" Disappointment laces her questions.

Looking into those perfect green eyes surrounded by dark full lashes, I want to tell her it will all be alright. I want to lie and say I won't kill anyone. "If I must. We will try to fool them and hope they run away."

"It's not their fault that Vanora put them under a spell or infected them or whatever it is she does." A crease forms between her eyes. "And why are they lesser exactly?"

"Because they don't have written language yet and no magic." I've never particularly liked the term either. "I know it's not their fault, but they may give us no choice."

She crosses her arms over her chest. "There's always a choice. Humans have no magic. Do you consider us lesser as well?"

"I didn't see you defending the wolves or the shadow

demons." My temper is rising. I want to calm myself and tell her all the things she wants to hear, but the truth is, I may have to kill those poor elves.

"The wolves attacked us, as did the shadow demons." Conflict flickers in her eyes, and she bites her bottom lip.

I lean over her so that she's flat on her back. I wish she didn't have to be any part of this, and at the same time, I want her to be here with me. "They have another name. Aracan elves. They are not less, but they are different. Humans have magic, but they have forgotten. Many elves will see you as less. I hope you know how I see you. I will do my best not to kill, but they are controlled by dark magic and may make it impossible, so I will not promise." I take a deep breath. "She didn't kill you because she fears killing you would only produce another chosen from your world to take your place."

Eyes as big as saucers, she stares, blinks, and looks away. She rolls out from under me.

A high-pitched screech of a seabird pierces the air.

"That's our signal." I cast a spell of mirrors and hope it holds long enough. When we rise from behind the embankment, we look like hundreds of armed and armored elves marching into battle.

The ship is long with tall masts. Hopefully, it's as good as it looks bobbing on its moorings. There are no goods at the port as there once were when trades were made between villages and cities. Only the rubbish remains, when once this was a bustling center of commerce.

A head lifts above the ship's rail, and then another. A loud cry in an Old Elvish tongue sounds the warning.

If they knew we were a band of mostly injured and weak, magicless slaves, what would they do?

More heads and yelling.

"Hold." I lift my fist to stop our progress fifty feet from the forward end of the ship.

Jax does the same from aft.

It's been a long time since I studied the old language, but I cobble together a phrase telling them to abandon the ship and leave and no one will be harmed.

Tension hangs in the warm air.

Harper grabs the back of my arm. Her hand trembles. "I wish there was a way to cast the darkness from them."

Someone walks the ramp from the deck toward me.

When he reaches land, I raise my palm. "Hold."

His English is guttered and rough. "She queen. Her ship." He slaps his palm against his chest. Crouching in a battle-ready pose, he growls.

Hunched and hissing like animals, dozens jump to land from the ship. With their cheeks sunken and hollow, they barely look elven. Long hair in every color hangs loose around their shoulders in filthy dreads. With empty hungry eyes and rotting teeth, they are barely alive.

"Damn." My heart sinks, but there's little choice. I raise my sword and wait for the first one to attack.

Harper releases my arm, but instead of stepping back out of danger, she runs past our lines. She raises her arms, rainbows of light shoot from her fingers into the sky, and screams at the top of her lungs, "No!"

The Aracan stop and stare. Their tattered clothes cling to underfed hunched bodies.

"No one has to die today. You can leave. You can go

home or make a home. Vanora is poison, she will discard you when she thinks you are no longer useful." Harper might be the bravest person I've ever known. She has no weapons, save the dagger I gave her, and it is still tucked in a sheath at her waist. She has no training or diplomatic skills. Yet, here she stands, face-to-face with forty or more enemy soldiers, begging them to stand down.

I tuck in next to her, the hum of her magic almost as addictive to me as the woman herself. "I don't think they understand."

"Then tell them." Desperation makes her voice sharp.

I translate her words into old elven.

"Queen!" A roar rises from the Aracan. "Queen! Queen!"

Harper thrusts her hands forward, and the rainbow light floods across the witch queen's followers. It highlights their barely living state.

Some scream, as if in pain.

A few rush at Jax and his flanking forces.

Raising his rusty sword, his face full or horror, their leader rushes toward us.

I step in front of Harper, my sword held horizontally ready to block an attack.

The color drains from the Aracan elf's face, exposing his pocked flesh. His eyes shine with terror, and he throws himself on my sword, effectively slicing himself in half. Blood splatters and he collapses on the dock.

The rest of the forty or so stare blankly for a moment before running into the darkness beyond the port.

I dislodge my sword from the Aracan. My gut twists. Five more lie dead in front of Jax, Beran, and the others.

"Why would he do that? Did he fear Vanora more than death?" Harper kneels and closes his gaping eyes.

"Maybe. I don't know." I wish I could ease her sorrow, but there is nothing I can say.

"He's nothing but skin and bones. Doesn't she feed her disciples?" Harper's eyes flash with anger.

Cara steps forward, and taking Harper's hand, urges her from the ground. She pats her cheek.

Dorian says, "Her tolerance for the physical needs of others is very low. However, perhaps she thinks the supply of willing bodies is endless. She once thought she could win this war with only shadow demons. When she realized they couldn't do labor, she enslaved elves. She stole the lesser elves from the southern continent and Arcania. They may be easier to influence."

Jax wipes his sword on the clothes of one of the dead. "We barely drew our weapons. It was more suicide than battle. What kind of magic do you wield, human?"

"I only wished for them to be removed from Vanora's power." She steps back from Jax, who storms closer.

I step into his path. "Whatever the magic was, it saved us from having to slaughter them all. There's nothing we can do for the rest of them now." Looking into the dawn, I make out a few retreating figures running northeast. "I think they may be heading to the sacred forest."

Fancor pats Harper on the back and gives her a sympathetic look, as if he were her uncle. "They won't last long in there. They say the sacred forest never gives back anyone or anything that stumbles inside."

Jax snorts. "Fables and folklore. It's just a forest. If they're smart, they'll stay within and remember how to feed themselves on the berries, rabbits, and fish. If not, they barely had enough on their bones to last the week."

My spell has dissipated and Jax's is only a moment behind. Now, with the illusion of an army gone, we are just a ragtag group, looking little better than the Aracan.

I turn toward the ship named *Gaithgaisce*. "Bert, can you have a look and see if she's seaworthy?"

He nods and points to the name. "What does it mean, Nainsi?"

Nainsi lets out a long breath. "Windfoe, or fighter of wind."

"We'll have to hope she won't fight too hard." He calls the four elves with sailing experience to go with him, including Beran.

They board with Jax and two more armed men to secure the boat and discover whether or not we can sail it across a very unforgiving sea.

My charges bring our meager food to the port's edge.

Dorian shakes his head. "I'll take two hunters with me, and we'll see if we can find something more. This won't last two days."

"How long will we be at sea?" Harper's cheeks are already turning green, and we haven't set foot on the ship yet.

"At least five days, *mo chroi*. It's a wide sea, and we can't sail through the forbidden waters. It would be more direct, but too dangerous. We have to go southwest to the islands, cut through, then sail north along the coast to the north port." I wish there was another way.

"All of this because I went into the woods for some peace during a party." She sits on an old stack of pallets.

Cara sits beside her and pats her knee.

Dorian strings his bow and leans down to kiss his wife's cheek. "We would still be slaves had you not come to Tobhtá. Everything for a reason, my friend." With a squeeze of Cara's hand, he and two others go hunting south of the port.

I call to them. "See if you can find any berries or vegetables. Fish should be available, but we'll need to ration water and the rest."

Dorian waves in acknowledgment but doesn't turn back.

"Aaran," Bert calls from the railing. "You'd better get up here."

There's no fear or signs of danger, so when Harper walks with me, I don't try to dissuade her. Not that it would matter. I'm beginning to realize that trying to protect her is fruitless. She's in danger, and she will continue to be until we defeat the witch queen. Maybe I can teach her to control her magic rather than use it only when desperately wishing.

We walk up the ramp and find the deck clean and clear. "They have been doing some upkeep."

Bert nods. He points to the second ship. "No hope for that poor girl." The smaller ship is listing badly and will soon sink or break apart.

"Does that mean she can't get her army across the sea if she has more Aracan elves and we take this ship?" Harper runs her hand along the rail and jerks as a splinter pierces the pad of her finger. Using her teeth, she pulls it out and wipes the dot of blood on her pants.

Continuing aft, Bert disappears down a steep stair that leads to the hold.

Expecting to find some horror, I follow, keeping my hand on my sword hilt.

Weeping, quiet and childish, reaches me before my eyes adjust. In the hold, lit only by a few portholes and the growing dawn, it's difficult to see.

Jax and Nainsi stare down at seven small children huddled on some blankets. A girl of perhaps twelve or thirteen with arms crossed stands, guarding the crying little ones. Her hair is light brown dreads, and a streak of dirt marks the left side of her tanned face. She's wearing leggings that may have once been blue but have faded to gray with sun and dirt. They're too short for her long legs. She hisses at me.

"She either can't or won't speak." Nainsi shrugs.

Taking my hand from my sword, I kneel. "Do you know the common language?" I ask in both common and old elven.

"I know." Her voice is rough and cracked, as if speaking at all doesn't come easily.

"Your people have fled." It's information she needs.

"Dead?" She shifts teary eyes to my sword.

Holding up my hand to indicate that five had died. "Most ran away." I point to my chest. "Aaran." I point to her.

Her tears fall, but she narrows her gaze and growls. "Enemy."

Nainsi lowers to her knees. "No. You are safe."

The girl looks from Nainsi to me, then raises her chin to the sky and screams. The smaller children join her, and it's like a pack of wolves calling for a lost member. Their grief echoes around the wooden hold, making it hard to think.

"Stop," I command loud enough to be heard above the wailing. I hold up a palm for peace.

Seven sets of eyes stare at me through tears, but the keening stops.

This is not good. I look at Jax. "We could take them to the sacred woods and hope their parents find them." Even as I say it, I wonder if those starved creatures have any sense of parenting. I can't imagine running away with my child left behind.

"We can't leave them without knowing they are cared for, and their people will be too afraid to come out of the woods if that's where they went." Beholding the girl, Jax says, "A female child."

Of course, I thought it too. The Aracan elves can still have female children, or at least they could when this girl was born. "Those questions will have to wait. What do we do with them?"

Bert steps forward. "You can't leave them to maybe be cared for by their parents. They need food, water, a bath, and clean clothes." He lifts the smallest, a boy of perhaps four or five. "Will you set him in front of the woods and walk away?"

The child cocks his head and pulls on Bert's beard.

Fancor climbs down the stairs. "What on Domhan is going on down here? The noise was like the gates of Ifreann had opened." He reaches the bottom and surveys the space. "The lesser elves left their babes behind? Blazes!"

"They were not exactly in their right minds." Harper sighs. "I terrified them."

Wrapping an arm around Harper, Nainsi says, "They'd been under Vanora's dark magic. They may not even remember birthing these children if you broke that spell."

The girl takes the boy from Bert's arms and steps back. "Queen dead?" She clutches the boy, her grimy fingers threading through his blond hair.

"I'm afraid not, lass," Fancor says. "She still breathes, but our people are free of her magic."

Pointing to the stairs, she says. "Go?"

"Where will you go?" Bert's voice is soft and full of sympathy. He sits beside her. No longer the burly fisherman, he speaks as if she's his to worry over. "The rest have run away, and we don't know where to."

The boy in her arms touches Bert's round ears and laughs. It's a sound I didn't expect to hear today, and it fills my soul with hope.

Even Jax smiles. "We should get them above and feed them. There's little time before the tide."

"He's right." Bert stands and offers the girl his hand. "If we're leaving today, we only have an hour or so before the tide goes out."

An hour to decide the fate of seven Aracan children. I wonder if this was what the oracle had in mind when she sent me to find the human woman. Any hope of leaving the shores of Ear Talamh today is quickly fading.

Chapter Fifteen

HARPER

Guilt is something I'm intimately familiar with. I felt guilty for living when my father died, and guilty for not falling to pieces like Mom. When she got sick, I felt guilty for being helpless. Now, I've chased away the parents of these poor children, and there's no way to give them back.

Though, watching them eat a full meal does give me some satisfaction. It's a miracle any of these seven lived. Six boys under the age of eight and one girl of perhaps eleven. However, they are so malnourished that they might be older than they look.

Cara and a young man of perhaps sixteen whose name is Jarol set up a crate and some boxes on the deck with berries, edible leaves, and enough deer meat to feed the children, but not so much that they would overeat and become sick.

All the while, Bert commands the checking of sails and

inspection of the keel. He's in his element. Nainsi helps, occasionally looking proudly at her man. Aaran and Jax are deep in a discussion that likely involves the fate of the children.

I honestly have no idea if bringing them across the sea is a good idea, but how can we leave them behind to starve or worse? They were barely cared for by their people before my magic. We don't even know if those who ran remember having children.

The girl looks up and wipes her hands on her tattered clothes. She points to her chest. "Tal."

"Harper." I can't help feeling a little honored that she chose to tell me her name. It might have just been because I'm the one still sitting here while the rest argue and work.

She points to Aaran and Jax. "They kill us?"

I'm shocked by her use of English. "No." My heart breaks. "They don't know what to do with you, but they won't kill you."

"Why?"

I shrug. "They are good." I touch my mouth "How did you learn to speak this way?"

Cocking her head, she points to her ear. "Queen people talk."

I assume this means she listened and learned. It also means at some point Vanora had her followers here. Where are they now? I shake away all my questions to pay attention to Tal.

On the other side of the dune, the bodies of the Aracan who were killed on the dock are being burned.

Tal points. "No."

There's no good way to explain the funeral taking place. I call to Jarnol, "Will you watch the boys don't get hurt?"

He nods and takes my seat as I rise and offer Tal my hand. "Come and see." I know she's young, but suspect she's been witness to more death than most.

Rather than take my hand, she crosses her arms but follows me off the ship and across the dock. We climb the rough stone steps that go over the dune near the building where Aaran said the shipping business used to take place.

As soon as we reach the crest, the heat and horrid smell hits me. I take Tal's arm and pull her to the side where we are not in the direct line of the smoke.

The fire towers twenty feet above the ground. Ten elves kneel in a wide circle around the pyre, singing a dirge-sounding song and rocking with hands clasped in prayer. "We did what we had to do, Tal, but no one dismisses your loss."

She stares dry-eyed while I cry. She turns away and descends back to the port. "Queen killed."

Following, I jog to catch up. "Why didn't the queen kill you?"

She stares at the ground as if searching. "Too young to make dark. I girl."

I point at the ship. "What about the boys?"

"New." Rage burns in her dark brown eyes. "I hide. Too small before, but..." She runs up the ramp to the deck.

I cannot imagine what that girl has been through, and I'm positive I don't want to. My gut knots as she storms away with shoulders back and chin up. Swallowing down my emotions, I board the ship and find Aaran and Jax still arguing, only now they are joined by Fancor, Cara, and Dorian.

I step into the center of the circle, effectively stopping the conversation. "The children will come with us. You can't leave them here even if you know where their parents are. They've been through enough. Vanora killed all the boys because they were too young to turn. She couldn't control them. She left Tal alive because she's a girl. Tal hid the younger ones once she was old enough to understand they'd be killed. We're not leaving them here." Without waiting for a response, I walk back to the lower deck where the children are fascinated by Jarnol and his bucket of clean water.

Each one takes a turn approaching the water before darting away and laughing.

Smiling, Jarnol waits for the next one to let him try.

Tal walks to the bucket and cups the water. She rubs it on her cheeks and neck.

Gaping, Jarnol hands her the rag.

She snatches it and scrubs her face, revealing pink cheeks.

When she hands him back the rag, Jarnol grins, his white teeth gleaming against his dark skin. As all the boys follow Tal's lead and come to wash their faces, Jarnol helps them wipe the grime away.

Bert steps next to me. "Well done, Harper." He lifts his chin toward the dispersing group on the upper deck.

My cheeks heat.

By the time provisions and people are loaded and the ropes released from the moorings, we barely make the next tide as it pulls us out to sea. Who knows what terrible fate awaits us in the depths of the ocean? I stare over the railing, my stomach lurching with the rocking of the ship.

Even though I have little idea of the position of things, somehow pulling away from shore feels as if I'm moving farther away from my life, my mother, and any sense or memory of normalcy.

"I will do whatever I can to get you back to your mother and the life you had before." Aaran wraps his arms around me from behind. His magic hums around me.

My stomach immediately settles. I press my hand over his. "Thank you, but I thought you weren't going to linger in my thoughts anymore."

He never said so, but he's been closing off his mind more and more.

He kisses my neck where it meets my shoulder. "It's difficult to do what must be done when I feel every emotion you experience. Even when you're brave, and you always are, I worry that you will put yourself in danger."

"My father once told me that I'm a survivor." I lean back into Aaran's hard chest. "I was eight, and we went to Bunker Hill to go sleigh riding after the first big snow of the winter. I'd been down a few times and couldn't get enough. It's as clear as if it happened yesterday. I ran up the hill, my legs burning from the effort, but I didn't care. I reached the top, put my sleigh in the snow, and down I went. But with all the other riders, the snow started to melt and turn slushy. I hit a rut, and the sleigh stopped short. I went flying ass-over-head and landed twenty feet down the hill. The next thing I knew, my father was lifting me out of a drift. His eyes were filled with worry, but I laughed. It had been like really flying. He checked my arms and legs for damage and my head for bumps and declared me a survivor."

"You've managed to dodge death several times since I've met you." His thumb slowly rubs just under my breasts.

"But if I die, you'll return to Earth and find some other woman." It's not fair to be jealous of that woman or to feel betrayed by the idea of her, but there it is. My truth. I'm expendable.

He pulls in a sharp breath as if I'd hit him in the gut. "I didn't make the prophecy, and I don't know if it's true. I didn't even know if you would be real when I went through the oracle's portal. All I knew was I had to hold the magic in place and get you to come back with me in a short period."

I'm not sure why the idea of being replaced bothers me so much. If I could be swapped out for another human woman, I could go home and leave the problems of good versus evil behind. Would Aaran tell that replacement that he loved her too? Will he forget me as soon as I'm no longer part of his prophetic destiny?

Two of the boys run across the deck.

Aaran kneels and gently takes each by the arm. He says something in their language, and they nod with wide eyes, then walk back to where the other children sit watching the land grow smaller.

I'm sure he told them not to run on deck. "Did you tell them there are monsters in the sea?"

A sad smile touches his eyes. "They've had enough monsters in their lives. I told them we didn't want to have to all jump in after them so they shouldn't run and promised them a place where they can run for miles at this journey's end."

"That must sound like heaven to children who've likely been prisoners their entire lives." Did they even know who their parents were within the group of Aracan who ran away or were killed at the docks? Tired and sad, I step away from the rail and go below, where I've been given the smallest of three cabins.

The captain's suite is quite large and has been given to the children. Cara and Dorian will stay with them and keep them safe.

Bert and Nainsi said they would stay on deck, but Jax insisted they take a cabin as it's the captain's prerogative.

I'm happy with a quiet place, even if my stomach doesn't really love being below deck. With Aaran's magic, I step inside, and the nausea is gone.

Stepping in behind me, Aaran fills the space.

My pulse thrums fast and hard as I turn to face him.

With one hand around my back and the other cupping my cheek, he stares into my eyes. "You are not replaceable. Whatever Vanora or the oracle might think, if you die, I die. Even if I lived, it would be a life of torment."

There are no words to fill the silence after his declaration. I want to believe him, and I know he believes what he says. "Thank you."

A short angry laugh pushes from his beautiful lips, and he shakes his head. "I love you, Harper. Maybe that's prophesied, and maybe not. Maybe I'd be forced to carry out my duty and find another human in your absence. I don't know. I'm no oracle. I'm an elven man, and I have lost my heart to you, a human woman. It wasn't smart or planned. This would be easier if I didn't care for you."

All I can do is blink up at him. It takes me a few beats to gather enough breath to respond. "I love you too, and probably wouldn't have come here to help your people if I hadn't already been in love with you."

Magic shimmers in the air between us like fairy dust. His eyes shine with so much emotion that I can't look away or even move. I'm mesmerized by how much he loves me.

I rise on my toes, cupping the back of his neck, and suck his bottom lip between mine. I kiss his top lip, then tilt my head and cover his mouth, exploring with my tongue along his teeth, and when they part, I touch his tongue.

On a growl, he hugs me tight and devours my mouth. Plundering with abandon.

Pressing my breasts to his chest, I can't get close enough. I wish our clothes weren't in the way. My clit pulses, needing more than kisses. I wrap a leg around his and pull tighter.

Cupping my ass, he presses his thick cock between my denim-covered legs.

The boat rocks hard to the left, throwing us off-balance and onto the soft mattress.

Aaran breaks the kiss and lands on his forearms in time to ensure his weight doesn't crush me. Smiling down at me, he cups my cheek. "As much as I want you"—he grinds his hips forward—"and I'm sure you can feel how much I do, there are over a hundred people above and below decks."

Of course, he's right. The timing is not good for a morning tryst. Still, it's hard to release him. With a long breath, I let go. "You're right. Maybe someday, we won't have a world to save." My heart breaks a little. Without a world needing us, will we even be together?

My hands glow rainbow colors. "Aaran?"

Aaran grips my hands, and his loving expression is replaced by a frown. He rises, then helps me to stand, and we rush to the deck.

Beran's voice rises above the sounds of the sea. "On the port side!"

On deck, we run to the left side of the ship. The rocking of the ocean has increased since we set sail. It's all I can do to keep my feet and move with the rocking to reach the railing.

Several elves are at the rail, and others hold the children away from danger.

Beran points to the water a few hundred yards away.

Something long and large with scales slips through the waves. It reminds me of all those fake photos of the Loch Ness Monster. "What is that?"

Jax looks a bit green, but nocks an arrow and waits for the thing to rise up again. "Sea dragon. More slug than lizard. They shouldn't be this far south. The witch queen is gaining her strength back, and she knows we've freed her disciples."

"You don't know that," Nainsi argues.

Jax lowers his bow and his jaw ticks. "There have never been sea dragons this far south. You don't think that fancy rainbow light magic went unnoticed by Vanora, do you? Don't be a fool. It was a kindness to free them, but it gave her our location." He turns a vicious frown on me, and his eyes burn with accusation.

Dorian takes a bow from a soldier and nocks an arrow, his eyes focused on the water. "It's not as if there were that many options for her to choose from. Stop blaming Harper for everything you think has gone wrong."

While I appreciate the solidarity, I can't help but agree with Jax. I don't know what I'm doing with my magic. I'm reckless with it and have yet to think through the consequences of my actions.

At the moment, the sea monster churning up the ocean seems like a more immediate issue than how we got here or whose fault it is. "What do they do besides make the ocean rough?"

"Some say they can sink a ship, and some say they can seduce the crew into jumping off the deck." Nainsi shrugs.

A triangular head rises from the deep, and the sea dragon roars, showing three rows of sharp teeth. Its roar is like a combination of a lion and a gorilla. I have watched too many nature documentaries.

In the distance, another hump cuts through the waves.

I point. "Is that another one, or is it that big?" I'm not sure which would be worse.

"Another, I think." Aaran stares out at the horizon. "I think more are coming."

The ocean looks like river rapids, and the bubbling is getting closer.

The sea dragon leaps from the water and shoots its body across the bow, tearing the rigging holding the forward sail. Eight feet long, with spines along its underbelly and scales, it's a monster out of a nightmare. Glowing red eyes are deeply set into its triangular head. It looks like a snake, and it glares right at me.

It shatters a piece of railing as it crashes against the ship and falls back into the sea.

More are coming fast.

Bert shouts, "Lower the sails!"

Beran replies, "We can't outrun them without the sails."

Aaran's arrow lodges in the head of the monster before it hits the water. "Turn south. Hopefully, they can't bear the warmer water."

Jax and the other soldiers shoot arrows at every scale that breaches the surface as our ship turns left and cuts through the waves. Water crashes over the sides as we spear the next towering wave and then another.

The archers stumble aft and continue firing.

I rush to the children who are sloshing from one side of the deck to the other with every wave. "Hold on to each other. We're going below." I grab the youngest, named Fort, and pull him to the stairs.

He grips Bor's leg, the oldest boy, who has hold of two more sprawled across the deck.

I keep pulling until I have Tal's hands in mine and all seven children are below. I grab the door to their room and the ship tips hard, sending them down the narrow hall. I grip the doorknob and hang for a moment before we're righted, and I come down hard on my knees. "Hurry. Before the next one."

They scramble back to me, and I lock us inside the room.

We get to the center of the large bed and huddle together. I put myriad dusty pillows along the walls, hoping it will cushion our fall should we climb another wave or be tossed over.

A sea dragon flies past the window, its sharp teeth bared and its roar shaking the glass. The children scream. It's all I can do not to join them. Instead, I hug them tight in a group hug, my arms aching with the effort to keep them safe.

The children yell something in their native language.

I don't know what they're saying, and can only coo to them softly, telling them everything is going to be okay. It might be a lie. I have no idea if we're going to survive this. However, I have to believe that if we die here, we go someplace good. Surely the babies will go to heaven or someplace like that. Will I go to heaven if I die in this other world? I shake away the ridiculous thought and renew my grip as another wave sends us all flying to one side of the bed. Another flings us toward the windows. I grip the wooden frame with my ass pressed against the glass and pray the pane holds my weight long enough for the ship to correct itself.

The ship sounds as if it's breaking in two.

All their hands grip at me from different angles. I'm pretty sure this is exactly like some nightmares I've had about hell, but I scream, "Hold on." As if they know what I'm saying.

We flop back to the mattress in a jumble of arms and legs. Lem's foot smacks into my eye, and someone's elbow catches me in the ribs. Everything moves from side to side like water in a bathtub when you stand out of it.

The swaying becomes gentle, and the only noise is from crying children and my own breathing. Kissing the forehead of a little one named Gnal, I dislodge myself from the pile and listen for signs of danger.

Standing with my back to the bed, I grab a broken leg from the shattered desk and hold it in one hand, then pull my knife from the sheath at my side. I wait.

The crying becomes sniffling behind me.

The door bursts open.

I stand ready to defend these babies with my last breath.

Aaran's welcome form fills the doorway. Blood stains his shirt at the shoulder, and a long scratch blooms red on his cheek. He lets out a breath, as if he'd been holding it for a long time. "Thank the old gods." He pulls me into his arms.

I drop the wood and hug him.

Little hands wrap around our legs and waists.

Chapter Sixteen

AARAN

By nightfall, we are far enough south that the chances of sea dragons are very slim. That's not to say that Vanora's other minions aren't seeking us, but for the moment, the sea is calm.

Maybe I should be below holding Harper and sleeping, but I can't leave the deck until I feel we are out of danger. With a sword at my side and a bow and quiver next to that, I stare up at the stars. Arcania glows purple on the horizon.

The deck creaks, and in a long white shirt and shoes, Harper is picking her way past the sleeping forms of our companions to the bow where I've made my resting place on higher ground. She lies down next to me.

"What are you wearing?" I wrap my arm around her as she settles in with her head on my shoulder.

With a shrug, she tugs the fabric. "I found it in a box at

the back of the closet with some other clothes. I've washed our clothes in salt water. At least the blood and sweat will be gone."

"Thank you. You didn't have to do my washing." I changed when I went to Cara to heal my wounded shoulder. I had an extra set of clothes in my bag, while Harper was already wearing her extra clothes.

"I was washing anyway. How is your shoulder?" She adjusts her body and settles again.

Keeping her head on my biceps, I turn to face her. The bruise under her eye has darkened, and she looks as if she's been in a fistfight. I skim my thumb along the mark. "My shoulder was healed and is only a dull ache now. How are you?"

She smiles, and my heart tightens. "I feel as if I've had a fierce battle with seven children and a rolling sea."

"You should have let Cara heal you." I send the little magic I have to ease her pains. The day has drained my magic and my energy.

Pulling back, she shakes her head. "I'm fine. They're just bruises. You need to recover, and that's not going to happen until the sun comes up tomorrow. If nothing attacks us between now and the next time we lie together, you can heal me."

Why does it feel as if that's unlikely? "You looked like a warrior when I opened the cabin door today. If I'd been a sea dragon, I'd have run."

"You're teasing me?" She hides her face in my arm.

"No." I wait for her to meet my gaze again. "Nothing was going to harm those children on your watch. The oracle may be wrong about a lot of things, but they were not wrong about you, Harper Craig. You are fierce and brave. You risk everything to keep strangers safe and think nothing of your own safety."

"Oh, I think about it. It's just usually too late when I do." Sighing, she closes her eyes and cuddles against me. "I looked at the stars when I first came up the stairs, but they're not my stars, and I find no comfort in them."

On my back, I pull her against me. "Sleep, *mo chroi*. Find comfort in me and know that your stars are there, if only a bit farther away." Maybe one day these stars will feel like home to her.

As the sun rises, I sit and let the warmth and magic fill me. I would have loved to remain with Harper in my arms, but the deck stirs with waking elves.

The breeze has hold of the main sail, and we're moving west, though a great deal farther south than I would have preferred. This journey feels longer with every step forward.

Her hand slides up my back to my shoulder. "You're worried."

Blocking my mind, I turn to find her black eye swollen nearly closed. The side of her face is red, black, blue, and puffed to the point where she's hardly recognizable. I touch the injury.

She winces and pulls back.

"This needs healing, as do your ribs. You're in no condition to train." Lifting my fingers, I keep my touch light and send healing magic to her skin and the cells beneath.

Harper lets out a long breath and relaxes into the comfort of healing. "Train? What am I training to do?"

With the sun's power flowing through me, I direct more to her ribs and open my eyes to find her staring back, looking much more herself. "That's better. You'll train to fight, defend, and most importantly, control your magic. Though, I'm concerned the witch queen can detect your magic here. That training may have to wait until we're safely home."

She smiles. "Thank you. I feel much better. All those arms and legs flailing around during the battle, I had more bruised skin than not." Standing, she stretches, and I admire the bare legs below the shirt she found.

I touch the soft fabric, then her calf. "It's not a bad idea to look through the ship more carefully to see what we can find."

"How will you train me to use magic that you said you don't understand?"

Holding her hand, I lead us to the lower deck and down the stairs with a wave to Bert at the ship's wheel. "We have to discover your abilities together and find ways to use them at will, rather than in states of panic and need only."

In our small cabin, she toes out of her shoes and pulls the shirt over her head. Reaching for her jeans, which hang over a cupboard door, she turns away from me. Her perfect round ass and hips make my fingers ache to touch her. The side of her breasts and the pointed nipples make my mouth water.

Unable to resist, I wrap my arms around her and pull her tight against my thick cock. "You are so lovely. One day, I will make love to you day and night without worry of monsters or demons."

Abandoning her clothes, she turns into my embrace and leaps off her feet to wrap her legs around me. She grinds her center forward and digs her fingers into my shoulders to pull us tighter together. "Are you making promises or just wishes?"

I grip her ass and lower us to the bed, still made as no one slept in it. I long to rumple sheets and love this woman until we're both spent and unable to think of danger or despair. "I can promise you that this is what I wish for."

Her smile is better than sun magic. "Just sex or are there other things? Not that I'd mind sex with you day and night. Just curious if we'd take breaks for food and air."

The list of things is so long, I'd be embarrassed to enumerate them all. "You are my air and my sustenance." It's true, but there's so much more. "I'd show you the caves where warm springs soothe all your aches. We'd picnic by the lake and swim. It isn't the land I was born to, but Tús Nua is very beautiful and untouched by Vanora."

Her smile falters and I regret mentioning the witch. "Why hasn't she touched it? Is your mother that powerful, and if she is, then how did Vanora capture the old city?"

Pushing desire aside, I pull back.

Harper tightens her grip with both arms and legs. "Don't pull away whenever I ask hard questions."

I brush her hair, wild from sleep, from her brow. "You want to have this discussion while you're naked beneath me?"

She giggles and releases her hold. "Maybe not. I do want

to know the answers." Once I stand, she pulls on her jeans and shirt.

While I fold the clothes she cleaned for me, I say, "The oracle's magic was enough to keep the witch queen from the western continent. When she took you from Clandunna was the first time I've heard of her breaching that magic."

"But the curse reaches Tús Nua. And that fact that she created a portal and came through it to get me is a bad sign." She straps the dagger to her belt as if she's been wearing a weapon all her life.

"The curse has affected most of Domhan. Though it would seem the Aracan took longer to be harmed. I wonder about the fairies, but they keep to themselves. Dwarves were only a few years behind us. They have not seen a female born in almost twenty-five suns. I'll admit, we have been consumed with the plight of elves." I have many things to discuss with my parents when we return.

She cocks her head. "Shortsighted. Are you certain that whatever we're doing will save the other beings living here? What about the animals? Have only male deer been born, male rabbits? Is the food supply growing scarce?"

In truth, I have no idea. "This might be a question for the oracle or my mother."

"Your mother seemed kind and strong. Is she science-minded or more politician?" There's only curiosity in her tone.

I open my mind to search for blame but find none.

She bats me out of her mind. "You can't pop in here whenever you don't believe me or want more information." She points to the side of her head. "You either want the connection or you don't, Aaran Riordan. There is no halfway."

Despite her desire for information, her anger wins, and she moves to storm from the cabin. I reach out and block her path. "I apologize. You're right." I open my soul to hers and let her feel all I feel.

She melts against me. "You can block me in battle if that's easier." Whether angry or mollified, she's sensible, my beautiful human.

"My mother is very complicated. She doesn't always share her knowledge, perhaps because she doesn't want to burden us with things we can't control. The prophecy is something we can act on."

Cheek to my chest, she nods.

"I have not noticed a lack of female animals, and we had a filly born just before I left home to find you." The idea of the curse going that far haunts me. "It would be a disaster if those short-lived creatures didn't bear both sexes." I wish we had a few dozen horses to carry us home once we reach land.

Pulling back, she grins up at me. "I heard that. Horses would be nice, though I've only ridden a few times, and that was when I was a teenager."

"I'll teach you to ride." I actually can't wait to see her astride a horse. She'd be magnificent. "Today, swords and knives. Perhaps a bit of archery. Later we'll talk about your magic with Jax."

She rolls her eyes, and I don't need to know her mind to gain her feelings about sharing time or details with the warrior. "He doesn't like me."

"He is cautious about things he doesn't understand. You are a puzzle to him. Perhaps talking through your magic will change that." I shrug. "However, that's not my purpose. He's very knowledgeable about magic."

"Then why is he a warrior and not a mage or whatever you call your magicians?" She props her fists on her hips. Adorable.

"His magic is strong but focused on healing, accuracy with a bow and arrow, and physical strength. Still, he's a wealth of information, as I'm guessing is Cara." I give her a long look that fills me with more joy than I deserve, and I'm wasting precious time to be alone with her. "My mother and father are both strong with magic. My younger brother, Liam, is a warrior, while I have a bit of both."

"And your youngest brother?"

"Raith." I sigh. "It's unclear where his gifts lie. His magic is strong, but often unfocused, and sometimes it goes wrong. He means well and tries, but his mind is a jumble of many thoughts at once."

Eyes wide, she stares. "And he's been sent to collect a human woman?"

I share her fear. "It's part of the prophecy that all three of us had to go."

She blows out a long breath but doesn't share her thoughts aloud. Inside, I hear her relief that it was me and not Raith who came for her.

My agreement has nothing to do with the uncertainty of my brother's magic. It's unimaginable that Harper wouldn't be in my life. "Let's get you a sword."

Holding up a finger, she drops to her knees. "I found this when I was looking for something to wear during laundry." Head halfway under the bed, she mutters a curse before backing out with a wooden box in tow. Its polished wood has a fine layer of dust broken up by several clean places where Harper has handled it. She unhooks the latch and pushes back the cover.

Within lies a sword that gleams in the sunlight coming through our small window. The hilt is wrapped with fine leather, and the blade is perfect, as if it was meant to be a gift but had never been delivered. It's smaller than my broadsword, so it might have been made for a woman or a child. My first training sword was similar, though not as fine. An amber stone gleams from the base of the hilt.

"This is very fine." I pick it up and feel the perfect balance of the workmanship. Next to the blade is a fine leather scabbard embossed with an intricate pattern I've never seen before.

"Too good for me to learn on. We can put it back." She waits for me to return the weapon to the case.

"I think it's perfect for you to use. It's a lighter sword than anything else we have, but well made." I test the blade before handing it to her. "Be careful, it's quite sharp."

She wraps her hand around the hilt and keeps the blade pointing toward the ground.

Leaving the fine leather sheath in the box, we head up to the deck.

Many stop to watch us. They've not seen Harper with a sword before.

Frowning, Jax crosses his arms and leans against the railing. It's hard to say exactly what the warrior is thinking. Like my brother, Liam, he keeps his emotions and feelings under the mask of discontent.

Pulling my sword, I stand ready with the point directed toward her.

After a moment of thought, she imitates me. "Now what?"

"Have you had any defensive training?" I tap my blade against hers.

Keeping her grip, she backs up a step. "I took boxing and some martial arts classes at the gym, but never anything with weapons. Also, those classes never had the intention of harming anyone."

"What were they for then?" Jax pushes from the side and steps closer.

She looks at him. "Exercise."

I slap her sword harder, and it clatters to the deck. "Never take your eyes off your opponent."

Shaking her hand, as there's some sting in the vibration, her face gets red, and she picks up the weapon and holds it up.

Jax shakes his head. "You're holding the hilt too tight. Keep a firm grip, but not a death hold. Never be rigid. Everything must flow from you, not be forced. These classes you took were hand-to-hand, I'm assuming. Think of the sword as an extension of your arm."

The white of her knuckles eases and she cocks her head as if feeling the difference. When I step to the right, she counters to the left naturally.

It's a good sign that she has some innate tendencies and the willingness to listen to instructions from someone she's unsure of. Jax has not ingratiated himself. It's not in his nature, but she recognizes his value as a soldier.

I attack and she blocks. Again and again, I go through the motions, slowly increasing the speed and strength of my attack. Left, then right until I jolt forward, unbalancing her.

She stumbles backward, her ass hitting the deck.

Jax smiles for the first time. "Not bad." He helps her up. "Bend your knees more to stay centered. Don't look at Aaran's sword. Focus on his eyes, they will tell you what his next move will be."

That adorable crease forms between her eyes as she rubs her sore bottom. "How will his eyes tell me anything about the sharp object coming at me?"

"Try it and see." Jax steps back.

Those gorgeous green eyes stare into mine.

I slash.

Harper blocks.

Recognition dawns on her face.

Striking from the left, then the right, I move faster and try to put her off-balance again.

Feet light and steady, she blocks each move but continues to be backed into a corner.

"Good. Now attack, Harper," Jax commands.

Panic registers in her gaze.

I knock her sword from her hand and leave the point of my blade an inch from her throat. "The enemy will not stop, *mo chroi*. You cannot hesitate."

With a nod, Jax stares at her. "Still, not bad. You have some natural ability. From what I know of your world, there is little sword fighting. You have other weapons, guns." He says the last word tentatively as if he'd struggled to pull it out of his memory.

Harper picks up her sword. "That's true, but I'm not a soldier. My first fight was on the boat to that first gate, and I only attacked out of desperation to save Aaran. There are no guns here?"

"Magic was given to us by the old gods. They taught our ancestors how to use it. They showed us the technology of your world and gave us the choice between that and magic. The kings and queens of Domhan chose magic." Jax's eyes are bright with challenge. "Your technology will not work in this world."

"But your magic works on Earth. That hardly seems right." Harper rolls her shoulders and bends and straightens her arm several times.

"Does it?" Jax asks, looking at me.

I nod. "Nainsi and I both used our magic in Harper's world. And their sun renewed my magic when I overextended myself."

"Maybe I should have brought my phone and some other technology and tested them on this side." She rocks her head from side to side, stretching her neck.

As if the conversation about magic versus technology were at an end, Jax says, "I will bespell your weapons during training. You won't be able to do more than bruise Aaran if you can get a blade to him."

Once he has her agreement, he casts the spell.

I should have thought of that from the beginning, but I was sure I wouldn't harm Harper, and perhaps arrogant to believe her incapable of getting through my defenses. After another hour of swordplay, I'm proved correct, though she improves throughout training.

Sitting on a crate, she rubs her arm and shoulder, wincing with every move.

"I think archery practice will have to wait for another day." I sit behind her and take over the massage. "I doubt you could pull back on the string right now."

Moaning and leaning into my touch, she closes her eyes. "Give me an hour, and I'd like to try it."

Jax sits opposite her and narrows his gaze. "You were far better than I expected."

"Um, thank you?"

It's hard not to laugh at the way her voice lifts in question over his halfhearted compliment. Despite my attempt, a short chortle escapes.

Chapter Seventeen

HARPER

I'm not sure what else I'm supposed to say to Jax. He hasn't liked or trusted me from the moment he met me. Still, his instruction during training made sense and helped. He's abrupt and direct. As a Jersey Girl, I appreciate that.

With eyes narrowed, he assesses me. "Tell me about your magic."

With a shrug, I say, "I don't know much about it other than it comes when I wish hard for something and need it desperately."

His gaze flicks to Aaran, who is rubbing knots out of my shoulder.

"I have not seen Harper create magic when desperation wasn't in play." Aaran stops massaging my shoulders and neck.

I continue to stretch those muscles and tendons.

Jax stares at the decking as he props his chin on his fist

and his elbow on his knee. After a second, his other hand shoots up and he grips my throat.

Unable to scream, I reach for my sword, but he kicks it away. It's getting hard to breathe and my vision dims around the edges.

"That's enough," Aaran demands.

The hand is gone, and I gulp air.

Aaran pulls me against his chest, and his warm magic floods my neck and throat.

Jax sighs and says, "No magic to save yourself. Or maybe you didn't think I would kill you."

I rub my bruised esophagus, wishing I could get to my sword before anyone stops me. "No. I thought you would."

"Maybe you knew Aaran wouldn't let anything happen to you?" Jax's voice is soft, and he leans forward. The rage that always seems to be present in his eyes is gone, replaced by regret and interest.

Beginning to see what he's getting at, I think about it. "Maybe."

While Aaran's magic soothes my bruised neck, Jax reaches forward, and with one cool touch, the pain is gone.

It takes all my will not to flinch, but I won't give him the satisfaction.

My reward is his rare smile. "So, you wish for a way to combat danger that will harm another, and that is the only time you've seen your magic?"

"No." My head clears, and my heart rate returns to a normal steady beat. "When we were still in my world, and Aaran told me about the shadow demons, the idea terrified me. I prayed that I never lose my soul like that."

His gaze shifts between me and Aaran. "What happened?"

My cheeks heat with the memory of glowing like a rainbow.

"She glowed with the most beautiful aura I've ever seen, but it could only be seen in her reflection in the mirror." His voice softened. "I've never seen anything like her and how those colors glowed outward from her skin."

Blinking, Jax gapes at Aaran.

Wishing we were alone, I look over my shoulder, and I am unable to keep the blush from spreading to other places. Shaking those thoughts away, I return my attention to Jax. "I glowed in the mirror. I only started glowing without a reflection when we arrived here in Domhan."

Cara and Dorian stand a few feet away. Cara points to Dorian, poking him in the chest.

Stepping forward, Dorian says, "Cara thinks that while the magic in Harper is based on desire, she can be taught to conjure and use it."

With a slow nod, Jax draws a deep breath. "I agree. She killed a shadow demon, so there is defensive and offensive power." He leans in so close our noses are practically touching. "Think about the way you feel just before you conjure magic. What happens inside you?"

"I was afraid." Even though Jax is intimidating, my instinct to face him toe to toe takes over, and I keep my gaze locked with his.

"Be more specific," Jax commands.

Cara comes close. She touches her head, her chest, and then her abdomen. She grips and releases her hands before making a circle around herself.

"I understand." I think back to the least violent moment when my magic happened. It seems insane to even think the words *my magic*, but there's no denying the things I have seen and done. Closing my eyes, I put myself back in the hotel in New England. I remember the story about the shadow demons. "My stomach knotted, and my chest felt as if there was a weight on it. My pulse quickened, as if I were running away from danger, and I knew being turned into a shadow demon would be a fate worse than death."

The gasps from many force me to open my eyes. Everyone is staring at me with wide eyes and shocked expressions. Some look afraid, and others shocked.

I hold up my hand and colors flow over my skin as if I'm standing inside a rainbow reflecting every color like a prism. The colors shift from red, orange to yellow, blue, to green, and purple before white light radiates from my palm.

Whispering in my ear, Aaran asks, "Do you see the small crate near the anchor chain?" He points, and his finger cuts through my light but does not dim it.

"I see it." My heart races, but rather than try to calm myself, I accept the tension and excitement.

"Lift it off the deck and bring it here."

There's no lid on the crate, but at this angle, I have no idea what's inside or how heavy it might be. I extend my arm, palm away from me and call the crate to me.

It rumbles against the deck, rocking from side to side. It drags on the wood, moving an inch toward us before gaining some air between the two surfaces and jerking forward. A six-inch steel chain link clatters to the deck. I realize the crate is extra links and probably weighs over a hundred pounds. It crashes to the deck and shatters, scattering a few dozen links and making several people jump out of the way.

Embarrassed, I rise to clean up the mess I've made.

Jax grips my upper arm. "Well done. Why did you drop it?"

Three elves rush in to clean up the wood and metal.

His gaze burns into mine, and I remember the moment I lost control. "It was too heavy."

A morsel of amusement in his eyes, he says, "You lifted it when you did not know what was inside, Harper." He taps the side of my head. "Do not let what you *think* you know interfere with what magic can do."

Unable to look away, I study Jax. "You're right. As soon as I thought it was too heavy, I lost control."

With a curt nod, he releases me and rises.

When I turn to Aaran, Cara and Dorian are beside him. All three are grinning back at me.

Dorian says, "Very good."

Cara nods her agreement before they walk away.

"You did very well today, and I think you're winning Jax over." Aaran chuckles.

Fancor was watching from the steps to the upper deck, and his deep laugh breaks into our conversation. "You'll have that elf eating out of your hands in no time, lass."

Several elves laugh with the dwarf.

I turn to help with the mess, but they've already cleared it away.

Taking my hand, Aaran leads me back to sit on a crate. "Are you tired?"

"My body feels as if I've been run over by a truck, but my mind is reeling from what I just did."

"It's to be expected."

"I never felt drained from the magic I wielded accidentally. Even when I killed the shadow demon, I was freaked out by killing, but this is different." I rub my sore arms.

Aaran's ears twitch, and his eyes narrow as he looks out over the ocean.

The boat increases its rocking motion. I grip the rope on the crate to keep my seat. "What's happening?"

Clouds form and come together as the sea roughens.

"The witch queen has found us," Beran shouts. "Hold on. Get below." He ushers the children to the steps.

"Go with the children, Harper." Aaran stands in the center of the deck, legs wide, riding the motion of the ship as if he were born on a boat.

"I might be able to help." Even as I say it, my stomach lurches. "Or maybe not." I head for the stairs, helping others to get off the deck.

It makes no sense for anyone without working magic or a background in sailing to risk flying into the sea. Water crashes over the rail and pours down the stairs.

Sputtering, I grip the handrail. Sure that anyone who can't help above is safe, I rush to the cabin where I find the children already huddled on the bed. "Are you alright?"

They stare back with fear in their eyes, but uninjured.

Before I can join them and give them a false sense of comfort, the sky clears, and the ocean settles. "Stay here," I command, with no idea if they will listen or understand me.

I run from the cabin to the deck. "What happened?"

Dorian says, "I think she sensed your magic, but it was so brief that she can't pinpoint our location. She's searching." He points to the clouds forming to our east.

Jax stands at the bow of the ship arms crossed. "We won't be able to teach you how to use your magic while at sea." He frowns at me as if it's my fault.

"Can she detect all magic, or is it just mine?" I ruffle Bor's hair as he and the others rush past me to the open air of the deck.

"Your human magic feels different. Elven magic emanates from every drop of water, every leaf, or grain of sand. Maybe if she wasn't searching, but she'll feel you now. She knows how to sense it. And after what you did to her, she's angry as well as desperate." Jax returns his attention to the vast sea in front of us.

"None of that is my fault." I throw my arms up. What am I supposed to do? "I'd be happy to go home." It's not entirely true, but I'm trying to make a point.

Aaran takes my hand and leads me back to our room. Once inside, he lets go and paces the two steps the room allows. "Jax is not angry with you. He's frustrated with the situation."

"He could have fooled me. His scowl is starting to annoy me, and I was just starting to find him tolerable." Only barely. I mean at first, he was intimidating. After a while, I just got used to him, and he was in the party who saved me. Now, I'm losing my patience with his attitude, and my Jersey Girl nature is pushing through.

Stopping, Aaran stares at me, and a wide smile blooms on his already too-handsome face. "He's a good man."

It's not easy to stay angry when Aaran looks at me like this. "Stop defending him."

He wraps me in his arms and pulls me in. "You'll need to get along with him. We still have a long journey ahead."

"No."

"No?" He cocks his head.

"Jax needs to get along *with me.* I'm done trying to be nice to a man who, despite needing me, treats me like I'm the problem. I have no idea why I've done so this long. There will be no more adjusting of my personality to suit anyone else." I poke his chest. "And I'm including you in that. I'm not sweet. I'm not mild mannered. I don't like to be told what to do. I was terrified when I came into this world, but I'm done with that as well. If I die, then at least I put up a fight and didn't cower in the cabins with the children. No more, Aaran." I push out of his arms.

His smile never falters. "Alright."

"What does that mean?" I suspect he's mollifying me.

Closing the distance between us, he backs me against the door. "I don't want you to pretend to be anything, Harper. I loved you in your world when you were aloof, dismissive, and brave as a dragon. I loved you in my world when you stepped through an unknown portal to save a village full of people you barely knew. I love you in this moment when you think you're throwing off some guise that never existed. I have never asked you to be anything other than yourself. If you feel as if you've been stymied by events or people, you should do what you must to remove those issues."

I'm struck dumb by his declaration. Not to mention that he's standing so close, his heat is warming all my lady parts. "Oh."

He tucks my hair behind my ear and skims my lobe with his finger. "I was thinking of kissing you, but I don't want to block any human need you have for individuality."

"You're teasing me?" All of that, and now he's making jokes.

His smile is wicked.

Trapped between his hard body and the door, I do what any self-respecting Jersey Girl would do. I reach between us and grab his cock. Holding it tight enough to gain his full attention and wipe that smile from his face, but not cause him pain, I stare into his wide eyes. "We have two options: I can turn this into a caress, or you can keep making light of my concerns."

Grinding his hips into my hand, he lowers his lips until they're a breath away from mine. "It's not making light, *mo chroi*. I just find you even more irresistible when you fight back."

I caress his thick cock through his trousers. "When have I fought back?"

He raises one curved eyebrow. "When have you not? From the moment we met, you have fought, either me with that bit of steel, or others with your magic or wits. You may not have been raised to be a warrior, but you're the bravest person I've ever met. With you at my side, I know anything is possible, even defeating the witch queen." He crushes my mouth with his lips.

I slip my hand inside his fly and grip his hot flesh, working him from base to tip. My pussy aches with need. "Why is everything you say so hot?"

Tugging the button and zipper of my jeans free, he works the denim over my hips, only stopping when I push him back.

"Everyone above will know what we're doing," I say, but I'm not one hundred percent sure I care.

"Probably." He steps out of his boots and tosses his weapons and clothes on the floor.

God he's beautiful. His cock stands out from his perfect body, and I quake with need. I push the bolt on the door into place and pull my shirt over my head. "What if Vanora returns?"

"They'll sound an alarm from above." He lets me back him on the bed, and I straddle his legs.

When he reaches for me as if to bring me onto his cock, I shake my head. Leaning forward, I suck his thick shaft deep into my mouth.

His fingers thread my hair. "Harper." It's more growl than my name. He says it again and again as I release him and draw him deep.

My juices drip down my thighs and I can barely contain my own pleasure despite not having been touched. As his balls tighten, I crawl up his body and impale myself on him. I muffle my scream against his chest.

His groan rumbles in his throat. "All the old gods, Harper. You are magnificent in every way."

Grinding my hips forward, I take him deeper. I'm so close to coming, it's hard to breathe. I sit up and rise to my knees, then plunge, taking him inside me again and again. Faster and with his fingers digging into my hips to keep our pace, we both tighten and tumble over into ecstasy.

I collapse on his chest as my body shakes with the orgasm.

His legs shake beneath me as his warm cum fills me.

"Can elves and humans conceive?" I voice my thought as the rapture ebbs.

He draws a long breath and lifts me with his muscular

chest. "I imagine we can, and since you're not an elf with the magic to control pregnancy, we should be more careful."

My mind drifts to a trio of children who have my hair and his eyes. They play and smile as dragons fly overhead.

"What was that?" Aaran grips my arms and stares into my eyes.

I blink the lingering images away. "I don't know."

Gently but decidedly, he slides out of me and rolls us to our sides. "I don't think... Those notions..." He combs his fingers through his hair and sits on the edge of the bed. "It doesn't do either of us any good to imagine such a future."

I stand and grab a towel that was among the things I found in the abandoned room. I wipe our joined juices from between my legs before pulling on my jeans. I can't decide if I'm angry or hurt. Whatever I am, it's not how I want to feel after sex. I put on my shirt and pick up my shoes. "How do you know the vision came from me and not from you, Aaran? You're no better than Jax, blaming me for everything that happens in your life." I storm from the room and put my shoes on at the base of the stairs.

Half-dressed, he stops me with a hand on my shoulder. "I don't know. I'm sorry. I got a bit..."

"Freaked out. Yes. I saw that. Men are the same in any world. If my magic can kill a shadow demon, you shouldn't worry. I'm sure I can prevent your seed from taking hold inside me. I wouldn't want to ruin your plans to rule this world one day." My rage is burning so hot I can't stop my thoughts from rolling to the side of extreme.

I storm up the steps.

At the top, he grabs my arm.

Shaking loose, I say, "I might remind you and Jax that

you came and found me. I didn't want to risk my life for this world. Now you've got me here, you might add a little more kindness to your list of attributes, Prince Aaran."

"What are you talking about?" His face turns red. Good, I'm not the only one angry finally.

"You're the firstborn of the woman who is the rightful queen of the elves, or did I get that wrong?" My breath is coming fast as I stare at him. "I needed the booty calls as much as anyone. Don't give it a second thought."

Scanning the deck and the number of people watching us, he lowers his voice. "What is a booty call? I told you how I feel."

"You told me plenty. You love me, but not in the future when you'll have to go back to a real elf's life. You love me, as long as we don't have shared visions of a future that freak you out." Refusing to cry, I draw a shaking breath. "I will save your world if I can. As for the rest, you can fuck off, Aaran Riordan."

Chapter Eighteen

AARAN

There's nothing to do but watch her storm across the deck and up the steps to the bow. I'll admit, I could have reacted better to the vision, but it was so real. Me and Harper here in Domhan with dragons back in the world and three littles who looked like us. How was I supposed to react? I've never had feelings like this for anyone. It was bad enough to hear the things she was saying, but I felt her hurt from the inside.

Moving aft, I block her thoughts. She told me not to, but I think she's happy to have me out of her head right now.

As the sun begins to set, Fancor brings me a bowl of food. "That could have been better handled, lad."

"I know." I take the meager stew and eat. "It's complicated."

He slaps me on the back hard enough that I nearly spit out a mouthful of food. "No. It's not." He laughs. "You declared yourself, and then you got scared. Everyone on the ship knows that now. How are you going to make it right again?" He sits on the crate of extra wood next to me. It's for the galley, but there wasn't room below, so it's relegated to the deck. Not ideal, but better than people having to endure all weather up here.

"Maybe it's better if I don't. She's human. She has a mother and a life in her world." A few hours ago, I would have begged her to stay here, but now I'm imagining her going home. I'm feeling more undecided than my youngest brother. Maybe I've always been too hard on Raith after all.

Fancor rubs his face like a man holding himself in check. "Lad, that woman came all the way here to save your world. Do you think she did that out of the kindness of her heart?"

"I saved her mother's life. That's why she came."

He shakes his head. "Don't be a dolt. You don't believe that. She came because even then, she cared about what happened to you and the people you love. Did you lie when you told her you loved her? Was all of that just for the, what did she call it, booty call?" He chuckles at the foreign term.

"I didn't lie, but we can't always have what we want." My stomach gives a lurch that has nothing to do with the stew. I put aside the half-eaten food.

"Maybe the lass was right about you thinking your princely duties outweigh the duty of the heart." He nods, looking pleased. "She's a smart one, our Harper."

Once the dwarf leaves me alone, my thoughts do not give me a moment's peace. I am a dolt.

For the next two days, we journey west.

Harper bolts the cabin door each night. When I open my mind to search for hers, I find that closed to me as well.

Without complaint, I sleep on the deck. It's a small penance for my stupidity.

During the day, Jax, Nainsi, Fancor, and I train her with sword and arrow. She has good instincts, a fine eye for the target, and is willing to learn. We couldn't ask for a better student.

On the third night, I'm lying on the deck when a whiff of grass crosses the bow. I squint into the darkness and make out the shadow of land in the distance. The southern end of the west continent is finally within our sight. I breathe deep the hint of flowers and trees.

Silent as a cat, Harper steps onto the deck. I know she's there before I turn. Though her mind still blocks me, I sense her in other ways. My skin tingles and my heart beats faster when she is present. We are connected through deeper means than hearing thoughts. She steps to the rail and her shoulders rise and fall.

I move beside her. "You can't sleep?"

Shaking her head, she says, "Is that land?"

"We missed the islands completely. That's the continent. We should arrive at the gulf just north of Clandunna." I long to reach over and pull her close. My fingers itch for contact.

"Back where we started." She sighs. "Will we go by land once we arrive?"

"No." I hazard touching her back, and when she doesn't move away, I skim my palm up her spine to the base of her neck. "We'll need to send a hunting party out and gather provisions, but we'll take this ship up the coast to the north port."

She faces me. "I understand why you were scared."

"I'm sorry for the way I reacted. I do love you, Harper. I have prayed day and night that you know that." It's hard to breathe with my pulse racing so fast.

Like magic illuminating a room, her mind opens to me. Her love flows into me, and my soul sings in unison with hers. My throat is tight with emotion, and I open my arms to her.

Harper steps into my embrace and cries against my chest. Air rushes from her lungs. "I don't want to fight anymore. I don't want to be angry with you. I left my world to save yours. If we don't succeed, it is all for nothing."

As much as I long to hear her tell me she still loves me, I don't deserve that level of comfort. "We will do what we must. I promised to keep you safe so you can return to your mother. I will keep my promise even if we fight. I will love you, even if you despise me. I don't know how to atone for what I said." I lose my words.

"I don't despise you." She presses her cheek to my chest and wraps her arms around me. Together, we watch the horizon. "How far is the land?"

"Half a day's journey. We will arrive midmorning." Even after all this time in Domhan, she still smells uniquely of her world and her essence. I've missed her, despite being on the same ship and training together. I've missed the feel of her in my arms and the sense of her thoughts close by. "We should try to sleep. Dawn is only a few hours away."

After dislodging from my embrace, she lies down on my blanket pallet and turns on her side.

Lying beside her, I curl my front to her back and slide my arm under her head.

She snuggles into my biceps and sighs. "This is better."

It is. It's more than I deserve and everything I'll ever want. "I won't freak out again, *mo chroi*." I use her words so we're clear on what we are speaking of.

"I'll try not to lose my temper if you do." I can feel the niggling inside her mind. "One thing, though..." She rolls to face me.

I skim my hand over her cheek and thread her hair through my fingers and out of her face. "The vision?"

She nods. "Are you certain it came from me?"

"I honestly don't know if it was from you or me or some magic made by the two of us together. I know what we saw was beautiful and feels impossible at this moment." My throat tightens.

"It does. I can't argue with that. Do you think it was the future or just a fantasy?" Her green eyes seem lighted, though there is no moon, only starlight.

"Maybe a possible future. I don't know, Harper. Even seers will caution against believing their visions entirely. The past is set in place, but the future is always variable. And since there were dragons in the vision, even the past can be false." My gut is churning with the realization.

She gapes. "What does that mean?"

I embrace her and pull her close. Cupping her head, I

comb my fingers over her soft hair. "Dragon magic is complicated. They can manipulate time. That's how Delana trapped them in time."

"I don't understand."

Having her in my arms is so comfortable. It's as if this was always meant to be. I close my eyes. "We can ask my mother about the vision when we see her. She has far more knowledge of such things."

"Mmm..." Her breathing slow and steady she cuddles into me.

With Harper in my arms, I find peace and rest for the first time in three nights.

At first light, the entire party is awake and watching as we approach land. I'll admit that I'm anxious to get off the ship and feel dry, solid land beneath my feet.

Since there is no port in the Gulf Uaine, we have to drop anchor and take the small boat to the rocky beach. There is some sand, but many boulders jut from the beach. Jax has fished the area and is confident about our approach. If he's wrong, we could drown. At the very least, if we lose the boat, we'll have a hell of a time getting back to the ship.

Bert gives the command to drop anchor, and it feels as if everyone on board sighs with relief. Still, there's a long journey ahead, and not all of it is easy.

"What is it?" Harper stands beside me.

"I worry too much." It's my attempt to ease her fears.

She laughs. "I doubt that, considering what we've faced so far."

"Are you sure you would not be better off staying aboard?" I know I'd feel better.

She stares me down like the warrior she is. "No. I need to use some of the skills you've taught me these last few days. Besides, what if the ship is attacked? Will you be comfortable not being able to reach me?"

It is difficult not to adore her quick mind and how she always thinks one or three steps ahead. "You are too clever for me, and perhaps for your own good as well."

As she climbs over the rail and into the boat, she says, "You're not the first person to tell me that."

I'm not at all surprised. I hold my breath until she's seated in the dinghy, and then I head down the rope ladder to join the party of ten who will hunt and gather for the rest of the trip up the coast.

With two oarsmen, we paddle toward land.

Bert stays aboard the ship, but Nainsi is a fine archer and comes to hunt.

As he promised, Jax directs the boat to a sandy patch of beach where we ride a wave to safety. Once the boat is secured, Cara, Dorian, and two more head into the woods to the northwest. Jax, Nainsi, Harper, Beran, Fancor, and I keep to the west and south.

This part of the world is filled with contrast. The dark sea crashes against jutting gray rocks and soft white sand. A hundred yards away stands the greenest woods I've ever seen. From the cliffs where Harper and I arrived at Clandunna, these woods looked as if they'd been painted into place.

Birds squawk loudly, unbothered by our presence. With no paths to follow, we push through dense underbrush until we reach the heavy canopy. It's an old forest with gnarled roots rising above the soil. Overhead, the treetops sway in the breeze. The trunks creak and groan as if they speak to each other. Hopefully, they're not complaining about our presence.

It's hard enough on my legs to traverse this place. I'm wishing more than ever that Harper had stayed behind.

Without complaint, she walks carefully a few feet to my left. "I feel as if I'm still swaying with the ocean."

Patting her arm, Fancor grins. "It will take some time to find your land legs again." He stops, crouches, and narrows his gaze westward.

A twig snaps. I'm slightly annoyed that a dwarf heard the deer before I did. Signaling to Harper, I point. It seems a consensus to let Harper take the first kill. Everyone watches, eager to see what she can do.

She swallows, and her color grows pale and a little green. Still, she nocks her arrow, takes a firm stance, and waits.

The deer steps into view.

I whisper, "Just behind and above the front leg."

Harper is focused, but no less gray. Sorrow and pain reflect in her eyes as she draws the bow back and releases her arrow. It flies true, and the deer drops where it stood. Tears stream down her cheeks as she walks with her head high to the kill.

The rest of us follow and watch as she kneels beside the doe. Placing her hand on its neck, she closes her eyes.

I take a knee, as does the rest of the group. Thanking the animal for giving itself so we might live is an old practice, one

I haven't done since I was a boy and my father taught me and my brothers to hunt. I'm at a loss for why I stopped, and say the words in my heart.

Fancor presses his hand to his heart in the tradition of dwarven prayer.

When she pulls her hand away, she asks, "What now?"

"I'll show you, lass," Fancor says. "It was a fine, clean kill. The best first shot I've ever seen."

"It was a fine shot." I sense her trepidation to accept the compliments. It's the first innocent animal she's ever killed.

After dashing her tears away, she cleans the dear as Fancor instructs.

The hunt continues until we have three deer and a handful of rabbits. It's a shame to leave the skins, but it's the meat we'll need in the coming days, and we don't have time for tanning.

When the work is done, we wait on the beach for the gathering party to return.

Harper scrubs her hands in the saltwater before coming and sitting beside me in the sand. "I suppose you would consider this a good day."

Leaning on my palms in the soft damp sand, I love that she comes to me for comfort and conversation. "It was a productive hunt, and we will all get to eat during our journey north."

"I guess I'll have to cultivate a harder heart." She wraps her arms around her knees and stares out at the horizon.

The sun is directly above us, and all the blond and red streaks shine along her braid.

Unable to resist, I touch the bottom of the plait and

worry the soft strands between my fingers. "I would be very sorry for you to change anything about your heart."

"But it hurt me to kill that deer, even though I know we need the food." A tear rolls down her cheek.

I sit up so that I can look into her eyes. "It's not a bad thing to feel sorrow for the loss while accepting its inevitability. More than that, Harper, you reminded the rest of us that the deer is more than food. What you did today was beautiful and poignant. I was honored to witness those moments in the woods with you, and I am willing to wager that the others feel the same."

She looks at Nainsi, who sits only ten or so feet away.

With a sharp nod, Nainsi blushes.

"I was a little ashamed of myself when I saw you praying over the deer. It had been years since I thanked a beast for giving its life for my sake." My throat clogs.

Blinking, Harper turns bright red. "Oh. It seemed only right. I don't know the customs."

I press a finger over her lips then cup her cheek and kiss her. "It was beautiful. My father is going to adore you."

Her smile could light all of Domhan.

A rustle in the forest grabs our attention, and four elves laden with full baskets trudge onto the beach.

Once we are all loaded, we make our way back to the ship. My muscles ache from a hard day's work, but my arms are content with Harper leaning against me at the rear of the boat.

On a long sigh, she says, "It was a good day."

Chapter Nineteen

HARPER

I knew plenty of people who hunted, both growing up in Central New Jersey and as an adult. I just never had any interest in getting my food from anywhere besides the supermarket or a restaurant. Now, I'm standing on the deck of a ship in an alien land helping to dry meat so it will keep for the journey.

There was a moment just before I pulled my bowstring back that I considered not taking the shot. Then I thought about Tal and the other children. They have to be fed and cared for. I'm as responsible for their fate as any of the elves.

Once I made the kill, I struggled not to puke. I felt the life flow out of that animal. More than that. When the arrow struck, I felt a sharp pain in my chest and a flash of fear before peace and nothing. All I could do was thank that poor deer, and now honor her by surviving with the food she provided.

I cut long strips of muscle with my knife and drop them in a bucket of seawater. Someone else takes the meat to another bucket before hanging it to dry in the sun. A few weeks ago, I had Paul downstairs at the deli cooking most of my meals.

My mind drifts to my mother. I miss her. I know she's safe and healthy now, but I miss her. She wouldn't recognize me if she saw me today.

Aaran's soft warm breath tickles my earlobe. "I think she'd be extremely proud of you."

"Stop listening, or I'll block you again." It's a scolding, but I can't help loving that he's here for me whether I'm distraught over a deer or thinking of my mom. The image of those three children and the dragons tries to press to the front of my thoughts, but I push it back. I don't want to know the future unless it's a guarantee we'll survive the battle with the witch queen.

As I drop the last of the meat into the bucket, I step back. My hands are covered in blood, and my fingers ache from the unfamiliar kind of work.

Cara wraps an arm around me and leads me to a soapy bucket of water where I wash my hands and the knife. With her kind smile, she takes my still-damp hands between hers and closes her eyes. Her easy magic flows through me, like stepping into a hot bath and relaxing.

My muscles relax, and my pain subsides. "Thank you."

Releasing my hands, she kisses my forehead and walks away.

The hot sun bakes down on me. I suppose it's good for curing the meat, but I'm tired. I slip down the stairs to my cabin and strip off my sweaty clothes. In the small basin of water, I wash as best I can and pull the long white shirt over my head. It's so big, there's no need to unbutton it.

I climb into the bed and close my eyes. Visions of dragons and beautiful babies with green eyes and pointed ears fill my dreams. I never thought I'd want children, but now I'm not sure.

Part of me hears the cabin door open and close several times. I feel Aaran close, then farther away. The fragrance of warm spices and cooked meat wakes me.

Stretching long like a cat, I open my eyes. It's dark outside the window but the cabin is lit by an unseen source that I assume is magic.

Smiling down at me, Aaran holds a steaming wooden bowl. "You should eat something."

My stomach rumbles in agreement. Sitting up, I shake away the dreams. "It's the first time I've slept without nightmares since the black castle."

He sits beside me and hands me the bowl and spoon. "Maybe you were too tired for dreams."

"I had dreams." I eat the stew and avoid the fact that my dreams were focused on that same vision that caused our argument.

He blushes. "I see. Well, then better thoughts have taken the place of those horrors. I'm glad of that." Toying with the hair that has escaped my braid, he kisses my temple.

There's a lot of laughing and stomping above. "Everyone is fed and happy?"

"Yes. It's quiet at sea, and we have enough food to get us home." He pauses. "Well, it's my home. So many people and still a long way to go."

I finish the food and put the bowl aside. "We will make it. We have to."

His gaze slips to the sheets. "I've been thinking."

I search his gaze. He's sour on whatever has been on his mind. "What?" I push his hand from my hair.

Letting out a heavy sigh, he stands. He's too big for the small cabin, and one step brings him to the other side of the available space. "You and I have to get to Tús Nua. The fate of Domhan depends on that. It's been long enough that we could portal there."

"And leave these people behind?" I can't believe what I'm hearing.

"It's too important that we get home, Harper." He stares at me with his fists at his sides. "These people will be safer without you on this ship."

It's a lie. I feel it. "If that were true, you would have left them behind and there would only be a few of us aboard. She will come for them regardless of my presence. She'll do it just to hurt me, and we won't be here to protect them. No. I'm not leaving them."

"You are more important than these people. You have to survive." He leans over me, his arms on either side of me, pressing into the mattress.

I jab my finger in the center of his chest. "Aaran Riordan, look me in the eye and tell me that you believe one life is worth more than the next. Tell me that you'll be able to live with yourself if these people die at sea and we survive. Can you know that they died on a journey we started together, and go on with your princely life?"

"I don't have a princely life." He moves away and leans on the inside of the door. "I have a normal life."

"Answer the question." I sit up, cross my legs and watch him. I feel the split in his thoughts.

"My duty is to you and your safety. I swore to the oracle to bring you back."

"You swore to bring a human back to go to some gate and find a weapon. If I die, you'll go get another girl. If I live and these people, who have protected me and given their magic to me, die because they were with me, I will not be able to live with myself. My answer is no. So, unless you plan to drag me through a portal against my will, this conversation is over." I keep my gaze fixed on him.

The duality of his thoughts lessens. "I'm not convinced this is the right course, Harper. But I didn't drag you through the portal in your motor vehicle building, and I won't force you through one now unless all hope is lost to get all of us to Tús Nua."

"Fine. Only if it's a last resort." I scoot back on the mattress. "Now, you can come to bed if you want."

The coast is beautiful from the deck of the ship. My lessons continue, with me landing on my ass more than on my feet.

Before lunch each day, Jax trains me in sword fighting. He doesn't hold back, which I appreciate, as Vanora and her soldiers, whatever form they take, will not worry about my skill level.

Jax looks fierce with narrowed eyes and tight lips. He's as attractive as all the other elves, but there's a hardness in him.

If I had not seen him with his children, I would have thought him heartless. He brings his sword down.

I block the blow. The vibration of steel against steel jolts up my arm. My hand goes numb, and my sword clatters to the deck.

Glee shines in Jax's eyes as he raises his sword for the kill.

Dropping to the deck, I roll out of the path of his blade.

His eyes shift to something ahead.

Whatever it is, it's a boon to me. I sweep his leg.

The tall, proud elf falls to the hard wood with a resounding thud.

Grabbing my lost sword, I kneel on his right arm and point my blade at his exposed throat. As his eyes fill with shock at being bested by a mere human woman, joy fills me.

An instant later, he smiles. "Well won. I lost my concentration, and you did not."

I stand and offer my hand to help him up. "It might be the only time I win one of our sessions, but I'm going to keep this feeling with me for the rest of my life."

He looks from my face to my hand. Of course, he doesn't need help. I haven't injured him. Still, with a laugh, he takes my hand and rises. His attention shifts back to the distance ahead.

Gray smoke pours from the top of a large mountain.

"Is that a volcano?"

Fancor grumbles, "Bolcán."

"It is a volcano." Aaran's lips are pulled into a tight line, and his jaw ticks. "It's been dormant for hundreds of suns."

"Going out on a limb, I'm guessing this is not a good

sign." The stench of sulfur tinges the air and I slip my sword into the sheath at my side.

Bert calls up to Beran at the helm, "Turn to starboard. Let's give that a wide birth."

Doing as he's told, Beran shifts the boat to the right. "We've got half a day before we'll reach Bolcán. If we go too far east, we get into dangerous waters."

"If you've ever seen the sea boil, you know that's plenty dangerous enough." Bert goes to the upper deck and climbs the rigging to a crow's nest. "I don't see lava, but you can't be too careful around an active volcano."

With her hands fisted at her side, Nainsi watches her husband. "Bert used to make extra money fishing winters off the coast of Hawaii."

I nod, but the others stare at her blankly. She says, "It's a volcanic grouping of islands in the human world. He knows what he's talking about."

Jax grumbles, "So we have a choice between the boiling sea or the monsters of the forbidden waters."

"You said that oracle magic keeps Vanora off the western continent. Is that mountain erupting just a natural occurrence?"

Shaking his head, Aaran's shoulders rise and fall with a deep breath. "It's possible, but unlikely."

With an ugly laugh, Jax says, "It's more likely that Vanora has found a way past the oracle's wards."

"She's gone through Ifreann. Demons down there are beyond her control. How could she have managed such a feat?" Fancor looks up at Bert. "Does the sea churn? Do you spy any serpents?"

Climbing down, Bert goes slowly and carefully. When

he sets his feet back on the deck, he says, "Nothing looks amiss besides the mountain puffing smoke. Maybe Aaran is right, and it's a natural occurrence. We could sail past without incident."

My gut tightens. "It's an awfully big coincidence for it to happen now, after hundreds of years." The skeptic in me isn't buying it. Vanora is involved. I can feel her tainted magic like soured milk fouling the air.

Bert sends Jarnol to the lookout basket to report if there are any changes. We plan to give the mountain a wide birth, but not so far as to put us into the monster-ridden northern sea.

The smoke grows larger as day turns to night. The hint of orange brightens Bolcán's peak. "That looks like more than smoke."

Aaran is shoulder to shoulder with me at the rail. "This is not good. I don't suppose I can talk you into going below?"

"Not this time." I draw a long breath to steady my fear and call out, "Get below and hold on."

Jarnol yells, "The sea is capping!" He points.

"Come down!" Bert orders the teen. "We're close enough to see from the deck. Get below."

Like a cat, he scurries down the rigging. "I can fight." He rushes to the bow of the ship.

A rogue wave crashes against the side of the ship. We're pushed farther away from shore as we list to the starboard side.

Dark clouds gather, and a downpour begins.

Wrapping my arm through the rigging at the port rail, I keep my feet on the deck and my eyes on the mountain.

Bert stumbles up the steps and relieves Beran at the helm. He spins the wheel, which turns us into the waves. Another wave comes from the rear and swamps the deck. Bert turns us again. "It keeps shifting. I can't get out of the trough."

Waves hit us from every direction, tossing the ship around like a toy in a bathtub.

A fifty-foot wave hovers over my head. I'm going to die right here. I hope someone lives and will tell my mother what happened to me. My father's smiling face flashes in my mind.

Aaran wraps his arm around me.

Still hanging on to the rigging, I take a deep breath and hold it.

Bert screams, "Hang on!"

Water pummels my head. Darkness and cold salt prod at me, floating and being pushed and pulled in all directions. It reminds me of the portal. My lungs scream as I have no choice but to exhale. I hit the wood hard, ass first. Sputtering and gasping, I cough out seawater.

Miraculously we're still upright. Coughing and scurrying comes from every corner of the ship.

Aaran's soggy hair covers his face, and blood runs down from a cut over his eye. "Are you alright?"

I touch his cut. "I'm fine. You're hurt."

Wiping the blood out of his eye, he says, "It's nothing."

Bert gets us positioned so we're cutting through the wave rather than sunken at the bottom of a trough.

The sea tries to gobble the ship, but we continue to shift east, away from the boiling cauldron of saltwater and magma.

An explosion shudders the world. My ears ring with deafening bang.

The top of Bolcán flies off and explodes in ash and fire. Dirt pelts the deck despite several miles of distance. Fire slithers down the mountain, first one way, then the other, cutting a path.

Sound roars back into my head. The way the lava moves is different from any movies or documentaries I've seen about volcanoes. Its progress is too specific. "Does that seem alive to you?"

Aaran stares at the lava. "I don't think that's magma. Kron. Demon! Kron!" he screams.

The lava snaps away from the land like a striking snake. At least a hundred feet long with a diamond-shaped head and two dark eyes, the kron opens its gaping mouth and shoots fire at the ship.

Jax holds up his hands and mutters. Water slices the air and forms a wall between us and the monster.

The kron roars and pulls back, ready to strike again. This time it shoots fire high, and the tops of the masts and sails catch fire. Flames and ash fall to the deck. Elves run around stomping out small fires.

Aaran casts a spell, and biting cold shoots from his fingertips up the masts and fights back the fire's heat.

The kron slithers to the edge of the sea and rides the waves like a water moccasin. Even at this distance, the heat bakes my cheeks. My sword is useless. I don't think an arrow will be of any use. I'm helpless to save these people.

Beside me, Jax grips the railing. His skin is pale. The magic he used must have been very strong to drain his energy. "Use what magic you have, Harper."

"You said she'd find us. You said my magic needed to be honed." I don't even know what to do or how to summon a spell.

His voice is calm, and he looks me in the eyes. "She already knows where we are, and magical training can wait. Do what you do. Make your wish."

I want to save these people. I came all this way to do the right thing. After everything we've been through, it's unfair for us to fail now. The rush of power begins in my gut. Please let me destroy this demon and save these people. The hair on my arms stands up as my spine tingles with the rise of magic. Having no idea what will happen, I lift my hands and point them at the snake of fire cutting through the ocean toward us.

A shadow flows from my fingers, hovers over the kron, and wraps around it like a sleeping bag. Its screeching rents the air so loud my ears ring.

The shadow smothers the kron, which wriggles violently in an attempt to break free of my magic. A trickle of fire escapes to the sea, and my shadow leaps out like an amoeba and pulls the burning worm back in.

The demon shrieks and throws off the veil of my magic. Body coiled, its head rises and it snaps fiery jaws at us. Rearing back, it roars and shoots flames at the main sail.

In a second, the mast and sail are engulfed. Embers rain down, burning my arm. The acridness of burning hair mingles with that of rotten eggs. The heat is unbearable.

A wave of icy magic shifts the wind. It's the witch queen's magic. I'll never forget the sting of it.

I command more, stronger magic to smother the kron. A blacker shadow forms around my fingers and expands. I pull my arms back and throw it at the demon like a fishing net.

Pushing and binding the kron, my magic tightens, feeling as though it's tethered to a knot in my gut. I will the shadow to keep wrapping over and over, getting smaller with each round.

The screeching dies, and the fire within the shadow dims. The only sound is the rain pelting the deck.

Thank goodness. The shadow rises from the water, revealing an ashen snake dispersed among the waves. As the sea settles, the ashes sink until nothing of the kron remains. My magic fades until it's nothing but a bit of haze that blows away in the breeze.

I let out the breath I've been holding and collapse to my knees. I guess even my magic has a price. Jax gets blurry while I try to tell him I don't feel well.

Chapter Twenty

AARAN

Jax keeps Harper's head from striking the deck when she faints. He holds her like a child. "Shadow magic." Worry dims his eyes.

I kneel beside her while the last of the fires are dowsed on the charred ship. "Without it, we would all be burned to death." I take her from him and hold her in my lap.

Ash falls like snow, but the mountain is again silent. The rain slows to a sprinkle.

I kiss her forehead. "Wake up, Harper. Tell me you're alright."

Her right arm has a puckered, blistering burn. I run my fingers over it and send healing to her flesh.

Drawing a gasping breath, she sits up, one hand in a fist and the other reaching for her sword. She pulls away from me, but her fear shifts to relief, and she closes her eyes and relaxes into my arms.

Inches from us, Fancor slides to a stop. "By the old gods, let her be alive." His hair is scorched in several places, and his skin is covered in soot, which makes his eyes appear brighter.

"I'm alive, friend." Opening her eyes, she tries to smile. "I guess we won?"

Patting her hair, Fancor sighs, and it's more like a bear about to attack. "We lost four elves including Jarnol."

"Oh no." Harper sits up, but her eyes roll and she eases back into my lap. "He was only a boy."

"Ay, a good lad. He and the other three went into the sea when the big wave hit. We're lucky we didn't capsize. If not for Bert's skill, we'd all be drowned, and the kron would be loose in Domhan."

Voice sharp, Jax demands, "How did you know to use shadow magic, human?"

It's not a good sign that he's stopped using her name again, and I feel her annoyance with him.

"I don't know, elf. I haven't had any magical training. I did what you told me to do. I wished to save this ship and the lives on it. I wished for a way to defeat the demon. Why, is shadow magic bad?"

Jax's jaw ticks.

Despite needing Jax and respecting him, I'm not immune to finding his old ways aggravating. "No. There is no good or bad kind of magic. The user and the usage determine such things."

"The witch queen uses shadow magic to create her demons." Jax stands and surveys the state of the ship. He sighs. "Aaran is correct, as is Fancor. Without your magic, we would likely have all perished. I shall attempt to alter my beliefs." He stomps away and helps two elves push a burning barrel overboard.

"I feel like we just had a breakthrough." Harper sits up again, only slower this time.

"What is a breakthrough?" Fancor gives her his hand and helps her to her feet, then he hovers to ensure she stays upright while I rise.

Gripping his shoulder and my arm, she smiles. "Humans use that term sometimes to describe when someone makes a step in a mentally healthy new direction."

"Oh, yes." Fancor laughs. "I see." Still chuckling, he leaves us near the wooden rail, black with ash and soot.

Harper looks from one end of the ship to the other. "How will we ever get anywhere now? We'll be adrift."

I wonder the same thing, but kiss the top of her head. "Let's help clean up and then we can talk to Bert."

"We need to have some sort of memorial for the elves who were lost at sea." She bends down and tosses a burnt piece of railing overboard. "I hope we're not the next to be mourned."

Underneath her sarcastic tone stirs fear and sorrow that stab me to my core.

It's full dark, and most of the elves are asleep on the lower deck. We're all exhausted and sad over the loss of four souls. Jarnol was only a boy with his entire life ahead of him. I failed him and the others.

Harper squeezes my hand and whispers, "It's not your fault."

Bert sits between Nainsi and Fancor.

Jax kneels to my right. "How do we get to the western continent?"

Taking Nainsi's hand, Bert kisses her fingers. "We'll use the tide. It won't bring us as far as we'd hoped, but we're lucky to still be afloat. By all rights, we should have capsized, and then burned. Nainsi tells me there are shallows where a sandy bottom might save us from falling apart when we beach. I've made that our heading, and the tide should bring us to a grinding halt just after first light."

"How do you move us without the wind?" Harper asks.

"We're not the first ship to lose her sails. She has a manual rudder, so that helps. Not having electronics to begin with makes small disasters easier and everyday sailing more difficult. I'll try to tack us in with Beran's help. I suggest you all get a couple of hours' sleep. It's not going to be a three-point landing." Weary and determined, Bert rises and heads back to the helm. He and Beran exchange whispers.

Nainsi stands. "I'll stay nearby in case he needs me to wake you."

I can see there's no convincing her to get rest. She won't until her man is able. As if they're always meant to be together, one unit working together despite having been raised in different worlds, their differences do not matter to either of them.

Rather than separating, we all stay in the small circle with the magical light that Jax created to give off heat. The deck is still damp, but the rain helped wash away most of the ash and dirt.

I pull Harper close so she can rest her head on my shoulder as we attempt an hour or two of sleep before daybreak.

"These shallows that we're headed for, do they extend very far from land?" Harper's mind is already calculating all the things that might go wrong even without the witch queen's interference.

"I've never been to the area north of Bolcán except to visit the port, and that's a long way from where we'll stop." I avoid saying crash, even though that's what will happen. "On the maps, it's perhaps half a mile out to sea where the continental shelf ends."

She nods against my biceps. "We can carry the children and injured a half mile or so. Do you think we'll be able to rest once we reach land?"

"I can't say, but I'm not counting on it. We'll still be in the shadow of the volcano, Harper." There's more to say about that. Vanora found a way to the west. My heart pounds in my ears at the ramifications of what we saw in the fire.

"She's strong again. I felt her in the fire. I felt her in that kron." Inside, Harper shakes as if a shiver went up her spine.

Holding her tighter, I kiss her temple. "I know. I felt her too. She's stronger than before. To break through and control a fire demon is the darkest kind of magic. She has somehow grown more dangerous since she attacked you. Maybe we should have risked a portal after we got you back. I fear I'm not a very good leader." Even whispered in the dark, it feels like the truth. Doubting myself is not how I've lived my life. I'm the eldest son of Elspeth and Brion Riordan. My abilities should be sharper. My mission was clear, yet I deviated and put Harper at great risk.

She pushes me back to the deck and stares into my eyes for a long second. Her jaw ticks as if she's straining against scolding me. Leaning close, she whispers, "If you had left these elves in Vanora's clutches, you would not be the man I love. Besides, what if you or I had died in the next portal? You told me it was too soon when we first left Tobhtá. Even when it was safe, we could not leave them. Personally, I would just as soon never go through one again."

My emotions are rocketing in every direction. Her strength is both adorable and arousing. She loves me for the man I am, not the leader I strive to be. Her vision of me makes me want to rethink everything I know. I press my lips to the shell of her ear. "Thank you."

We lie awake for the hour we have to rest. Her thoughts mingle with mine, and it's a kind of symphony of give and take. I love the way she thinks and worries and pushes those worries aside to focus on the task at hand.

All we have to do is survive long enough to get these people to safety. After that, we'll figure out how to survive the next step, whatever that might be.

My father would have a plan for the entire journey. He would anticipate battles and risk additional lives to beat his opponent.

I wonder how my mother would handle this journey. I suppose when I tell her my choices, she'll explain where I didn't meet her expectations. Every step we take seems to bring more danger. We've lost five lives, and I must carry the burden of those losses. My entire life has been in preparation for this, and I pray I measure up to the task.

Nainsi stirs and listens to Bert for a moment.

Before she steps toward us, Harper and I sit up.

"We're getting close," Nainsi says, with the first pink daylight on her face. "Help me wake everyone?"

Fancor and Jax are up and stretching before we have a chance to nudge them.

"We should have tried harder to sleep." Harper raises her arms above her head and makes a squeaking noise and she shifts from foot to foot.

On a gruff laugh, Fancor says, "Sleep never came to anyone from trying, lass. We rested, and that's better than nothing."

The western continent looms before us, white sand with a smattering of ash from the eruption and rolling hills beyond the dunes. The clouds of the previous night have given way to a clear sky that hints at a warm, dry day. The scent of flowers reaches me and for a second, I wish I'd taken the time to learn the name behind the fresh smell.

One by one, we wake everyone above and the children below, and all assemble on deck. We gather as much from the hold as we have, which amounts to a day's worth of meat and some edible leaves. We're short on water, but that's a problem for later.

I stand at the top of the stairs on the upper deck. "Everyone grab something solid, and hold on to each other. We are going to hit bottom, and the ship may tip and break apart."

Many of the elves look back with fear, but on the faces of most, I see only resignation. They've been through so much that death is not a threat. At least, if they die here, Vanora will not have them or their souls.

Beran and Bert stay at the helm, while I join the others. Wrapping my arms around Harper, I hold the central mast.

"Brace yourselves," Bert shouts.

The sound of the keel striking land is like nothing I've ever heard before. The ship screams in protest. If I could, I would hold my ears to protect them from the cacophony of cracks and breaks. The wood roars as it gives way, and a shrill scream fills the air as we crash over the sand bar. We jerk to the left, then forward. Wood snapping and cracking follows. The deck buckles like water but doesn't break.

When we come to a stop, the ship lists to the starboard side, and elves tumble across the deck. Their screams replace those of the broken ship.

Harper reaches out and grabs Cara's hand before she can fall past. She hauls her up to us where Cara grabs hold of the mast and braces her feet.

Dorian rolls across the deck to the rail. From below us, he yells. "I'm fine. Hold on."

Still the ship creaks and moves until it settles.

Bert's voice breaks the momentary silence. "Beran will see how stable the shelf beneath us is. Hold on another moment."

The splash of Beran hitting the water and sloshing across forms a knot in my gut. It feels as if everyone is holding their breath.

"It's safe. We're lengths of the boat beyond the deep drop." Beran's voice is strong and calm.

"Well, that's step one." Harper eases down until she's sitting on the slanted deck.

Below us, Dorian is on his feet with one leg braced against the rail now at a forty-five-degree angle. He smiles at his wife, and she lets go, then slides down the deck on her bottom. He catches her, and they climb over the rail together and splash into the water.

Nearly every elf is off the ship before I take Harper's hand. "Together?"

She nods and we let go of the mast. If not for the half-burned rail at the end, it would be like a child's slide. I grip the edge with my boots against the rail.

Harper tumbles over the edge ass-over-head and lands with a hard splash.

My heart stops and doesn't beat again until she surfaces.

Sputtering to the surface, she laughs and grins up at me as she gains her feet. "I'm fine." She wipes water from her eyes.

I join her in the hip-deep water.

Bert is the last to leave behind the ship that saved us and was nearly our doom. He lifts one of the Aracan boys and Nainsi takes another as the couple leads our group toward dry land.

Tal slips one hand into Harper's and the other into mine. We walk together as if we were a family. Visions of my parents taking me for walks before Vanora upturned our world flit through my memories.

This is what I'm fighting for. This is worth dying for. We cannot fail, or there will be no more parents to hold their children's hands in Domhan.

"The witch queen." Harper stops and lets go of Tal. Her hands glow rainbow colors. "Run." She draws her sword and faces the darkening sea.

Tal runs toward the shore until an elf lifts her and runs,

carrying her. As if of one mind, the former slaves all run to the beach.

Standing with Harper, I hold my sword ready. Jax and his soldiers turn back, as does Fancor. Seven against whatever horrors are churning up the deep. "Let's back away. Try not to stir the water.

Harper grips her head. "She's angry about the elves we took."

Grabbing her around the waist, I pull her back with us as we slowly retreat. "Block your mind, *mo chroi*. Don't let her in." I send magic to her to help her close the door to her thoughts.

The shallow water roils. A terrible cackle rents the air. A black tentacle slithers toward us, and before I can get away, it wraps around Harper's leg and pulls her out of my arms. Another tentacle springs out of the water and slams between me and Harper.

Jax slices his sword through the air, but the tentacle pulls back. He leaps on top of the one holding Harper and stabs through it and into the soft sand.

Another rises from the dark waters and smashes my ribs, throwing me backward, then presses me under the water.

Sword lost in the water, I grapple for the dagger in my boot.

The creature releases me, and black blood pours into the water.

Sputtering to the surface, I gasp for air and cough out the water burning my throat and lungs.

Sword raised, Fancor runs after the tentacle pulling Jax and Harper out to the darkening sea.

More tentacles attack the soldiers. I can't tell if it's one monster or five. The one that attacked me lies inert under the sea, its blood mingling with the water.

Getting to my feet, I chase after Harper. My vision narrows on her, and I'm fixed on getting close enough to haul her back.

Jax lifts his sword and plunges it into the beast again and again.

I run past Fancor as he slices another tentacle with his broadsword. What remains, smacks him and sends him flying ten feet in the air.

Calling on my magic, I leap forward and land within inches of Harper. I wrap my arms around her and dig my feet into the sand. Slowing our progress to the deep, but not stopping, I think about a rope. In my mind, in my soul, my magic responds, and the thick strands bite into the skin of my fingers. "Fancor!" I wrap one end around my forearm and cast the rest to the dwarf.

His eyes widen, recognizing what I'm doing. He wraps it around himself, and holds, digging his sturdy feet into the sand.

"Jax, get ready."

The magical rope pulls taut, and our progress stops.

Lifting his sword, Jax slices off the tentacle, and we fall into the water on our backs.

I rise, and keeping hold of the rope, throw Harper over my shoulder. As I run, Fancor pulls us in, ready to keep anything else from reaching out and grabbing us.

A bulbous black octopus-like head breaches the deep before sinking out of sight. Perhaps four severed tentacles were too much, or maybe Vanora's magic is spent for the moment. When we collapse on the sandy shoreline, nothing comes after us.

Lying on my back with Harper lying against my chest, I hold her tight, as if something else might pull her away. "Are you hurt?"

She turns and her elbow grazes my ribs.

I suck in a sharp breath. My chest hurts almost as much as my ribs.

Touching my ribcage with the tips of her fingers, I can feel her wishing she had healing magic. There is no tingle from her. This is beyond her abilities. "Cara, Aaran needs you." Harper scrambles back out of the way.

My vision blurs. "It's hard to breathe."

Dozens of faces stare at me. I want to reassure them that all will be well, but I can't catch my breath. Harper's eyes stare into mine. Our minds open, and she says, "Stay with me, Aaran. I'm here. Just hold on."

Chapter Twenty-One

HARPER

It took most of the day to walk to a place that feels relatively safe, a hillside where a cluster of trees blocks us from sight of the volcano. Jax claims Vanora can't come this far, but I think he's hoping more than knowing. What good will it do to be terrified or scare the children? Better to watch for trouble and believe none will come.

Aaran has not regained consciousness. We made a pallet from parts of the ship to carry him.

Through Dorian, Cara says that he broke several ribs, and one punctured his lung. She healed him, but the injury is serious enough that he may need several days to recover. The seawater he inhaled could add to the problem.

I get the impression it would be better for him if we remained in one place, but it's not safe to stay. Vanora seems to grow stronger by the day.

The setting sun shines with myriad aqua and pink hues

that look as if they were painted there. It's hard to believe a place so beautiful can contain so much horror. However, human history and current events show that any place can be ruined by bad people.

Fancor builds a small fire, sits down hard, and grunts. He must have a few aches and pains of his own. Leaning low, he blows the flames higher, making sure the wood catches.

I was too busy being dragged away to see much of the battle. I saw those slime-covered tentacles bleeding in the water. I shake the image away and let the heat of the fire comfort me. "He hasn't woken."

Patting my hand, Fancor sighs. "He will, lass."

"I can't even hear his mind now." I've tried to communicate with Aaran's mind directly, but he's silent there too.

"He needs time to heal. He nearly died to save you and Jax. Most men would have dropped when the beast broke his ribs." He nods toward Aaran's prone body. "He kept on until he knew you were safe."

I don't know what I'll do if he doesn't wake up. I can't even bear the thought. "We can't stay here long."

"Just the night. We've agreed that we have to get past the Dá Lock River as soon as possible. After that, we can rest a day or so if needed." He picks up a stick and digs a little hole in the dirt. His focus on what he's doing, he asks, "Just before the beasts came, you felt something?"

Even the memory of the chill that comes with Vanora's magic makes me shiver. "I sensed her magic, the witch queen. It was just a nasty twinge, but I knew she was close, or her magic at least."

"That might be useful. We didn't listen. You were too concerned with the others when you should have protected yourself." Before I can correct him, he holds up his hands, palm out. The stick falls to the ground. "I know, Harper. It's your instinct to protect. I also know you don't want anyone to die to keep you safe. However, the entire world will perish without you. You have to remember that. Don't stand and fight, back away and let me or Aaran defend you."

"I don't think I can do that." In a backward way, my earlier argument seems selfish. "It was only a second or two in advance, Fancor. I barely had time to react, and I don't seem to be a run-and-hide kind of girl anymore."

He laughs. "Were you ever?"

His laugh is full of joy, and I find myself thinking of the dwarf as a beloved uncle. "The day Aaran jumped through a portal into my world and demanded I come here, I ran away. If time had been on my side, I would have driven as fast and far from him as I could."

"What changed?" He recovers the stick and draws something in the dark soil.

Trying to remember the moment when I knew I would help Aaran brings my mother's illness to mind. She's well now, and probably living a good life with her friends beside her. Maybe she'll meet a nice man and find love again. I've always wondered why she never dated. It's possible she thought I would disapprove. Maybe she was right. Now, I just want her to be happy.

Still, Aaran saving my mother wasn't the moment. Before that, I saw him sleeping on my couch that morning. He looked troubled even at rest. His pointed ears were peeking through his tousled hair. My heart contracted at the sight of him, as if I'd known him all my life. My gut told me to help him even when my head said no way. When he was healing my mother, I knew he wouldn't hurt her, just as I knew he might harm himself.

Fancor has scribbled three symbols in the dirt. One looks like a diamond with a star inside it. The next is like an open safety pin with the sharp end facing down. The last is a capital L shape, but the bottom part is tipped up at an angle.

"He changed me. Some things are hard to explain with words."

Fancor nods.

"What does that mean?" I point to his drawing.

"It's the protecting runes of my people." He stands. "Get some sleep, Harper. I'll watch over you both." He moves a few feet away and leans against a rock.

There's no telling him that he too needs rest, so I snuggle along Aaran's good side and close my eyes. *I'm here. I wish you would let me know that you're still with me.*

"There is no place far enough that I can't reach you, human. I will destroy everything you love while you watch. Once that is done, I will come for you." The witch queen's voice sounds loud and painful in my skull.

Wake yourself. It's only a dream. I know she's not really here, but she has entered my mind just the same.

"That elf spawn of Elspeth's will be the first. I'm almost glad he survived the Cuanuilebheist. Now I can kill him slowly. Now I can make you watch while he suffers. I will find those you left in the human world and destroy them."

Even in the dream state, my fury rises. I'm in darkness. There's no body to go with her voice as there was when Elspeth came to my sleep. It's only me in the dark. *"If you could make good on any of these threats, you would be standing before me in the real world instead of disturbing my sleep, Vanora Braddish—idle threats to frighten me and make me run. Maybe you think you can convince me to come to you as you did when I first arrived in this world. You make threats in the darkness, but you haven't the power to follow through."*

"You dare call me by my familiar name? I'm your queen. You are nothing but a tiny human who will die easily enough." Her rage manifests as a shadow demon that sweeps past me but doesn't hurt or drain my power. It's not real.

Rather than give her the satisfaction of seeing my fear, I laugh. *"More smoke and shadows from a pretender to a crown. You are no queen, and I am going to wake myself up."*

As I pull myself out of the dream, her rage-filled scream follows me. I sit up. My heart races, and my chest feels like an anvil is pressing down on it.

Fancor jumps to his feet and draws his sword. "What in the name of the old gods was that?"

"You heard that?" I look around at the rest of the party. No one else rises or stirs in their sleep. Even the soldier standing guard is unfazed.

Fancor tilts his head as if he's listening for more. "I heard something, but your lips didn't move, lass."

"Vanora was in my dream." Sitting up, I cross my legs and shake off the remains of the dream.

"Are you saying I heard her through your dream?" He takes a similar position facing me, and adds a log to our dwindling fire.

Watching the wood catch, I shrug. "I guess you must have."

"What did she say?" His dark-brown eyes are full of worry.

Like I might have any favorite uncle, I tell him the whole

story of my dream. It helps relieve some of the pressure in my chest.

His left brow lifts, and he stares into the fire. "I think you had the right of it. She's making empty threats. She wants to frighten you."

My laugh matches the sarcasm and strain within me. "She needn't have bothered. I'm plenty scared enough. Her invasion only made me angry."

"That's better than scared. She'd have been wise to learn more about you when she had you in her grasp." He shakes his head.

Giving that some thought, I consider the time I spent under her control. I've been pushing those memories away. The terror of the dungeon, the cold, the pain, and the helplessness were all too much, and I wanted them gone. But now, I let those days back into my mind, looking for clues. "She's self-absorbed, Fancor. She thinks of nothing but herself and how one person might benefit her or another might do her harm. She never considers the true value of a person. Of course, this is just my opinion based on observation." I'm no psychiatrist. Still, I've always understood people and their motives, even when I don't like the outcome.

"You have seen her at her worst. Who better to judge?" He pokes the fire with a stick.

"Even Ciaran means little to her. She'll use him up and find another. Though, for him, she plays the part of a lover. He must have been very strong and not very smart. Maybe he thought he could manipulate her and seize her power. He's fading now. She'll start looking for someone new to help her." I touch the runes still showing in the dark. "Could this be why she couldn't show herself in my dream?"

He shrugs. "I don't know. Maybe. They're meant to protect you from evil."

"Well, she couldn't touch me. Even the shadow demon was not real, only an illusion." I like the idea that his magic protected me. Maybe I'm kidding myself, but I like it just the same.

As the sun hits the hills, I feel Aaran's mind awaken, as if a shroud has been lifted.

I revel for a moment in the feel of his love within me. It's warm, and I didn't realize how much I'd missed it. Sitting up, I roll toward him.

No longer ashen, his cheeks are pink. His eyes blink open, and he winces before smiling at me. "Hello."

"Hello, yourself. You almost died, and you promised me you would keep me safe." My scolding is soft, and there's no way to hide my relief. I feel as if I can finally release the breath I've been holding.

Wincing again, he attempts to sit, but gives up a moment later. "Sorry about that. It seemed like the right thing to do at the time. In my defense, a monster was dragging you out to sea."

My heart leaps in my chest. I had no idea love could be like this. Any brush with romance I had in my past life was mere fondness compared to the all-consuming adoration I feel for this elf. "I will forgive you if you stay still and heal properly."

"Where are we?" He helps me lift his head to put a blanket behind him. His lips thin from the strain.

"We carried you all day yesterday. We're in the hills between the sea and some river." I'm sure someone told me the names of these places, but I can't remember.

"The Bog Hills and the river is Dá Lock Abhainn. We'll be safe across the river." He closes his eyes.

"We were supposed to be safe on this continent, but she has attacked by land and by sea." I shouldn't add to his worries, but it's best to be realistic. I do keep my dream to myself for now.

"Not land. She used demons from what you would call hell to attack."

I don't get a chance to tell him what I think of the distinction.

"You're awake." Nainsi rushes to Aaran's side. "Cara is well enough to add some healing magic. I'm going to help her. You'll be better in no time."

Bert grins down at him. "You gave us quite a scare. Especially when Harper couldn't reach your mind."

Aaran's eyes grow distant. "I was...elsewhere. I don't know how to explain it."

Nainsi frowns. "We are all much relieved you found your way back to us."

"Where are Jax and the others?" Aaran's jaw ticks.

"Relax," I press his shoulder back before he decides to leap up and damage himself again.

Bert waves at Cara so she'll come, then turns back. "They've gone to scout ahead and check that we're not followed. Fancor and Beran are guarding the camp, and we'll take shifts until we can safely move. Everyone is tired. Another day here would be a blessing."

"Not if Vanora knows where we are," Nainsi mutters, her hands balled at her sides.

Cara shoos Bert and me away and kneels beside Aaran with Nainsi. She places Nainsi's hands on his ribs and hers on top.

The tingle of magic flashes through me even from ten feet away. I feel the moment Aaran loses consciousness. I wonder if we had other choices. Should I have let him portal us away and left these people to their fate? Would Aaran be safe and whole if I had?

A flush of love flows over me from his mind.

He may be sleeping off the injury and the healing magic, but his mind is still with me. *You were right, mo chroi.*

It felt right at the time, but seeing him weak and pale, I wonder. Have his brothers already found the human women they were sent for? They may be with their mother, waiting and wondering if we're alive. I am the reason more people are dying in this land. How many have been turned to shadow demons since I arrived, and how many more before we get to the gate?

Even then, will the answers be simple? I doubt it. Nothing ever is, and this battle with the witch queen has been going on since before I was born. War, death, and loss are all Aaran has ever known. It's ridiculous to believe that I'm the solution.

My hand slides to the hilt of the sword strapped to my hip. My mother wouldn't recognize me with a weapon. Nor would she believe I have a dagger tucked in my boot. I barely recognize myself.

Jax jogs toward me. I have no idea how far he ran, but he's not out of breath. When he stops, he stares at my face for a long moment. "Are you well?"

I pull my shoulders back and lift my chin. "I'm fine. Aaran woke up. They're healing him now."

His gaze flits over the camp where elves rest or keep fires burning. Several cook on a main fire at the center of the group. "The path ahead appears clear. I saw no signs of Vanora or her creatures. The others should return soon. Hopefully, they'll have similar reports."

A bright red head crests the hill northwest. "There is Breck now."

Jax turns and walks a few steps toward his soldier. He stops and looks over his shoulder at me. "Are you certain you're well?"

"I have no idea, to be honest." The moment I say so, I wish I'd kept my mouth closed.

Jax gives Breck a nod, then turns to face me. "Tell me." He gestures that I should walk with him at the edge of the camp.

We're not friends. He barely tolerates me. But I respect him. The others will soothe me by telling me everything is going to be alright. At least from Jax, I'll get the brutal truth. We walk for more than a minute before I say, "I'm not suited to this kind of life. I have almost no training, and the magic I have is erratic and new. The most magical thing I did in my world was touch someone's hand and know that someone was going to die young or lose a baby. And here, I am some savior who's supposed to save a world and all its people. I don't even like camping."

"I prefer my own bed with my wife in it as well." He chuckles.

The sound is so strange I stop and make sure it was really from him. "Are you making fun of me?" I can't decide if I'm shocked or annoyed.

He shakes his head. "No. I can see how all of this is overwhelming and exhausting."

When he doesn't say more, I say, "I know that it sounds like I'm whining. You and your people have been dealing with this for thirty years. Your entire species is in jeopardy. I shouldn't complain. It's only...what if I fail?"

"You may fail." He crosses his thick arms. "We may all perish at Vanora's hand or be turned into soulless shadow."

"Great. That's reassuring."

He smiles.

I take a step back. "I had no idea you were this handsome."

Grinning wider, he nods. "I am a fine specimen. That's what Selina told me when first we met." His smile dims. "I cannot predict the future, Harper. I don't know what will happen to my people or if you and two more are the answer we've been praying for."

"Honesty." I sigh.

"Despite your lack of magical training and offensive skills, you have improved with a sword, killed a deer, and defended this party of strangers with your magic valiantly. If you had asked me when first we met if I thought you could save Domhan, I would have told you no. I would have said we'd be better off throwing ourselves on our swords now if this small woman from the human world was our only hope."

I hold up my hands to stop him. My gut is in knots, and I'm barely holding back a torrent of tears. "Alright. That's enough." I turn to walk away.

He stops me with a hand on my shoulder. "Let me finish. Today, I see a woman who has overcome an entire belief system to help a people not her own, and she has won battles that might have been lost without her help. I see strength in you, Harper Craig. Far more than I, and maybe you, gave you credit for."

I brush away a tear.

"Now, I think this is a woman who the oracle has predicted will help rescue us. I see the possibility of a life where my sons grow up, and perhaps my precious wife gives birth to a girl. You give me hope that there will be a future. I don't know if you will succeed, but I will follow you to what-ever end is waiting. I believe you are one of three in the prophecy."

Chapter Twenty-Two

AARAN

The sun is setting when I wake up again.

Harper sits, eating from a leaf. She smiles at me, but her eyes are distant. "I'm glad you're awake."

Testing my ribs, I take a deep breath. "I feel better."

"You had a collapsed lung. It looks like you're breathing easier." She finishes the meat. "Are you hungry? They've saved you food."

Anchoring my elbow, I ease myself to sitting. Only the echo of pain in my side, I settle against the rise behind me. "I am a bit hungry."

In a flash, she's up and walking away. A moment later, she has a large leaf filled with meat and berries.

I eat, but her expression worries me. "Are you ill?"

"No. Just thinking about something Jax said." She smiles, but again it doesn't touch her eyes.

"What did he say?" I must speak to Jax about being

kinder to Harper. She needs her confidence bolstered, not torn down at every opportunity.

"He said that he believes in me. Well, and a lot of other things, but that was the most important." She moves to sit beside me against the hill, her shoulder pressed to mine.

"That's—" I'm not sure how to respond. It was the last thing I expected her to say. "Extraordinary."

"Right? I know. I was feeling less, and he helped." She snorts. "I expected him to agree with all my doubts, but while he understood them, he pointed out some of my strengths as well." She shrugs. "I'm glad you're better. Cara said you will be ready to journey by morning."

"Cara said?" I eat my food, which tastes better than I expected. I must have been hungrier than I thought.

"Well, through Dorian, but you know what I mean."

When I can't eat anymore, my eyes drift closed. I wrap my arm around Harper's back and keep her close. "I suppose that's the closest I've ever been to death."

"Too close."

"I'm sorry I scared you." Honestly, when the darkness took me, I was scared too. I was letting everyone down, but it was peaceful in the place between worlds.

"Don't do it again." She kisses my cheek.

I wish I could tell her we're safe from now on, but that would be a lie. No one is safe, nor will they be until Vanora has been dealt with.

Stars begin winking into existence, and the moon rises next to Arcania.

Tal walks over and lies down next to Harper. Silently, she closes her eyes as Harper pulls a tattered blanket over the girl. Within a few minutes, the boys make their way over and pile in to sleep like cats.

When Fort plops his head on my ribs and I have minimal pain, I'm relieved.

The oldest, Bor, snuggles in behind Fort.

"This is unexpected," I whisper.

"They've been staying close to me. Last night, I didn't sleep much. They found their way over in the middle of the night. Fancor took them to a spot closer to the fire, so you wouldn't be disturbed." She brushes Tal's hair from her eyes. "I think they've adopted me as their protector. They're badly in need of some love and care."

The children are smarter than we gave them credit for. No one exudes more love than Harper. It pours from her, filling everything with her soft attention. The fact that she bestows her love on me is a miracle. I can only hope that if we live long enough, I'll become a man who deserves it. "There is no one better suited for the job."

She sighs and leans her head on my shoulder. "Will your mother ensure they are taken care of until we can bring them to their families? I know they're not your people, but they're only children."

Kissing the top of her head fills me with warmth and gives me the false impression that I'm somehow taking care of her. "No harm will come to them."

"That's not exactly what I asked." She closes her eyes.

"No. I know, but I don't have all the answers, Harper. Nothing has been ordinary since I met you." The last light of day slips away, and the air cools. I'm not even strong enough to add heat to the fire. My magic is busy healing my wounds.

As if summoned, Jax walks over and shakes his head at

me with a pile of children sleeping all around and Harper dozing at my side. He sends heat to the stones surrounding the fire. It will keep us warm through the night and allow the burning wood to die out. It's better not to have those fires as beacons for the enemy. "I'm a little jealous, Riordan. I miss my family."

"You'll be with them soon." I want to say that the worst is behind us, but I have no idea if that's true. "Maybe we can gather some horses. The wild ones like the great spring."

"Perhaps. Sleep now. I will keep watch. At daylight, we should leave this place." He turns away and scrutinizes the surrounding dark hills.

"When will you sleep, my friend?" I feel as if I've been away from the group for months, though they told me it was only two days and a night that I was unconscious. Wherever I was is shrouded in mist now. Like a dream that I can almost remember but can't quite reach. I don't know who has slept and who has not. I only know what I've been told, which is very little.

"Fancor will take my place in a few hours. Your charges are safe, Aaran." He walks to the top of the nearest hill.

"Thank you," I say softly.

His warrior's ears twitch, and he nods once.

Aside from a few stiff muscles from the heads, arms, and legs of children hemming me in, I'm myself again when the sun rises. Its heat and energy fuel my magic. I may need a few days to be at full strength, but I'm on my feet, and that's a big improvement.

Most of the freed elves are well enough to walk on their own.

Some carry the children or corral them in the right direction as we cross the hill country on our way to the river.

Harper stays by my side. I feel her worry. When I was elsewhere, I still felt the connection to her, but I suspect she did not. "Have you been working on your sword skills while I was unavailable?"

The way her lips twist in that don't-mess-with-me way makes me want to kiss her hard until she's panting. "I trained while you slept yesterday. Jax knocked me on my ass twice, but I nearly got the drop on him."

"You know he's been training as a soldier most of his life. Perhaps besting him shouldn't be your aim." I love how ambitious she is.

Grinning like she has a secret, she says, "I'm happy with nearly, but I would love to beat him one time when a volcano isn't distracting him."

"Take that as a big win, *mo chroi*. I doubt I could win a sword fight with Jax, and I've been at it since I was eight suns."

"Eight. We really do come from different worlds. At eight, I played soccer, with my father coaching and my mother screaming encouragement from the sidelines." Her memory leaves a soft, sad smile in its wake.

"What is soccer?"

"A game where two teams battle for a ball. Without using their hands, they try to get the ball in the net of the opposing team." She kicks her right foot out as if she has a ball.

"You'll have to teach me sometime." A little jealous of her energy, I send a revival spell to my legs since they're already sore and we've only gone a few miles.

Green rolling hills stretch on for as far as I can see. As we climb the next ridge, the glimmer of sunlight hitting water gives me hope. Still half a day away, and then the ferry across. It's going to be hard going with so many to get across.

"Tell me about the river?" Harper picks up Bor and carries him.

The child rests his head on her shoulder and toys with her braid.

Before I can answer, Nainsi says, "Dálock Abhainn. It means Two Lakes River. It's wide, and at this end, there are only two ways to cross. The ferry above the first lake or the Dagda Bridge, a full day's journey north." She tightens the band holding her braid at the bottom and pulls her lips into a tight line.

"Why do you look so dour? Is the ferry a bad choice?" Harper is a keen observer of others.

Shrugging, Nainsi sighs. "We have little choice really. Sometimes the water near the first lake is a bit rough, and there are a lot of us. But the bridge would be a day north and then an extra day south on the other side." She picks up Tor as he's running by. "We don't have the resources for the extra days."

"We're already long overdue." Ignoring the fact that my muscles are weak from lack of use, I trudge up the next hill, and the next.

It's a great relief when we're past the hills, and all that

lies between us and the river is meadowland and high grasses for miles. Not exactly easy travel, but at least it's flat, and the summer has left the ground mostly dry.

Deep into the grasses, Harper stops. "I have something in my shoe." She puts Bor down and takes a step back to kneel.

I lift my arms and stretch, then squat and try to loosen my leg muscles. When I look back, Harper is rising.

She cocks her head and looks for something across the grass. "Magic?"

There's a dull popping sound, and a hole opens beneath Bor and sucks him away. I leap to try to grab his hand, but the hole closes just as the pain of a vortex hits my arm.

With wide panicked eyes, Harper hollers, "Bor!"

The popping sound comes a second time. I grab Harper before she can be pulled away by another opening in the ground. Pushing her forward, I scream, "Run!"

"But Bor," she protests.

"You can't help him now. They want you. Run!"

She does as I say and sprints northwest as I follow.

I call out over and over to the group. "Run. Portal magic. Run for the river." I'm just behind Harper. "Turn right. Get away from the group."

"You should leave me." She keeps running hard, her arms pumping.

With a pop, another portal appears beside me with Harper only a toe's length in front. She teeters on the edge and screams. She's falls back toward the empty space.

Digging deep for my magic, I shoot energy toward her and leap across the chasm. I wrap my arms around her waist and we tumble forward, away from the portal.

She jumps to her feet and continues to race toward the north.

Fancor hollers, "We'll be at the ferry."

"Go without us. Get them to safety." I keep my focus on Harper and listen for pops of whatever magic this is. Behind us, elves are screaming and calling names. I have to fulfill my mission. As much as I want to help those heading west, my first duty must be to Harper. In my peripheral, the tall form of Avon is there one moment and gone the next.

Jax calls his name.

Still, we can't go back or even look back. I've never seen portals formed in the ground. I don't know where they go or how such magic was achieved. The only thing I'm certain of is that I can never let Vanora capture Harper again. I failed her once; I will not do so again.

Breathing heavy, Harper begins to slow.

I run beside her. "We can't stop yet."

Her cheeks are scratched and bleeding from the tall grass whipping her as she runs. Tears run with the blood and sweat. "I can't run much longer." She grips her left side. "I still feel that magic."

We splash through wet ground. Calling to the bright sun, I draw in more magic and let that filter through me to her, releasing her stitch.

She dashes forward. At the far northern edge of the grass, the land grows dryer, and here Harper stops. She cocks her head as if listening for something. "It's gone. I don't feel that magic anymore."

I take her hand and pull her farther north, away from the wetlands and our friends.

After a few hundred yards, she bends over and grabs her knees. "Now what?"

Catching my breath, I say, "We head for the bridge. Whatever that magic was, it ended at dryer higher ground. Maybe she can't cast it here, but we can't go back and risk her feeling your presence anywhere near the others. They will cross at the ferry."

"It didn't feel like Vanora's magic." She pauses and winces as if remembering the pain from her capture and torture. Gaze distant, she searches behind us and tears roll down her cheeks. "So, we just abandon them to whatever fate?"

I hate the pain in her voice. "No. We let them defend themselves. Fancor, Jax, and the others will protect them with their lives. If you go back, you're putting them in more danger."

"Why? How?" She dashes away her tears and faces me like a warrior.

"Whoever sent those portals knew where you were. The first one appeared just where you were standing a moment before. The second was just under you before I snatched you back. Even with you running, they almost pulled you in. They must have been able to feel you in that soft wet earth, Harper. We can't go back." With every fiber of my being, I want to tell her that everything is going to be alright. I want her to feel safe and at peace. But that's not the truth. "We need to get across the river and then to the spring. It's at least two days. The others will likely be rested and fed by the time we reach Tús Nua." At least, I hope that's true.

Eyes clear, she nods. "I thought Vanora couldn't use her magic here. You said the oracle protected this continent."

"Clearly she's finding other ways through and if that wasn't her magic, then perhaps she has an ally we didn't count on." There are so many possibilities, and my head is full of theories. Hand in hand, we walk north, and her mind settles into acceptance.

Moving away from my touch, she keeps walking toward the Dagda Bridge. "Do you think your mother will like me?"

The question seems so random, I chuckle.

Harper gives me a sharp look.

"I think at the very least, she is grateful you have come."

If her frown is to be believed, that was not the response she was looking for.

"Does it matter if my mother likes you or not? She will show you kindness and deference regardless." The river appears at our left, and I walk to the edge. I send my magic to check for dark or shadow bewitchment. Finding none, I kneel and drink.

Harper sits at the edge and takes her shoes off. She drinks several handfuls, and then puts her feet in the cool water. Sighing, she leans back on her elbows. "It matters."

Sitting cross-legged next to her with my arm touching her shoulder, I let her energy mix with mine. I could gather the information I want from our link, but I don't, and she doesn't offer it up. "I cannot imagine my mother or father disliking you, but I'm quite biased, as I love you more than I ever dreamed possible."

"Thank you." She closes her eyes and lies back in the green grass. "What will happen once we reach your home?"

"I imagine there will be a big feast." I can almost taste the pheasant and wine. My stomach rumbles.

"Will we go directly to this gate of yours?" She removes

her feet from the river and moves back far enough that they can dry in the sun.

"It depends on if my brothers have returned with the other women."

Sitting up, she wipes the water from her feet and pulls her shoes on. "I almost forgot that I'm really just a tool to open the gate and that there are two other tools. Perhaps you would have been better off if one of them had been your goal. They might have jumped right into your portal, and you would have been back to the oracle and safe in a few minutes."

I understand that she's tired and scared. I also know that I am responsible for everything that has happened to her since we met. Still, her words cut deep. Before she can walk away, I take her hand. "I didn't go about anything right. I thought I could command a stranger to jump through my portal without any explanation just because I am the eldest son of Elspeth Riordan. I was arrogant and intolerable. I have since put you in great danger. I never dreamed Vanora would be able to break through the oracle's wards. Even the vortex that she made in those woods, and the damage she did, I explained away as being too far south for the wards to be secure. I have been wrong about everything from the start, and I'm beginning to question my competence for leadership."

She plops down, cross-legged in front of me. "You were bossy and carrying a sword which is strange in my world. However, you soon grew charming. You also saved my mother, for which, I can never repay you. Everything that happened since then was not your doing. I know you feel responsible, but you cannot take responsibility for the actions of others. You have gotten me to this point. In a few days, we'll reach your home. Maybe there we will be safe for a time."

The exhaustion in her voice pains me. I want her to be safe, to feel safe. I long to hold her through the night without having the need of guards and wards. "I wish you had seen this land before Vanora. I was only a child, but it was greener then, brighter, and magic vibrated in the air. When Vanora took the old city, her magic permeated and dulled Domhan."

Standing, she looks around. "It's quite beautiful now."

Rising, I nod. "One day, my mother will step back into the tower and make it white again. Her magic will fuel that of the world, and then you will see what you have saved, Harper Craig."

With a resigned sigh, she walks north along the river as I trail a step behind.

Chapter Twenty-Three

HARPER

By the time we reach the bridge, the sun is setting. My legs are like rubber. I'm not used to running long distances, and clearly not as if my life depends on it. That was more terrifying than being imprisoned and tortured, where at least I knew what was happening. Portals sucking people away were worse.

Bor. That poor baby is in evil's clutches now.

Aaran holds me back while he checks for dark magic on the bridge. He's been doing this every few miles. Once he's satisfied, he offers me his hand to cross. "On the other side, we can rest under the bridge for the night."

Two visions war in my brain. The first is the unsavory people who often live under bridges in the urban areas back home. The second is a childhood tale about a troll and three goats. Thoughts of my father and his warmth and fun-loving ways flow through me.

On the west side of the bridge, the air is lighter. It's easier to breathe. I inhale deeply and gently let it out. "That's nice."

"Yes. That is Mother's magic, and some of the oracles." He rounds the stone pylon and heads down the embankment.

I wait, as if a troll might appear, then laugh at myself and ease toward the river.

No goats or monsters of any kind lurk in twenty feet of dry land under the bridge, and the riverbank is two feet above the rushing water. As the sun lowers behind us, Aaran and I gather rocks rounded by the water. Rather than burn wood that might smoke us out, we pile up the stones, and Aaran uses magic to heat the rocks. He digs in his pack, pulls out a warm blanket, and lays it on the ground. "It's not exactly lush, but we should be dry and warm through the night."

I lean against a pylon, and the magic heat drives away the coming chill of night. "It's perfect."

He's still healing. Tired from the long day, he drags his feet and his shoulders slump when he walks to the bank. "I'll try to use magic to bring up a fish or two. We can cook it on the rocks."

Even though eating unseasoned fish from rocks sounds horrible, my stomach rumbles. "Are you sure you have more magic to use?" I hate seeing him weak.

"This doesn't take much, and we have to eat." Eyes closed, he lies on his stomach and reaches into the river. His skin brightens, and the pulse of his warm magic flushes over me.

A minute later, he pulls a fish big enough to feed us both

from the water. In his elvish language, he says something that might be a prayer before he brings the fish to cook. Adding heat, he places the fish on the stones with a sizzle.

"You're just going to cook it head and tail and all?" My hunger is failing.

"Without a pan, this is the best way to keep it moist. I won't make you eat scales or bones." He winks.

Despite myself, my cheeks heat. "You can't make me do anything."

"True," he says, and smiles without looking up from his cooking. "What were you thinking when I said we'd sleep under the bridge? I felt something, but I couldn't tell whether it was happy or sad."

"My father used to go on business trips when I was a girl." He had blue eyes and brown hair, always looked powerful in his business suits when he came home from work. Then he would change into jeans or shorts, and that felt better to me.

"The bridge made you think of your father's work?" Now he looks, but his expression is confused. He flips the fish over.

Shaking my head, I explain. "When he was gone for a long time, he'd bring me home a gift. Once he brought me a book with children's poems, stories, and fairy tales. It was hard-covered and had characters from rhymes and stories on the front and back. I loved that book. There was a story about a troll who lived under the bridge and three goats that wanted to cross. This made me think of that story, which made me think of my father. And I suppose thinking of him makes me both happy and sad."

Aaran's knife glints in the glow of the stones. He cuts

open the fish, slices out some flaky white meat, places it on a leaf and hands it to me. "It probably would benefit from spices, but we'll have to make do."

Too hungry to argue, I eat the fish, and while salt would be nice, it's not bad.

Fed and having washed our hands in the river, we lie back on the blanket. I rest my head on Aaran's shoulder and close my eyes.

"Tell me the story," he says.

"Hmm?" My muscles tick as they relax from a day of overexertion.

He wraps his arm around me and kisses my cheek, and it feels as if we've always known each other. "Tell me about the goats and the troll."

Eyes closed, I conjure up the tale of *The Three Billy Goats Gruff* and tell him what I can remember, right through the demise of the unfortunate troll. "I'm not sure if we're the goats or the troll."

He chuckles, and my head bobs on his warm body. "I'm not sure who's the hero of that tale."

"When I was little, I cheered for the goats, but now I can see the flaws in the lesson. I can't say if that's the point of the story or not. Most of the nursery rhymes and fairy tales from my childhood are either gruesome or ambiguous when you think about them." This is not the first time I've realized this. It was a topic in one of my literature classes in college. "A lot of them were written during times of war and disease."

"It's interesting. Not much different here. There were many tales of children being whisked away by monsters in my childhood as well." He falls silent.

"Perhaps because there *were* monsters, and it would frighten you into staying in places your parents thought safe.

"Perhaps."

As the sunlight brings the first gray and purple to the day, I pull out of Aaran's arms. At the water's edge, I slip out of my clothes and into the river. The cold water makes me squeak despite not wanting to wake him.

"Harper?"

I squeeze my eyes closed and wish I had been able to keep silent. "I'm just washing up."

An instant later, he's at the edge of the embankment stripping out of his clothes.

The cold washes away, and even after seeing him naked before, I heat from head to toe. He's beautiful, hard, and muscled. Whatever harm the wound and two days' rest did, it hasn't affected his toned body.

He steps into the river, and without being fazed by the chill, dives under. Like a merman, he swims toward me.

Instinctively, I step back. The round stones under my feet are hard to grip, and I slip. My head goes under in an instant. I come up sputtering and cough up water. When I stand, Aaran wraps his arms around me.

"Are you alright?" He brushes my hair from my face, and it takes several attempts to get the wet strands out of my eyes. "Why did you back away?"

Clutching his shoulders, I don't have a good answer. "I

don't know. This felt new somehow. You're..." I search for the word. "Changed. Not in a bad way, but still, not the same."

With his muscled legs wide, he lifts me until he can kiss my throat without leaning over. "Back in familiar light magic. I'm feeling much better. If we didn't have to get to the spring before dark, I would make love to you here on the banks of the river. I would hear you scream my name a dozen times."

My breath hitches. Wrapping my legs around his hips brings his cock along my slit. I rub along his shaft and moan. "You do feel better."

A few minutes to forget everything else. It's not too much to want. The aches of my body and the memories from yesterday, I just want it all to go away, so I won't hurt so much.

With a frustrated groan, he carries me from the river and lies on top of me on the grassy shore. I love the weight of him pressing into me. His mouth is electric along the skin of my neck and chest. He looks into my eyes, and his shine with so much love, it's hard to breathe. Lowering his mouth, he devours mine. His tongue seeks mine and slides over and around until I'm squirming beneath him.

Threading my fingers through his damp hair, I suck his tongue, then make love to his lips. On fire, I lift my hips so he can feel how wet I am, and it has nothing to do with the river.

A *kraa-kraa* breaks the silence as the shadow of a bird flies over us.

Aaran stills.

"Oh god, is it the blackbirds? Has Vanora found us?" My pulse races, and I try to judge how far it is to get under the bridge and out of sight.

Shading his eyes, he looks up. "We're safe." He sighs, lifts to one arm, and grabs my clothes. "You should get dressed. That's not a blackbird. It's a raven. Mother and the ravens are connected. I'm sure she sent it."

Taking my clothes, I scramble out from under him and run under the bridge to dress. "Your mother, she sees through the raven?"

He rises slowly and pulls on his pants. It's hard to look away from how male and perfect he is. Shrugging into his shirt, he says, "When she wishes."

The raven lands on a rock at the base of the bridge. "*Kraa-kraa.*" With shiny jet-black and curious eyes, it looks at me, then at Aaran.

Taking a knee, he pets the bird.

It fluffs and bends its neck for more attention. Then it flaps its wide wings and cocks its head.

"Tell her we're on our way." Aaran gives it one last pat and turns to me. "We can make the Naomh Spring before dark if we leave now. It's a full day's walk."

The raven flaps its wings and takes flight. It speeds west until it's only a speck in the purplish sky.

Sitting, I pull on my shoes. I can't decide if his mother knowing her son and I are intimate bothers me or not. She was very kind in the vision, giving me hope and making me want to hang on. All of that may have changed now that she knows. Mothers are protective of sons, especially those meant to rule one day.

Aaran's shadow blocks the rising sun. "Stop worrying. You're giving me a headache." He grins at me so brightly that I know he's not serious about the headache.

As cool as it was at night, the rising sun makes the plains fairly hot. "Does it snow here?"

"It does. More here than it did in the east. It's beautiful at home when the snow is fresh." A hint of his worry that they may never see another winter in Domhan niggles at me through our connection.

Wishing I could assure him it will be fine doesn't make it true. We may all die, and then perhaps we won't care what happens to this world. "I'd like to see Domhan covered in snow. I always love how the world gets quiet when it snows at home. Fewer cars, the birds are silent, and the snow mutes much of the commotion in Princeton. I bundle up and sit on my patio with cocoa and watch until I'm wet through."

"I would like to see that." He narrows his gaze and stares ahead.

Something is moving toward us fast. "Oh, god. What now?" My gut knots, and I crouch, ready to run.

"We're safe, *mo chroi*. I think Mother has sent some transportation." He continues walking.

Following, I narrow my gaze to see what he means by transportation. The black spot approaching becomes a beautiful horse, bigger than any I've ever seen.

It lowers his head affectionately toward Aaran, and

Aaran runs his hand up the beast's nose, then pats his neck. "Hello, Gaofar. It's good to see you." Grabbing a handful of thick black mane, Aaran swings onto the horse's bare back.

"Hand your pack up." He wings my pack over his shoulder and extends his hand to me. "Come on."

Drawing a deep breath, I wonder if my sore muscles can take the pounding of a horse's hooves. I take his hand, and he swings me up in front of him. A small squeak escapes as I adjust to the change in altitude. "This is the biggest horse I've ever seen."

His arms cradle me on either side. "Have you ridden before?"

"It's been a while. We went on trail rides when I was little, and I took lessons as a teenager." I take hold of Gaofar's mane and hope my grip and Aaran's arms are enough to keep me astride.

"This will be like riding air." We start at a light trot. "Gaofar is the king of the horses of Siar Fàilte."

"He's very beautiful, and my feet are grateful for the ride." I lean into Aaran's chest. "I'm a little worried about my ass though."

His chest shakes as he laughs. "Hold on tight."

They must have a signal that's imperceptible to me. Gaofar leaps into a gallop. I yelp at the sudden change, but an instant later, realize this is not an ordinary horse. His gait is so smooth and easy that it's as if we're flying. Still holding on, I relax into the ride.

The countryside whizzes past in a blur of green, brown, and blue. I breathe in the scents of this strange world. This is the first time since leaving my home that I feel safe. Perhaps I'm fooling myself, but a sense of ease surrounds me. Maybe we will live through this, or this could be the calm before the storm. Whatever it is, I'm relieved to slip out of fight-or-flight mode.

I don't know exactly what I expected from the spring that feeds a second large river on this continent, but it's more of a stunning oasis. The land before was beautiful, but this is another level of green and lush. Kelly-green grass covers the ground, and several rock outcroppings have water running down them as if the rocks are capping a water spout. Flowers bloom in lavender and yellow along the base and on the bank. The spring itself is fifty feet wide and twice as long. A lake, big enough that I can't see what's on the other side, lies just south of the spring.

"This is the most beautiful place I've ever seen. Well, excluding the fairy glen." My cheeks heat with the memory of that magical night, though it seems like a lifetime ago. "Does this spring feed that entire lake?"

As we walk along the north side of the spring, he says, "There are many springs underground that also feed Naomh Lake."

As we turn south, Nainsi, Bert, and Fancor smile at us. Bert waves.

Three gray horses nearly as big as Gaofar munch grass near the spring.

Fancor strides toward us. "We were getting worried." He pats the horse.

Aaran lifts me down to Fancor, who eases me to my feet.

I throw my arms around him. "I'm happy you are here."

"Well, that's nice." He pats my back and blushes.

I hug Nainsi and Bert. "Where is everyone?"

Aaran lets Gaofar join the other horses, then shakes hands with Fancor and stands beside me, waiting for the answer.

Nainsi says, "The true queen sent carts and horses to transport us early this morning. Jax and the soldiers accompanied them to Tús Nua. We wanted to wait and reach the city with you."

My heart aches a little from the sweetness of this gesture. "I'm happy to see you." I feel Aaran's trepidation before he speaks.

"How many did we lose to those portals?"

In a long silence, Bert and Nainsi look at the ground.

Clearing his throat, Fancor crosses his thick arms. "It's a damned shame to get that close and..." He takes a breath. "We lost eight. Avon, four freed elves, and three of the littles, including Tal."

It feels as if my heart will spill out on the green grass. I clutch my chest. "They were meant for me." I crumple to the ground. That monster has three of those babies. "It's bad enough to be an adult in her clutches, but the children. Tal is so strong, but how does a child survive amidst such evil?"

"They were taken to hurt you. There's a difference, *mo chroi*," Aaran says.

Nainsi crouches to meet my gaze. "We'll get them back." She sounds so certain I almost believe her. "Right now, you need to pull yourself together, and we all need to go to the city. You must give the people hope that we can defeat the witch queen, Harper."

"I don't know if I can pretend to be something I'm not. I'm nobody's hero, Nainsi. Those people in town are expecting some kind of magical miracle. Won't they be disappointed when they see it's only me?" I feel as if the world is crashing down around me. This is all too much.

Her lips pull into a straight line. "Do you think they are the only ones under the thumb of evil? My parents died for this cause. Many more will die before this is over. If you can't stand up and walk into the city as a sign of hope, then we may as well send you back to New Jersey."

"Nainsi." Bert's voice is soft but admonishing. "Enough."

She takes a deep breath, and her expression softens. "Forgive me. You have been through a lot since you came here. More than you should have endured. All I'm asking is that you be the Harper Craig who walked through that portal in the woods outside of Clandunna because she had to save the village."

It seems like a lifetime ago, but it was less than a month ago. Home seems like a distant memory. Sometimes it feels like I was in my condo a moment ago. Right now, it could be a lifetime in the past. It all feels the same. I shake my head to clear the stupid thoughts. Wiping my face, I stand. "You're right. I came here to help. Everything I went through, and whatever our friends are enduring now, would be for nothing if I give up now."

Nainsi pulls me into a brief, fierce hug, turns, and mounts one of the gray horses.

Grinning, Aaran takes my hand.

"You're not disappointed in me?" My courage faltered. He should be disgusted.

With a shake of his head, he leaps onto Gaofar's back.

Once I'm securely seated in front of him, he whispers in my ear. "Fear is normal. Worry over our friends is expected. I never had any doubt that you would stand up. Never."

That's more than I can say. I had nothing but doubts. I lean into his chest, and we ride for Tús Nua.

Chapter Twenty-Four

HARPER

Tús Nua is walled with pale-gray stone that seems to have no beginning or end and makes me wonder if the entire thing was carved out of a slab of marble. The city glows white in the sunshine. A horn sounds from the ramparts above the gate. A bright blue flag flies high. In the center is a gold crown with three jewels beneath: one blue, one green, and one yellow. It flaps in the breeze while another flag rises to its right. This flag is also blue, but the circle in the center is a simple gold crown with only one palisade at the front. It rides above an elaborate R, also stitched in gold.

The gates are open, making me wonder when they close them. Will I be trapped inside once we cross the threshold?

It's impossible to look anything but astonished as thousands of elves crowd the street to get a glimpse of us. I can't decide if they're happy to see Aaran or me, then someone calls out Aaran's name and a great cheer rises. Somehow, that makes me less nervous. They don't care about me, and that suits me.

Pride swells inside Aaran, and he waves at the crowd, which parts for the horses. The castle has three white towers, and the largest rises from the center of an enormous building.

"I can see that you have been raised very simply." I don't know what I was expecting, but it wasn't this. Perhaps something grander than the houses at Clandunna, but not a castle nearly as big as the blackened tower where I was held.

At the bottom of a white marble staircase, Aaran slides from Goafar's back and reaches up to help me to my feet. He takes my hand, and we climb up stairs that seem to never end. Every twenty or so there's a stretch of flat marble and then the steps again.

Bert and Nainsi are behind us. Bert says, "I guess there are no elevators in this place."

Nainsi chuckles.

"What in the blazes is an elev iator?" Fancor falls in step beside me. "Hang on, lass. You're nearly there."

"Yes, but where is there?" I command my legs to stop shaking and squeeze Aaran's hand.

After twelve rises of steps, we reach the last, which is steeper and twice as high. At least any shaking is from my muscles and ass about to seize up rather than fear. At the top, we stand at the front of a courtyard at least two hundred feet wide and a hundred feet deep, and my breath catches.

The front of the castle is pure white, with the three towers resembling a crown. Below the crown, scenes of battle and triumph are carved into the stone. Beneath that are six pillars, and at the center, an enormous arched door with three diamonds carved over the top. Soldiers dressed in blue and gold livery flank the door.

In the center of the courtyard stand a man and woman dressed in the same blue as the flag. The woman is Elspeth Riordan. Her bright blond hair catches the breeze, and her smile is warm and welcoming. The man doesn't smile. His hair is tinged with red, and his eyes are the brightest blue I have ever seen.

When we're a few feet away, Aaran releases my hand and bows before rushing into his mother's arms. "It's good to see you." He hugs his father, then steps back. "Mother, Father, this is Harper Craig. She has been through a great deal on our behalf. I bid you welcome her to our home."

He's so formal I barely recognize him.

Elspeth stares at me.

I have no idea how to curtsy, so I lower my head as some sign of respect. "Thank you for helping me when I needed you…" I don't know how to address her, so the sentence hangs in want of a name.

Widening her grin, Elspeth pulls me into a hug. "I'm so relieved you are here and well. It is a great gift that you also brought with you so many who need our help."

My heart sinks. "Some, but not all."

She brushes my hair from my face in a way that reminds me of my mother. "You have much to tell us, and we want to hear everything. First, you need food and rest. May I introduce my husband, Brion? You needn't look for titles. They are rarely used in these times. Elspeth and Brion will suffice."

Well, that's not happening. I shake Brion's hand. "Nice to meet you, sir."

Lips twitching with the hint of a smile, he bows his head. "I'm relieved you have come, as are all who suffer under Vanora." He turns to Fancor. "You travel with a dwarf."

Fancor makes a deep bow. "My Lady and Lord Riordan. I am Fancor, son of Fan. I offer myself to the cause. To be honest, I have no intention of leaving until either Harper is safely home or the witch queen is vanquished."

Even if I didn't already adore the man, it would be impossible not to like him. I don't know why he's accepted me as his to protect, but I'm touched by his devotion.

Brion gives Fancor a long look. "Then you will stay as our honored guest."

Fancor pulls his shoulders back and lifts his chin. "My thanks."

"Nainsi." Brion pulls her into a hug, then shakes Bert's hand. "It's good you see you both. When we heard you had come through with the prophesied and Aaran, I was not at all surprised and a good deal pleased."

Elspeth hugs Nainsi and beams with pride. She shakes Bert's hand. "Bertram Donaldson, the years have been kind to you. I can see you have made our girl very happy."

"It is she who has made my life worth living, Elspeth. It's good to see you again." Bert keeps Nainsi's hand in his as he makes his greeting.

Once the hugging is finished, we are escorted through the arched door.

Aaran stops to speak to one of the guards who stands at attention at the entrance.

Elspeth says, "This is Lila. She will see to your comfort while you are here."

I spare Lila a distracted smile but focus on Aaran's mother. "Where are the elves and children we traveled with?"

Eyes widening a fraction, Elspeth studies me with her lips pulled into a line. "Many of them are ill, and all need to be treated for the loss of magic. We've set up a hospital room in the east ballroom. I can assure you they are comfortable."

"I would like to see them before I go to my...room." I nearly say cell but stop myself. I don't know why I feel trapped suddenly.

Halfway up the steps rounding in the other direction, Fancor stops. "Ay. I would rest easier if I saw them as well." Ignoring the surprise on the valet's face, he jogs down the steps and stands beside me.

A grinning Aaran joins us. It's clear he's happy to be home. "What's happening?"

"Harper wishes to see the guests who arrived earlier today." His mother's tone is sharp. I think she's used to everyone agreeing with her at all times.

That's too bad.

Smiling even wider, Aaran takes my hand. "That is a good idea. I'd like to see them as well. Where is Jax?"

Brion scans the situation backlogging the foyer. He stares at his wife a moment, then his expression softens. "Jax is with his wife and sons. They have rooms on the second floor. We expect Jax and Selina to join us for a family dinner this evening."

Lila breaks the awkward silence. "Why don't I go and ready the room for Miss Craig? Aaran can show them the way to the east ballroom so they can visit with their friends. Then perhaps he will show them to the guest quarters?"

"Perfect." Aaran seems oblivious to everyone's emotions and demeanor. He takes my hand, and we stride from the foyer down a wide hallway with elaborate trim that shines golden.

Two guards follow us.

I whisper, "Why are we followed?"

"It's just a precaution." Aaran walks so fast that Fancor and I have to jog to keep up.

Several guards stand in front of an open double door. Inside are rows of beds, some filled with sleeping elves. Four cots are grouped in the corner, but the children lie on the floor between them.

Fort yells, "Harp," and dashes toward me.

A guard steps between me and the boy.

"No." I round the guard and intercept Fort, lifting him into my arms. "He is not a danger to anyone," I scold. My heart breaks even more for Gnal, Bor, and Tal who are not present.

The guard backs up a step.

Tor and Lem hang on my legs, hugging me.

Aaran picks them up. "You look fine. Clean and in new clothes."

The soldier Aaran spoke to at the front door steps forward and whispers in his ear.

Smile faltering, Aaran shakes his head. "If that's so, Mother will see it. It's unlikely. There was no time."

"Time for what?" I demand, as if I have a right to know. I should remember that I'm in a fortress, and I have no idea how to behave.

"I'd like to know as well." Fancor ruffles Fort's hair.

When the soldier with dark eyes and hair pulls his lips tight and steps back, Aaran says, "Elspeth Riordan has declared a watch on those who were under the witch queen's control. She fears one or more of them might be passing information to Vanora."

"Are you telling me that they are all prisoners?" I'm half a second from going and finding Elspeth and getting very Jersey Girl with her.

Aaran puts a hand on my shoulder. "They need attention and care. They are only under a watch. Tomorrow, they will each be evaluated, and they'll be free to stay or go as they please. In the meantime, they are fed and have water for washing as well as clean clothes and beds." As hard as he's trying to sound optimistic, it's not working.

I go over to the children's' corner and put Fort down. I push the cots together and place the five-year-old on one. "Sleep now. You're tired."

The other three climb in, and all four curl with arms and legs overlapping like cats. Without Tal they'll need each other even more.

I close my eyes for a moment and repeat Nainsi's words in my head. *We'll get them back.*

Spotting Cara and Dorian near the tall windows that face east, I rush to them and hug each of them. "Are you well? Have they taken good care of you?"

Cara cups my cheek and Dorian says, "We're fine. Everyone has been kind. It's not surprising they worry we're spies. No one has heard from us since Vanora cleared our town and dragged us to the castle."

I don't suppose it would do much good to rage against

this. I didn't get to know each and every freed elf personally. It's possible one or more could be dangerous. Not wanting it to be true doesn't work as a defense. "I will be back tomorrow."

Beran steps into the group. "We'll be safe. You gave us hope. That's more than anyone else has done for us in many years."

Reluctantly, I agree to leave them in the ballroom with the guards.

Fancor grumbles the whole way down the hall. "Why are they a threat, but not me?"

"You weren't held captive by Vanora," Aaran suggests.

"I was." My anger rises. "Why not put me under guard?"

When Aaran doesn't answer, Fancor says, "We need you, lass. Elspeth needs you, as do all the people of Domhan. If you're compromised, all is lost. Besides, I would venture to guess that our hostess did a quick scan when she hugged you on the terrace."

"What?" I snap a sharp look at Aaran.

"He's probably right." Taking my hand, he kisses my fingers. "She's being cautious. We've been a land at war for over thirty suns."

I suppose that's a decent excuse.

Aaran takes me to a door that looks like every other wooden door in the second-floor hallway. He tells me he'll see me at dinner. When he leaves, he shuts me inside a very opulent room. Cream and pale pink cover the enormous bed that boasts gold curtains hanging from the ceiling at the head. They flow to the floor like a canopy for the mound of pillows. A plush cream rug covers the marble floors, and a stone fireplace is dark, but I imagine it's very cozy when the weather is cooler.

A small vanity with an ornate mirror atop and pink upholstered chair sits near one of two windows that look out to a view of mountains as tall as the Rockies. It's midafternoon, and sunlight streaks across the floor.

My clothes are too dirty to sit on anything, so I stand near the window and admire the view. It's strange being without Aaran. He's probably with his parents, catching up on all that has happened.

I'd like to go explore rather than stand alone in a room far too grand for me. The door bursts open, three elven women walk in, and startled, I squeak.

Lila is carrying an armful of clothes. Her light-brown hair is pulled into a tight bun at the back. Tall and thin, like most of the elves, she smiles, but then frowns. "I am Lila. I thought you might benefit from a long hot bath. I'm guessing it's been quite the journey. I brought you some clothes, something to wear to dinner. It won't be formal tonight, so just a simple dress. Then I have a few leggings and tunics that should fit you." She puts them all on the bed.

The other two go through a door, and the sound of water running fills me with joy. I never thought I would cry over running water, but I'm close to tears. "Thank you." The dress is burnt-orange velvet. It's soft and beautiful and will go nicely with my hair. It's easily the nicest thing I will have ever worn. The rest looks comfortable. Black or brown leggings and white tunics. Another maid rushes in with several pairs of shoes and boots, which she places on the floor at the bottom of the bed before rushing out.

Lila's eyes grow wide as she stares at my tears. "If these don't please you, I'm sure we can find something else."

Swallowing the emotions, I draw a breath and shake my head. "No. These are perfect. Thank you."

Once the tub is full, Lila hurries the other maids from the room. "Whatever we've done to offend you, miss, it was not intended."

"It's been so long since I had clean clothes and a hot bath, that I wasn't sure such things existed anymore." I wipe my tears. I think I've cried more since coming to Domhan than in the ten previous years combined. Maybe if I'd cried more over my father and mother, I'd be tougher now.

With a warm smile, Lila nods. "Do you need help washing?"

"No. I'll be fine. Thank you." The bathroom is awash with cream tiles with dark veining and gold fixtures gleaming in the sun shining through the high windows. The tub is carved into the floor, and rose-scented steam rises from the milky water. Under the window is a washbasin with a dragon painted inside the bowl. Through a door at the far end is a toilet not much different than those I've seen in historical renderings.

I strip out of my clothes and drop them on the floor before sinking into the luxury of a tub big enough for three or four people. One end has a cushioned headrest and a soft seat as well. Two white towels wait on a chair, and beneath the chair are soap and shampoo. I should have brushed the knots. I let the water soothe my aches and pains while I unwind my braid.

Once my hair is washed, I float in the water until my skin grows pruned. With a sigh, I find the plug and pull it, letting the water drain as I stand and wrap myself in the softest towel I've ever held. I swaddle my hair with the other and stare into the foggy mirror.

Whoever the woman looking back is, I barely recognize her. She's too thin, and her eyes are larger than I remember. The cut of my biceps and triceps has me turning to take a better look.

I stumble into the bedroom and flop on the soft mattress. I'm damp, but at least I'm clean. I moan over how soft and fluffy the bed is. "I may never get up."

Lila must have put all the clothes away. The only evidence is the dress that hangs on an armoire across the room. Unable to decide if I'm curious about the city and my surroundings or too tired to care, I close my eyes and the decision is made.

A chill in the room stirs me awake. There's a noise and I sit up, grabbing my towel.

One of the maids is building a fire. "Sorry to disturb you, miss. I saw you were sleeping an hour ago and thought I'd come back so you could rest. The nights get cool here. I didn't want you to catch a chill."

I blink and rise. "Thank you. My name is Harper."

She smiles and uses her forearm to brush her curly blond hair from her face. "I'm Mari. Lila will be in shortly to help you dress and do your hair. Dinner will be at eight."

The sun is low, almost touching the mountains. "What time is it now?" Suddenly, I miss my phone.

"Nearly six." Once the fire catches, she makes a little curtsy and rushes from the room, carrying a metal bucket.

I sit at the vanity and pull the towel from my hair.

"Oh dear!" Lila shouts from the doorway. She comes over. You should have called me to brush your hair before you napped. She takes a brush from a drawer in the vanity and works the soft bristles gently through my wild hair.

"We can just pull it into a ponytail. There's no need to fuss," I say, but having someone brush my hair is a luxury I can't turn down, so I sit and let her brush to her heart's content, while I close my eyes and enjoy.

"We can do better than that." She opens and closes the drawers a few more times. "The rumor going around the city is that you and the future king are lovers."

I snap out of my relaxed state and open my eyes. "I don't know what that means here. Are you asking me if I'm having sex with Aaran? Is Aaran to be king? Is Elspeth queen, or has she been deposed by Vanora?"

Pausing from her work, she meets my gaze in the mirror. "Elspeth Riordon is our queen. Vanora is a pretender who would destroy this world. Riordon is the royal name, and Aaran is the eldest child. I wouldn't presume to ask you about your sexual encounters." She returns to brushing.

"The royal name. I didn't know. I mean, I knew she ruled. I suppose I knew Aaran's part as the eldest son, but he always seems so down to earth. I guess I don't see him as a prince." Aaran would make a fine king. He's kind and smart. I, on the other hand, have no business dating or screwing, or whatever we're doing, the future ruler of a people. "Vanora tortured me and left evil behind that nearly killed me. I wasn't venerating her. I only want to know the status of things."

She twists and pins my hair before taking it all down. "I think it's beautiful down around your shoulders." She holds up a finger as if a thought has come to her. Pulling a shiny comb from the desk, she slips it into the right side of my hair, letting my ear show. "So no one forgets who you are."

"I'm no one," I remind myself as Lila goes to the closet and brings the dress back.

"You are our only hope." She helps me into the dress and buttons the back. With two straps to hold it up, and not much else, it leaves my arms bare. The soft fabric slips along my skin and shows every curve. We both look at me in the mirror. She says, "I think you'll do fine." With a smile and a nod, she bustles out of the room.

I slide on a pair of little shoes that are the same color as the dress. They fit my feet as if they were made just for me. Outside, the last of the day's light slides away. Summer is nearly over back home. I wonder if Mom went to the Jersey Shore and had some fun. She used to love a frozen drink on the boardwalk with her friends. I hope she's happy. Missing my mother is perfectly normal, and nothing to cry over. Shaking it off, I leave the confines of the room and step into a long hallway.

Left or right? I have no idea. I decide on the left and follow it to a set of stairs that go straight down, not curved like the ones that brought me to my room. At the bottom, I hear voices to the right and follow them, but soon realize I'm heading into a large group of soldiers.

I spin on my heel, rush back the other way and through a set of doors that open into a long hall with portraits on the walls and a piano in the corner. A violin rests on a stand, and several chairs are lined up against the wall.

Maybe it's a gallery or a music room. Posed paintings of blond-haired men and women cover the walls at even intervals. At the far end is Elspeth's portrait. She looks off past the artist to some pleasant scene.

"Should you be here?" A gruff masculine voice startles me.

I gasp and turn. "I didn't know the room was restricted."

He works his jaw from side to side. His dark-brown eyes stare at me as if he can see through me. He's handsome and fierce at the same time. In my experience, a deadly combination. "I am Rían Redmond, Captain of the Guard. The room is not forbidden, but if I'm not mistaken, you're expected at the family dinner."

This is the man who Aaran stopped to speak to when we arrived. I can't decide if he can be trusted. "I'll make my way there now." I head for the door closest with no idea where I am or how to reach the dining room.

The sharp clip of Rían's boots hitting the marble floor follows me. How had he been so silent when he entered the gallery?

I call over my shoulder, "Are you chasing me?"

"No. I'm seeing you safely to your destination." He pauses. "Which it is clear you have no idea how to reach," he says with laughter in his voice.

I still don't trust him, but I stop. I can't run in this dress and little slipper shoes. Turning toward him, I force a smile. "Captain Redmond, would you be so kind as to show me the way to the dinner I'm in peril of missing?"

"Peril indeed." He nods and gestures for me to return

through the gallery and down a hall that is tucked under the stairs. I hadn't noticed it before. Soon he opens a door, and we step into a larger hall.

A loud metal bang sounds from somewhere in the castle, and I jump.

"You've nothing to fear here, human. The witch queen cannot touch us." His chin is high and proud.

"Forgive me, Captain, but I've heard that before. The witch queen can't wield her magic on the western continent, and then a volcano erupted, and a two-hundred-foot fire serpent tried to drown us. We made it to the shore, and a sea monster nearly killed Aaran. We reached your marshland, and portals sucked away eight of my friends including three children. I think you have no idea what Vanora can do." I rein my anger, and take several deep breaths.

He studies me for an uncomfortably long time. "We will do all in our power to keep you safe. A squad is already being assembled to rescue those taken from your party." It sounds like a pledge. He points to the right. When we reach a double door, he rushes to open it for me.

"Thank you." As I pass, I ask, "Will you be leading that rescue, Captain?" It's a much smaller dining room than I expected. The table could seat perhaps eight and is set for seven.

Brion strides over. "Are you joining us for dinner, Captain?"

"I have already eaten, thank you. Miss Craig was turned around on the west side of the castle. I offered my assistance."

Aaran rushes over and kisses my cheek. "You look beautiful." He looks at Rían. "Stay. Hear the full story of our journey. I wouldn't mind hearing your thoughts."

"I would like to hear more, if you're certain I'm not intruding." He looks at me. "I've decided, at Miss Craig's urging, that I should lead the rescue party."

Elspeth's eyes widen before she smiles. "Then you'll want to be here to ask all your inciteful questions, Rían. Do join us. Harper, you look extremely well in that color. Were you able to rest?" She takes my hand and leads me to a chair to her left. She's draped in a blue gown, and a gold feather pendant shines in the magic lighting.

Flames shimmer and give off a lovely crackle and light woodsmoke odor in a fireplace with a thick wooden mantel. It spans the length of the table. At the far end of the room is a sitting area. Servants are filling glasses with wine and water. The walls are dark wood panels and the ceiling is painted with scenes of elves frolicking and happy.

"Thank you. I had a bath and a nap. Everyone has been very kind."

Fancor gives me a warm nod of approval before sitting across from me.

With Aaran on my other side and Brion at the head, we are five for dinner plus Rían, with two empty place settings. "Where are Nainsi and Bert?"

"Gone to see her family. It's been ten years or more. We'll see them tomorrow." Aaran lets his gentle thoughts float into mine. He's at ease, and it helps me calm a degree or two.

Selina and Jax rush in. "I'm sorry to be late," she says, her cheeks flushed. Seeing me, she rushes around the table and pulls me from my chair into a warm hug. "It is a great relief that you are here and safe. I will never forget what you did for the people of Clandunna."

She is so happy to see me, I don't let go. I wait for her to break the hug first. "I'm happy to see you as well."

She holds me as if she fears I might disappear. Finally, she releases me. "Are you well?"

"I'm fine." True or not, it is clearly what Selina needs to hear. "I'm sorry about Avon and Lare." Especially Lare.

"I'll not give up hope for Avon's safe return." Pulling her shoulders back, she takes her seat across the table.

The first course is served, and Aaran begins our story from the moment he stopped time while I was waiting for my driver's license.

I listen, dreading my part of the tale.

Chapter Twenty-Five

AARAN

With Harper's hand slipped through the crook of my elbow, we walk through the grand corridor and into the garden. To me, this is my home, but her eyes are wide and her mouth slightly agape with every new sight.

A maze of rose bushes leads to a center fountain. Late summer means that many flowers are blooming and the air is heady with lovely scents.

One of the maids runs after us and wraps a shawl over Harper's shoulders.

"Thank you, Mari."

Mari makes a quick curtsy and runs back inside.

"You already know the names of the staff?" Everything about Harper is lovely and kind. I don't deserve this woman. I've taken her from all she knows and nearly gotten her killed a dozen times.

"She made my fire." She clutches the cream-colored

shawl tight. "Did you think the captain believed our story? He looked...I don't know, skeptical."

Mother was right about the dress, but the color be damned; it caresses Harper's curves well enough to make my mouth water.

"Rían is a soldier through and through. He's not one to show emotions. He believed us and will think over what he heard. Tomorrow, he will likely have questions." I turn us down a path that leads to a gate.

She shivers.

Stopping, I pull her into my arms and rub her back. "I was going to show you something, but perhaps we can do that tomorrow when it's warmer."

"It has been a long day. Can we go back to my room for the night?"

I freeze, not certain I'm understanding her correctly. "You want me to stay the night with you?"

"Is that frowned on here?" She looks at me and toys with my unbound hair where it lies on my chest.

"No. I didn't know if you'd be comfortable having everyone know that we're intimate." By the old gods, I'm an idiot. Suddenly, I feel like a child afraid of being caught stealing from the larder.

Her moss-green eyes are mesmerizing, even as she shakes her head at me. "Since Lila already asked me to confirm that we're lovers, I'd say that cat is out of the bag."

My cheeks heat despite its ridiculousness. "I'm not familiar with that phrase, but I take it that a cat would run rampant once freed from the bag?"

She nods. "If you don't want to stay the night, just hold me until I fall asleep."

Is it possible she doesn't know how I feel? I've told her. I've said it more than once. Could she think anything has changed because we've come home? "I would spend every second, day and night, with you if that were possible, Harper."

"I would like to remember lying on a mattress with blankets and not waking with dirt in my nostrils and hair." She makes a face that is at once not pretty and also adorable, with her lips twisted and her nose wrinkled.

"I'm not sure you realize what it means to have my full strength back." I lift her and sling her over my shoulder like a sack of flour.

Slapping my back, she laughs. "What are you doing?"

"I'm taking you to bed." Using elf speed, I run through the garden, the lower level of the house, and up the stairs in a few seconds. I slow in the hallway.

"What the fuck was that?" She pushes until I let her slide to her feet. Her hair is flying in every direction. Looking wild and excited, she pokes her finger in my chest. "Since when can you move like that?"

"Since I was a boy of about twelve suns." I open her bedroom door, and once we're inside, I bolt it closed.

"Why didn't I know that?" Standing with her back to me, she points at the buttons at the back of her dress.

Caressing down her shoulders to her hips, I love how this frock hugs her curves. One by one, I slip the little pearls free from the russet loops. "You look beautiful in this."

"Answer the question." There is my human woman who ran from me and my portal, then brandished a stick of metal to beat me with in her automobile.

"There was no need for it when we first met, and after I

used so much magic the day we saw your mother, I never had enough to risk expending it on a whim. Besides, you'd be ill if we traveled like that for too long." On the last button, I push the strap from her shoulder and kiss her warm, soft skin.

Turning toward me, she lets the material slide from her body to a heap on the floor. She steps free and kicks off the shoes as well. Only small bruises remain on her ribs and arm. Every inch of her is pure perfection. With sultry eyes, she wraps an arm around my neck and lifts on her toes to kiss me. "You're probably right, but I don't mind that you got us here quickly tonight."

I press one hand to the small of her back and the other cups her bottom, pulling her against my painfully hard cock. "I didn't want you to think any hesitation on my part was because I don't want you. Believe me, Harper, I want all of you so much it hurts." I press my hips forward, letting her feel what she does to me.

Her soft moan is like a drug as she wraps her legs around my hips. Pupils dilated, she grips my neck and shoulders and devours my mouth. Her silken tongue slides along mine in a desperate dance.

Sharing her need, I grip her ass and press her back against the wall. I lower my head to her throat and kiss my way to her pulse and suck her earlobe between my lips. "I wanted to take it slow. You should be worshiped." Even as I say it, I grind against her open legs.

"We can do that next. Now I need you inside me. I need to feel you, Aaran." Fisting my hair, she meets my trouser-covered thrusts.

Slipping my fingers into her wetness I tease her sensitive

pearl until she calls my name and pulls my hair. "Do you know what other magic I have that you've not seen?"

"Other than that you're going to make me come in a few minutes?"

Pressing a finger inside her and then a second, I conjure my magic. "That's your magic, not mine, *mo chroi*. I know a little trick." I will my clothes off and an instant later, I'm naked, my bare shaft poised just under where my fingers tease her wet folds.

She grips my bare back. "This is a very useful piece of magic." She rocks against my hand and makes the most arousing sounds.

"I should take you to the bed."

"No. Now. Here." Her eyes are intense, and her voice is commanding.

Gripping my cock, I slip the head inside her and let gravity draw her down. My growl is half animal.

Her legs tighten, and she presses on my shoulders to lift herself and take me inside again and again. Her body pulses around me, and she bites her lip to keep her cries muffled.

I stop to give her time to enjoy her orgasm.

Digging her nails into my shoulders, staring fierce and feral, she demands, "Don't stop. I need you."

It's taken all my will to be gentle. After finally bringing her to a safe place, I don't want to scare her. My longing is too great. Maybe her needs are the same. I clutch her smooth ass and pound into her hard and fast.

She meets every thrust with the tip of her hips, which brings me that much deeper. The sex is animal, elf, and human. It's a desperate need and pure love. This want is more than any I've felt in my life. My legs shake, and the tingle begins at the base of my spine. "Harper." I devour her lips, tongue, and teeth.

Both of us grunting and moaning. Holding on as long as I can, I reach between our bodies and rub her bud.

A long low keen rents the air as she comes hard around my cock, pulling me over the precipice.

I mean to pull out, but it feels too right.

Meeting my gaze, Harper tightens her legs around me, locking me inside her as my pleasure overtakes me. I press my forehead to hers. "I love you. I'm not sure about the wisdom of risking a child now, but I cannot regret something so beautiful."

Her smile is soft, and the ferocity has gone from her. "You can take me to bed now if you want."

As if she were made of the most delicate porcelain, I lay her on the mattress. "I'll be right back."

Following me with her eyes, she bites her bottom lip.

My cock is back at full attention by the time I reach the washroom. I wet a cloth and return to clean her. Pulling the covers over her, I kiss her cheek. I wash up before getting under the covers and wrapping Harper in my arms. "Would you consider staying in Domhan, Harper?"

She rolls to face me, our heads on the same pillow. "What would I do here? I have no useful skills in this world."

"I don't think that's true. Look at how the freed elves and the children adore you. When this war is over, you will see there are many goals you could pursue here. As far as being queen, my mother is not giving her throne up anytime soon." I brush her hair off her face and still marvel at how soft her skin is.

"I suppose that's true." Her focus grows distant. "How long will you live if we survive this?"

Not liking where this is going, I say, "It doesn't matter." Her sharp look is enough. "Some elves reach five hundred. Most at least three hundred."

With a sad smile, she sighs. "I will be dead in seventy or seventy-five years, if I'm lucky. What will you do then? Perhaps this is why our peoples separated in the first place."

She could be right, but I'm not giving up. "We have to go to the oracle in two days. Will you hold your decision about the future until after that? We can ask them about how and if such a joining could work." At her nod, my entire body relaxes. I have two days to convince her. "Maybe they'd be willing to allow us to portal painlessly so you could visit your mother, and we could spend part of our lives in your world."

Pressing my chest until I roll to my back, she swings her leg over me and straddles me with her thighs. "If you lived in my world, I would say yes, Aaran. I love you. But the Jersey Girl in me thinks this is impractical. Is love enough?"

I want to scream from the great Cumhachdach Mountains that it is more than enough, but it's Harper making the sacrifices, not me. "Once this is all over, and my brothers and I are all alive, I could pass my responsibilities to Liam and come and live with you in your world."

Astride me like a goddess, she cocks her head and stares for a long minute. "You would do that? You would leave this castle and the one we'll take back from Vanora?"

Letting my thoughts flow freely, I push how much I love her through, so there is no mistake. "I will do what is needed to make you happy. Liam is more than capable."

With a long sigh, she leans over and presses her cheek to

my chest. "I will think about it and see what your oracle has to say." She kisses between my ribs, then lower. "We may die, and none of it will matter." Trailing her lips and tongue to my belly button, she dips inside and kisses lower, with her mossy eyes focused on mine. "Until then, we can have these moments."

My body burns for this amazing human woman. I'll never get enough of her.

Harper shares a wicked smile and sucks my cock deep into her mouth.

Her name grumbles from me, long and low. "That's..." There are no words. My hips press for her to take more, and she does.

Lifting away, she lets me pop free while gripping my shaft in her fist. She sucks me deep again and again and slides her fingers gently along my balls.

Unable to bear any more of this beautiful torture, I reach under her arms and lift her up and over my body until her sex hovers over my waiting lips. Grabbing her ass, I pull her tight, sucking and licking until she's riding my face and repeating my name like a prayer.

On a long keen, she comes apart, and I lap up every drop of her sweet nectar. Before I can roll her to her back, she skitters away and impales herself on my cock.

"By the old gods, Harper. You'll be the death of me." I clutch her thighs to keep her still, so I don't come too fast.

She presses her fingers to her sex and circles the pearl. "It's not a bad way to go." She rises and falls, over and over, until we're both panting. Riding me like she's the goddess and I'm her steed, she has perfect rhythm and never falters. Harder and faster.

My body tightens, and I shoot my seed deep inside her on a groan of pure rapture while her sheath milks every last drop from me. With a shaky breath, she folds forward. Her hair spreads out like a silken veil across my chest. "I love you, Aaran."

Those words are everything. I kiss the top of her head.

An hour past dawn, we head to the east ballroom. It is a different scene than the day before, and I feel Harper's trepidation ease. There are still guards at the door, but not as many.

It appears that every healer in the city has come to help.

My mother sits with Cara and Dorian by the large windows. Despite the rainy day, light filters in. We stop to see the children. They're playing with four wood-carved dragons. Clean and dressed in new clothes, they're hardly recognizable. It's wonderful, but hard to think about the three who are not here and safe.

"What do you have there, Nond?" Harper asks the oldest boy.

"Drac." He flies it over Fort's head and lands on a bed.

"Are you hungry?" She rubs her stomach to make them understand.

Nond shakes his head, his focus on the toy.

Off to the side, two young elves watch over the children. One is Lori, if my memory serves. She's only been working here for a few months. I met her once when she was first hired. "They all ate very well, miss. Yesterday, two meals, and they broke their fast with eggs and toast only an hour ago." Her voice is soft and kind, just as a nanny's should be.

Harper shakes the hands of the nannies. "Thank you for watching over them. They've been sleeping with us this last week. I worried they'd be lonesome. And with their family..." She swallows down the building emotions.

Lori's eyes swim with her own. "We'll see they're distracted and cared for until they can be reunited with their families."

Once Harper has thanked them again and said goodbye to the children, we cross toward my mother.

Smiling, Beran rushes toward us.

I have to blink several times to recognize that this is the same dour man I've traveled with these weeks.

He pulls Harper into a hug. "My magic has been restored. You can't know what it's like to have this part of me returned. It's as if I were blind and had my eyesight given back."

"I'm so happy for you, Beran." She holds his hand and grins back at him. "Was it difficult to restore?"

"No. It was done with a reversal spell, but this is only simple for certain elves." He takes a deep breath. "Your father healed me, Aaran. I'm forever grateful." He shakes my hand.

"I'm pleased for you, my friend." I've never seen a person altered so much for the better in so short a time, but I can imagine having one's magic stripped away would be a horrible half-life without being enslaved. "I've asked the captain of the guard, Rían, to speak with you. He'll ask about fortification and such at the black tower at Tobhtá."

More sober, Beran nods. "I'd be pleased to help in any way I can."

We continue to the windows where Mother and Cara are practically nose to nose. Every few feet one of the freed stops us to offer thanks. It takes twenty minutes to make the thirty-foot walk.

Mother looks pale and tired, and it's still early morning. Her hands rest on Cara's head and throat. She lets out a long breath. "I'm sorry. This magic will require some research to reverse, Cara."

Cara nods, her expression somber and resigned.

Dorian presses his hand to her shoulder. "Thank you, Ma'am. We're grateful for my magic's return and all your kindness."

"Mother, you look like you need a rest." I kiss her cheek.

Cara nods.

"I just need some fresh air and sunshine, but that's not what the gods have given this day. I'll step onto the veranda." She squeezes Cara's hand and walks to the doors at the end of the long row of windows.

Harper stays with Cara, but I follow Mother. The drizzle doesn't affect a few feet of cover outside. "I'm glad the freed will have their magic back."

She nods. "We found one whose magic is dark. He has been taken to the lower-level cells until Rían returns from patrol and can evaluate the cause."

The captain has a gift for knowing if Vanora's magic holds a person or if they've chosen a dark path. I ask, "Who is it?"

"His name is Cormac." She breathes deep, as if denied

clean air. "He claimed he's not a follower of the witch queen."

I picture the quiet man who carried injured children and helped in many small ways during the journey. "I never noticed anything off-putting about him."

She shrugs. "Better to be cautious. He'll be well treated until an evaluation can be made."

"And if he follows Vanora of his own free will?" A few months ago, if I were in her place, I'd be tempted to rid the world of all dark magic. Now, I know that all shadow is not evil.

"We'll hold him or banish him. I don't know yet, Aaran. I don't want to become what we're fighting." She slumps on a bench, and her lips tighten into a straight line.

"No. I agree. Vanora destroys what she can't use. We have to be better than her."

Mother stares at me. "You've changed. Is it the human woman?"

Sitting beside her, I say, "In part. Harper's magic is filled with light and shadow. She has taught me that all things can be used for good and evil. Maybe I haven't changed so much as I've grown up a bit."

Her smile is lighter and full of pride. "Are you in love with this human?"

"I am." I can't lie to my mother, though I'd hoped to keep this from her for a while longer. "Her soul's song sings to mine in a way I never dreamed possible."

"I see."

"You're displeased." I ready myself for a different kind of battle, though I feel as committed to winning this as I do to defeating Vanora.

"No. She's a smart, powerful woman who clearly adores you. She came here to help us when she didn't have to. That shows courage. What more can a mother ask for her eldest son?" Rising, she kisses my forehead.

"I will return to the human world if Harper won't agree to remain here. Liam will take my place at your side. He's a fine soldier and will learn diplomacy." It feels as if I'm disappointing her, but this is not negotiable. I need Harper, and once Domhan is safe, I'll choose her over duty.

Looking out over the Cumhachdach Mountains that rise to the west, Mother sighs. "I will accept whatever you decide, Aaran."

"You're not going to try to talk me out of this or demand we stay here?" It's hard to believe she'd let me go without a fight.

As she cups my cheek, her smile is sad, but pride shines in her steel-blue eyes. "All I have ever wanted for my sons is for them to find happiness. I want you to live, have babies—some girls would be nice—and enjoy every moment." On a deep inhale, she steps back. "Vanora must be our first task. After that, you are free to do what will make you and Harper happy."

I hug her tight. "Thank you, Mother. I hope Father is as understanding."

Laughing, she breaks our embrace. "You might want to hold off on this discussion with him. However, I think he'll be swayed."

Feeling a hundred times lighter knowing Mother approves and the freed are healing, I leave her and the veranda to find Harper and claim her time for the rest of the day. I just have to tear her away from the children.

Chapter Twenty-Six

HARPER

Aaran practically dragged me away from the ballroom, but it was his happiness that persuaded me more than his request. He leads me through the garden and past a gate at the far northern corner. "Where are we going?"

"I told you there are many springs that feed the lake. I want to show you my favorite place to think and get away from things in the house." He holds my hand and walks fast, as if the spring might disappear.

We traveled for so long, I'm a little worried about where he's dragging me. At least the rain has stopped, and the sun is trying to break through. "Is it far?"

He scoops me into his arms. "No."

Gripping his neck, I'm struck by all the joy welling inside him. "What did you and your mother talk about?"

"You, of course." It's a winding path to the caves. He's

careful to duck under a low-hanging branch. "It's wonderful to have you in my home."

"You never mentioned you grew up in a castle. You also never told me you will be king one day. Though, I suppose, I easily figured that out on my own." I rest my cheek on his shoulder and listen to the thumping of his heart.

"It didn't matter when we met, and then it mattered too much to risk you pulling away." His eyes flash with fear, and then his smile is back in place, and he lifts me a bit higher and runs down the path.

Unable to relax until he slows, I hang on for my life. "Why are we running?"

"I am running. You are a passenger." He slows and presses his lips to the top of my head. Putting me on my feet, he points to a bush as if I should be seeing something.

"What?"

Reaching out, he pushes aside the greenery, and sunlight streams through the canopy of trees and reflects like diamonds on a bubbling pool. "This is my favorite place in Tús Nua."

Yellow flowers bloom along the ground like a carpet. I immediately remove my shoes and feel the soft tickle of their petals on my feet. "This is beautiful."

"I've never shared this place with anyone." He sits on the grass and flowered carpet and lies back, staring up at the leaves.

Lying beside him, I thread my fingers through his. "I love it. Thank you." His thoughts stray, and I catch a hint of worry. "I wonder where you brothers are."

"They'll find a way, just as we did."

"I hope their way is easier than ours was."

"If that were the case, they would have arrived already. My brothers are resourceful. They will get here."

"Of course they will," I say with more confidence than I feel. "Can we go into this spring?"

"Yes." He pulls me to my feet, and we sit at the edge of the water.

I trail my fingers along the surface, and the water is warm. Vanora's sour magic hits me like the snap of a whip. I pull my hand back and grab Aaran's arm. "She's here."

"Who?" He looks around but lets me pull him away from the water.

The bubbling stills and reveals Vanora's beautiful, terrible face, now with a thin red scar on her left cheek. The water distorts her, but her glamor is in place. Though it cannot hide the scar I gave her. Her black hair flies in all directions, as if taken by the pool. Her hazel eyes glow with evil. "I see you, little human. Where are you though? You thought you could get away from me? I am all-powerful. Nothing you can do will stop me. Take my slaves, and I'll capture twice their number and make them suffer for your crimes. Now, where are you?" She squints as if trying to recognize some landmark.

I want to scream for her to go away and leave this place, but I hold my tongue. I might say something that gives her information. Right now, all she knows is that I'm near this pool of water.

"If you step in, I will make your end easy. There will be no more worry or suffering. I might even spare the Riordan's firstborn. Is he there with you? Aaran, push the human into the water, and I will spare your life. I will leave your brothers alive as well. One little worthless human for three strong elven men. It's more than fair." She laughs, but it's the most grating sound.

Instinct has me linking my hand with Aaran's. I pray Vanora will never sully this place again.

Aaran's strong pure magic flows through me.

We step closer.

"That's right. I feel you now, human. Just step in and let me take away all the pain and torture these elves have put you through." Another cackle.

The magic builds, and I draw a long breath, then break free of Aaran and slam my hand into the pool.

He screams. "No!"

There's a moment of knowing surprise on Vanora's reflected face before she and her magic disappear from the pool.

Scrambling away like a crab, I make it ten feet, then lean on my elbows to catch my breath.

With a growl, Aaran pulls me into his arms. "You shouldn't risk yourself that way, *mo chroi*. I don't know what I'd do if I lost you."

"We couldn't just leave her floating in your spring. She had to go." Vanora in the water, magic in the damp ground, magic on the flats. The fire demon. "That's how she followed us. When she has her strength, she can sense me through the water."

He stares for a long moment until the realization hits him too. "We have to go back to the house."

"Castle," I correct. "We need to tell your mother what we've learned. I don't know if it's good or bad, but it's knowledge."

"I think we need to see the oracle sooner than planned." He hauls me to my feet, and we run back down the path.

Within the hour, we're riding to see the oracle. The countryside is awash with every color of green, and flowers bloom as if painted on the landscape. At this speed, it's all going by like a blur, but I try to take in some of the beauty of Domhan.

I don't know what to expect. But my imagination has run amok with notions of a withered old woman wrapped up like a nun in black. Tucked in front of Aaran on his horse, there's nothing for me to do but worry. I should learn to ride again. When we get back to the castle, I'm questioning Rían about his assessment of Cormac and four others whose magic's return revealed loyalty to Vanora. I'll visit the prison and judge for myself. Staying in Domhan would mean giving up an entire life. However, it also means gaining a new one. I'd make a terrible queen.

Aaran leans close to my ear. "Stop. You'll make me go the wrong way if you keep thinking a dozen things at once. Besides, Rían is preparing to leave, as you commanded, to find those taken in the marshes."

"I commanded." I laugh, though I'm pleased that the captain is going and a rescue is nearly underway. "I merely asked if he was going." I should remember that he hears my thoughts if I'm broadcasting. While I could block him, we're beyond that now.

"I know you worry over Tal. I can't stop thinking about

how she put her trust in us. I failed her and the others. Rían will find them and bring them home if he can."

I don't need our connection to feel his guilt and sorrow. Pushing away the darker thoughts, I say. "You're following your parents. I hardly think you can make a wrong turn. How far is it?"

"The oracle is near the mountains."

"That's more than a day's ride." My gut twists, and my poor ass will not make it that long in a saddle.

"Don't worry. There's a shorter way." He guides the horse into a trot, then a walk, as we turn left and stop at the mouth of a cave. Once dismounted, he helps me down before tying the reins to a tree.

Elspeth and Brion secure their mounts before entering the cave.

It's dark and damp within. I can't see anything and stumble on the uneven ground.

Gripping my arm firmly, Aaran whispers something in elvish, and the cave illuminates, though I see no light source. I'm almost used to this whole magic to do everything business.

Gray ground, gray walls, and a musty smell leave me wondering why in the world we've come to this empty cave. "Are we waiting for something?"

Warm and loving, Aaran wraps an arm around my shoulder. "Mother must summon the bell, and hopefully the oracle will agree to see us."

"Agrees? What do you mean? She might tell us to go away?" The idea that anyone in this world would turn me away after what I've been through to get here sends indignation rushing from my brain. I open my mouth.

Aaran gently lays a finger over my lips. "Patience, *mo chroi*."

Brion gives me a sharp look, but he can't hide his amusement and his lips twitch, ruining the effect. "It's unlikely the oracle will refuse to see us."

I keep my they-better-not response to myself.

Elspeth steps to a plain wall, and her magic skitters over my skin, powerful and warm. It's the strongest magic I've felt, other than Vanora's, and it makes me wonder how the witch queen ever gained the upper hand.

Part of the stone shimmers, revealing a one-foot-square opening in the cave wall. A patina brass bell hangs in the alcove.

Elspeth pushes the bell, and it chimes deep, then in a higher pitch. It sounds as if there are several bells all ringing at the same time rather than just the one old one, which reminds me of an old cowbell.

As suddenly as it first rang, the sound stops.

My heart drops as nothing changes in the cave.

Aaran grips my shoulder tighter, either in warning or from anticipation.

The back wall of the cave spins and glows a white-blue.

Elspeth says, "The oracle will see us." She looks at me and smiles. "Try not to speak unless asked a direct question. I find these encounters go better if we let their wisdom come to us unhindered by a lot of questions."

Despite thinking that she might as well ask me to stop breathing, I nod. I have questions that need answers.

I brace for the pain of a portal and follow Elspeth through. It isn't terrible, painful, and nauseating. There is no harsh jarring or feeling of my flesh being ripped away. This is more like floating through a thick atmosphere. Then we step onto soft ground, and two women dressed in formal blue silk robes stand before a white castle built into the side of a mountain. The door is twice as tall as a man and equally as wide.

Elspeth covers her left fist with her right hand and lowers her chin. "Forgive our early arrival. Our first prophesied human has arrived and made a rather discouraging discovery."

Brion and Aaran make the same gesture with their hands, and we all follow as the heavy wood doors open with no sign of anyone pushing or pulling. The walls are all white and unadorned. Through another door, ten elves sit behind a high desk that wraps the circular room. There is one opening to the center, and we walk through while the two who brought us in find their places. All ten, men and women, are dressed in the same blue of Elspeth's flag. With hair and skins of all shades, they all look peaceful, as if nothing is amiss. Sconces burn all around the chamber.

The intimidation of the oracle is awe-inspiring. I've never seen anything so serene be so terrifying. It's pretty clever how they've set this up to put visitors on edge. It's working on me, and Elspeth's advice seems sound. I keep my mouth shut while Elspeth recounts what I told her about Vanora using water and fire to reach the Siar Fàilte continent.

In the center, a woman who might be thirty or a hundred and thirty stares at me. Her long white hair is unbound, and she wears a ringlet around her head with a round sapphire in the center of her forehead. "Harper Craig, step forward."

My legs shake, which pisses me off. I lift my chin and do as she asks.

A flash, and she's on my side of the desk, a foot from me.

It takes all my will not to back up. "Nice trick."

Her lips twitch. "The oracle deciphered a tablet that brought us to you and two more of your kind. You must defeat the witch queen or Domhan will perish. Do you understand?"

Is she kidding? "I nearly died more than once to get here. Of course, I understand."

Aaran's voice is in my head. *Gently, Harper.*

The oracle turns her attention to him. "You are bonded." She closes her eyes, as do the other nine.

I get the impression a conversation is happening that we're not invited to.

After several uncomfortable minutes, she opens her eyes. "The oracle will protect the water. We have no sway in the fires of Coire. It is hoped your sisters and brothers will not encounter Bolcán or anything like it."

"I don't even want to tell you how many times I've been told we're safely out of range of Vanora, or how each time, the information was wrong. Are you certain that the witch queen can't reach us here unless she goes through hell to get here?" In the back of my mind, Aaran advises me to ease up on the questions and sarcasm, but I push him away.

Staring into my eyes as if she can read everything in my mind, the oracle says, "No. She is resourceful and wants what we possess. She will always try to find a way."

Since I'm getting honesty from her, I ask, "What is behind the Watchers' Gate?"

"That is beyond our knowing. The gate was sealed by

the old gods when your human world and Domhan parted ways. That is before any who live as the oracle were born. In your world, we're stories passed down from mother to daughter, father to son. Myths and legends of no import. Those stories made it possible to bring you here. No magic could have worked if the hope of reunion didn't remain inside your soul. You must come to us for training to gain control of the strong magic the oracle senses." She closes her eyes again and the others follow.

Several minutes pass, and I begin to wonder if we're meant to leave now.

When the oracle's eyes open, they're brighter, as if lit from behind. "Do you wish a union with the Riordan?"

"Oh. Okay. Change of subject. Um, is that relevant?" I have to make the leap that the Riordan is Aaran, and I feel like this might fall under the none of your business column. I'm sure I appear braver than I feel. I just can't stand a bully, and this intimidation thing is annoying me.

She steps close, touches my shoulder, then we're standing on a wide stone veranda that looks out over the land below.

I take a moment to regain my balance. The castle looks very small but brilliant white in the sunshine. Rolling hills, the river, and lakes shine in the distance. It's too far to see, but I imagine the ocean beyond.

Aaran stands beside me, and his parents as well.

All the members of the oracle stand in a half circle around us. She says, "The oracle seeks meaning to the prophecy. It alludes to a merging of worlds."

"The human world is not ready for elves and dwarves or any other beings to start walking the streets of our cities.

They would see it as an invasion." The thought of it is horrifying. Humanity can't even get along with each other, let alone other species of sentient beings.

"We are aware. But there are some, like the fisherman and you, who think differently."

I nod in agreement. "If we survive the gate and the war, I would consider staying to be with Aaran." My cheeks are so hot that I have to force myself not to fan at them. "I would need to be able to see my mother from time to time. There are a lot of details to work out."

Aaran slips his fingers through mine. "If living in Domhan cannot make Harper happy, I will live in the human world to remain with her."

"What?" Brion raises his voice beyond what feels acceptable. "You can't leave here."

Turning to his father, he says, "Once Domhan is safe, I will do whatever is necessary so that Harper and I can be together, Father."

Brion's jaw ticks. "We will discuss it."

"No. We won't." Aaran turns back to the oracle. "My duty is to Domhan, but also to the woman I love. If we were not meant, I would not love her, nor she me."

The oracle's voice sounds like many again. "Look out over this world and what you risk your lives for. Do what must be done. Give hope where none exists, then live in your love with our blessing. Hope is all we have until the other two Riordans bring forth the prophesized. There must be six."

If Aaran's brothers fail, all of this could have been for nothing. She said six, so it's not just three human women, the brothers have to survive as well. If they go through half of what we did to get here, there are no guarantees any of Domhan will survive.

Beyond the veranda, the scene brightens as if all the world were put into Photoshop and the colors enhanced. The image stays with me as everything goes black and the four of us are suddenly standing at the gateway, back at the base of the mountains.

S tanding in front of a full-length mirror in my bedroom, I stare at my reflection and wonder who that woman is. Hair curled and left loose, eyes bright with both excitement and exhaustion, and in a pale-green gown made of silk.

An hour ago, I stood in the dungeon and talked to Cormac and the others. They are comfortable and well treated. They don't deny that they serve the witch queen, but they also claim they gave her no aid in finding us during the journey.

Now I look like some kind of princess in a gown. The borrowed necklace dips almost as low as the gown's scooping neckline. Touching the dark emeralds and gold, I pray I don't lose the thing.

I feel Aaran before the door opens. It's gratifying when he stares agape at me.

"You're even more beautiful, which seems impossible." He kisses my cheek.

I brush the deep blue of his lapel. "You look very hand-some. Is this formal dining a nightly thing?"

"Tonight is a celebration of our return." He leans in and

presses his lips to the curve of my neck. He breathes deep as if I'm a rose in bloom. "Most nights are family dinners, and we do generally dress for them, but not in gowns and suits."

"Can we just eat in the kitchen and not dress for dinner?" The idea of it every single night sounds as if it will get old very quickly.

Looking into my eyes, he runs his knuckles along my jaw. "We can break every tradition, as long as you promise to be by my side, *mo chroi*."

"The firstborn son of Riordan is going to break the rules?" Arms on his shoulders, I step close and thread my fingers through his hair.

"You don't even know how many I've broken already. My father would have brought you here directly and not given those slaves a second thought. My brother Liam might have done the same. They're soldiers. They only care about the mission." His expression dims as some internal battle rages.

Staring until I capture his gaze again, I say, "I don't think that's true. Your father spent most of the day healing those freed elves, which I'm guessing is not in his normal job description. Perhaps you are just being hard on yourself." I kiss his chin, along his jaw, and let my breath tickle his ear.

"If you keep doing that, we'll break another rule tonight and be late for our own party." He grabs my ass and drags me against his growing shaft.

"I like the sound of that. Do that magic thing where you vanish all our clothes."

Longing and duty war in his bright blue eyes.

With a sigh, I save him. "We'll go to the party and leave far earlier than is customary. Then you can do all the things to make up for making me wait." It's not even right how naughty this idea feels.

His smile and sexy thoughts slide through me. "It's going to be a long night."

Hand in hand, we turn toward the door. I say, "It's going to be fun teasing you all night until you bring me back here."

He growls and bites my neck hard enough to leave a mark under my hair. Good thing I didn't go with an up-do. "Be careful, love. I can give as good as I get."

A victim of my own teasing, I ache in all the best places. "Don't I know it."

Did you enjoy *A Crown of Light and Shadow?*
Please leave a review. It's the best way to help out the author.

FREE Novella
Follow the link to read all about the stern Captain Rían
Redman and his quest to save the captured elves and
children. He'll find more than he thinks in
A Crown of Blood and Duty.
https://dl.bookfunnel.com/8cs5hbl1wi

RÌAN

The mission is simple: rescue the elven children stolen by
the witch queen before they vanish forever. Freed once by
the human woman from the prophecy, then retaken, they'll
be held at the black tower. Failure isn't an option.

But when a fairy steps out of the shadows to warn us that
we've come to the wrong place, plans must be abandoned.
Fairies never leave their island. They don't meddle in elven
wars. And they definitely don't look at me the way Niamh
does. She is dangerous in ways I didn't anticipate, distracting, defiant, and far too tempting. I'm here to complete a
mission, not lose my heart to a fairy who doesn't belong in
my world.

NÌAMH

I watched Rìan Redmond long before he knew I existed. As
my father studied the elven realm through his scrying

mirrors, the captain of the guard was always there—steady, loyal, untouchable.

Seeing him in the flesh makes my pulse race, but this isn't a fairy tale. I left the safety of my island to help free the children trapped by the witch queen, and I won't turn back now. If fate insists on tangling my heart with a stubborn elven soldier along the way...who am I to argue?

Join my Newsletter – A wonderful way to stay in touch and always know what's new and exciting in the Andrea Rose, Andie, and A.S. Fenichel book universe is to sign up for my weekly newsletter. You'll automatically receive a free book, but beyond that, you'll love all the sales, news, and book talk.

www.asfenichel.com/newsletter

What to read Next: I hope you loved Aaran and Harper's story. If you want to know what's next, you can check out *A Crown of Wind and Water* and see how Liam finds his human from the prophecy.

A CROWN OF WIND AND WATER
Book 2
Reign of the Witch Queen

**A reluctant heroine, a hardened soldier,
and a love powerful enough to change fate.**

LIAM

I'm a soldier, not a diplomat, and certainly not a kidnapper.

But the oracle was clear: my brothers and I must retrieve the human women destined to destroy the Witch Queen or watch our world fall to darkness.

I expected a warrior.

Instead, I find Wren. She's small, sharp-eyed, and furious when I try to take her. She floors me with one well-placed kick and walks away like she hasn't just defied an elven soldier sent by fate itself.

I should be irritated.

Instead, I'm intrigued.

She may look fragile, but beneath her quiet strength is a power I don't fully understand—and a will of iron that makes me want her at my side far more than is wise.

WREN

My great-grandmother used to tell stories about the fair folk with bright eyes, pointed ears, and beauty dangerous enough to steal a girl's heart. I thought they were just stories.

Until one of them tries to abduct me from the dentist's office.

Liam is impossible to ignore—lethal, arrogant, and devastatingly beautiful, but I'm nobody's idea of a hero. I'm barely five-foot-two, I design jewelry for a living, and I want no part in an elven war.

Then he and my mother reveal the truth about the magic running through my blood, and I may be the key to saving an entire world.

Against my better judgment, I agree to travel to Domhan. But before I can reach the portal, a dragon attacks—ripping Liam and me away from Mom and hurling us one month back in time.

Now the fate of the elven world rests on my shoulders, but

I'm more concerned about finding my mother in this war-torn world.

No dragon.

No witch.

Not even destiny is going to stop me.

Also by Andrea Rose

FANTASY ROMANCE

Reign of the Witch Queen Series

A Crown of Light and Shadow

A Crown of Wind and Water

A Crown of Fire and Ice

A Crown of Stars and Sea (Prequel Novella)

A Crown of Blood and Duty (Novella)

Writing as A.S. Fenichel

HISTORICAL PARANORMAL ROMANCE

Witches of Windsor Series

Magic Touch

Magic Word

Pure Magic

The Demon Hunters Series

Ascension

Deception

Betrayal

Defiance

Vengeance

HISTORICAL ROMANCE

The Wallflowers of West Lane Series

The Earl Not Taken

Misleading A Duke

Capturing the Earl

Not Even For A Duke

The Everton Domestic Society Series

A Lady's Honor

A Lady's Escape

A Lady's Virtue

A Lady's Doubt

A Lady's Past

A Lady's Christmas

A Lady's Curves

The Forever Brides Series

Tainted Bride

Foolish Bride

Desperate Bride

Single Title Books

Wishing Game

Christmas Bliss

An Honorable Arrangement

CONTEMPORARY PARANORMAL EROTIC ROMANCE

The Psychic Mates Series

Kane's Bounty

Joshua's Mistake

Training Rain

The End of Days Series

Mayan Afterglow

Mayan Craving

Mayan Inferno

End of Days Trilogy

CONTEMPORARY EROTIC ROMANCE

Single Title Books

Alaskan Exposure

Revving Up the Holidays

Writing as Andie Fenichel

Dragon of My Dreams (Monster Between the Sheets)

Turnabout is Fairy Play (Monster Between the Sheets)

Soul of a Vampire (Brothers of Scrim Hall)

Soul of a Reaper (Brothers of Scrim Hall)

Soul of a Dragon (Brothers of Scrim Hall)

Soul of a Wolf (Brothers of Scrim Hall)

Soul of a Demon (Brothers of Scrim Hall)

Soul of a Phoenix (Brothers of Scrim Hall)

Soul of a Monster (Brothers of Scrim Hall)

Mantus

Riding With the Panther

The Manticore's Mate (Catskills Mountain Monsters)

Promised to the Satyr (Catskills Mountain Monsters)

Wild for the Wyvern (Catskills Mountain Monsters)

Big Enough to Bite (Harmony Glen)

Biting Bigfoot (Harmony Glen)

Bitten by Love (Harmony Glen)

Dad Bod Handyman (Lane Family)

Carnival Lane (Lane Family)

Lane to Fame (Lane Family)

Changing Lanes (Lane Family)

Heavy Petting (Lane Family)

Summer Lane (Lane Family)

Hero's Lane (Lane Family)

Icing It (Lane Family)

Mountain Lane (Lane Family)

Christmas Lane (Lane Family)

Texas Lane (Lane Family)

Building Lane (Lane Family)

Humbug Lane (Lane Family)

High Voltage Lane (Lane Family)

For Letter or Worse (Lane Family)

**Visit Andrea Rose's website
for a complete and up-to-date list of all her books.
http://andrearoseauthor.com**

About the Author

Andrea Rose is a pen name for author A.S. Fenichel. She also writes as Andie Fenichel. Andrea gave up a successful career in New York City to pursue her lifelong dream of being a professional writer. She's never looked back.

Andrea adores writing stories filled with love, passion, desire, magic, and maybe a little mayhem tossed in for good measure. Books have always been her perfect escape, and she still relishes diving into one and staying up all night to finish a good story.

With over 60 published books, Andrea Rose/Andie Fenichel/A.S. Fenichel has written historical romance, fantasy romance, contemporary romance, and mixed-genre romances. She has authored several series, including Reign of the Witch Queen, Everton Domestic Society, Witches of Windsor, and more. Strong, empowered heroines from Regency London to modern-day New York are what you'll find in all her books.

A Jersey Girl at heart, she now makes her home in Southern Missouri with her real-life hero, her wonderful husband. When not reading or writing, she enjoys cooking, traveling, history, and puttering in her garden.

Visit Andrea Rose's Website:
http://andrearoseauthor.com

Send Andrea Rose an Email:
andrearoseauthor@outlook.com

Join Andrea's Newsletter:
www.asfenichel.com/newsletter/

instagram.com/asfenichel

facebook.com/a.s.fenichel

tiktok.com/@asfenichel

bookbub.com/authors/andrea-rose

pinterest.com/asfenichel

x.com/asfenichel

amazon.com/author/andrearoseauthor